# The Alchemist

✣

Also by Donna Boyd

*The Awakening*

# The ALCHEMIST

Donna Boyd

THE RANDOM HOUSE PUBLISHING GROUP

NEW YORK

The Alchemist *is a work of fiction. Names, places, and incidents either are products of the author's imagination or are used fictitiously.*

*A Ballantine Book*
*Published by The Random House Publishing Group*



*www.ballantinebooks.com*

*Library of Congress Control Number: 2003091250*

*ISBN 978-0-345-46236-7*

*Cover design by Barbara Leff*
*Cover illustration by Phil Heffernan based on a painting by Raphael © Scala/Art Resource, NY*

*Manufactured in the United States of America*

*First Hardcover Edition: January 2002*
*First Trade Paperback Edition: July 2003*

## *NEW YORK CITY*
## *THE PRESENT*

Even now he could see it: the shower of blood that had sprayed from a surprised carotid artery, arching gracefully against a sun-drenched sky where it seemed to be captured for a moment in time and space, glistening drops of liquid life that spun and danced like melted gold in a viscous suspension before raining in a sweet gentle mist onto his face and skin and hair. He had expected the blood to sizzle against his skin, to bore perfectly round holes through flesh and bone, to burn the oxygen from the air and char his lungs to useless, crumbling remnants with his first desperate gasp. But it had been only a warm shower, slippery and rich with the elements of life. Lovely, really. A drop or two had landed on his tongue as he drew in a breath of wonder, and he tasted salt. He had savored the taste, and swallowed. Ah, that was the real alchemy.

The headlines were saturated with outrage. Words like *brutal, vicious, unimaginable,* and *horrific* were repeated so often they lost their power, like a rosary whose charm had been worn away by too many worrying fingers. Around the globe the airwaves pulsed with images that were only the remnants of loss: blood-splattered stones, masses of wailing mourners brought to their knees. Around the world, evil had become a palpable thing.

He was the island against which the stormy waters tumbled and surged, raged and lapped. To say he was unaffected would be a lie. But he was serene. When the worst is over, one often is.

* * *

The offices of Dr. Anne Kramer were located in a high-security building on Central Park West, an exclusive garden property that was protected by a stone wall and ironwork gate that was more than ornamental. The walls were upholstered and the floors were marble, the draperies heavy damask and the carpets oriental. There were few mirrors, and each expensive, carefully selected work of art had its own lighting. The furniture was dark and highly polished; voices were hushed.

There was a German cabinet clock in the corner of her office that ticked off the minutes with mechanical precision, and celebrated the hour by bringing to life a musical diorama of dancers at its base. The legend was that the brass pendulum on that clock had not stopped swinging in three hundred years. Even when it was shipped overseas, its owner had hired someone to supervise its movement, placement, and regular winding, so that it would not stop ticking. It had been ticking still when it was transferred to Anne's office. Now she timed her appointments by it, and the steady rhythmic sound was as soothing as the heartbeat of eternity, quiet, predictable, inevitable.

Her space was designed to be an oasis in the midst of chaos, a stalwart harbor at the edge of the storm. But even here the murmur of upheaval seeped through, in the form of the telephone, the television, the shocked, distressed faces of those who passed in the corridors or paused at the water cooler to exchange a few hushed and strained words. Unbelievable, they said. Unforgivable, they agreed.

He waited in her consultation office, a slender, elegant figure of a man with aristocratic features and thick silver hair. His face was composed, his skin golden-colored and unlined. He could have been anywhere between thirty-five and seventy. He had the kind of effortlessly maintained good looks that, like his casually tailored European clothes, were the trademark of uncounted generations of extreme wealth. His hands were folded lightly atop his trademark gold-knobbed walking stick, and his attention was on the television set that Anne normally kept behind the closed doors of a Louis Quatorze armoire. He did not look up when she came in.

Anne was briefly annoyed that he had made himself so much at home in her office as to open the armoire and turn on the television set, then she recognized the reaction for what it was—a defensive response to the invasive stresses of the day. Politely, and because she could not control a certain amount of grim fascination for the story herself, Anne waited until the newscaster finished announcing the details of the funeral services, which would be held on Sunday. But before he could go on to revisit the gruesome nature of the crime or to explore in painstaking detail the effect it was having on everyone from construction workers to schoolchildren around the nation, Anne closed the door firmly and stepped into the room.

"I'm sorry to keep you waiting, Mr. Sontime. I'm Dr. Kramer."

The sound on the television set was abruptly silenced and the red "mute" message appeared against the background of more news footage. She hadn't seen him touch the remote control.

He got to his feet and smiled, offering his hand. "It was good of you to see me at the end of a very long day."

Long, strong fingers, as smooth as marble. His grip was not warm, but firm, his skin not dry, but supple, raging with life. When he took her hand, Anne felt captured.

She faltered. He looked at her with eyes that were as green as the bottom of the ocean, and for a moment her mind went blank, wiped completely clean, a stutter in consciousness. It was not recognition, it was not shock, and yet it was somehow reminiscent of both. And when he released her hand, it was gone.

Anne took a steadying breath and moved around to her desk. She was not easily caught off-balance, and was mildly disturbed by the fact that this man had unsettled her so effortlessly. Randolph Sontime was renowned for his personal charisma; it was no one's fault but her own if she had allowed herself to fall victim to it.

The clock ticked rhythmically, yet its sound was uncharacteristically ominous, mimicking the pounding of her pulse. The time was six minutes after five.

Her patient resumed his seat. She started to take her notepad and pen to the chair adjacent to his, where she normally interviewed her patients, then abruptly changed her mind and sat down behind the desk. It was bad practice, she knew, to put that kind of barrier between a therapist and a client, but she did it anyway. Long day, she kept repeating to herself. Another hour and it would be over.

Absently she fingered the chain that held the pendant she wore beneath her sweater, a nervous habit that she checked immediately. She folded her hands deliberately atop the desk, leaned forward, and tried to look as welcoming as possible. "Let's talk about why you're here, Mr. Sontime."

"A woman who gets directly to the point," he observed. "I approve." He had a beautifully musical voice, with the hint of an accent she could not identify and, in fact, had to strain to discern.

He nodded toward the television, where the camera was focused on a mountainous shrine of flowers on the steps of a cathedral in Paris. "That is why," he said simply. "I am the assassin they seek. I killed that creature."

Her carefully trained features betrayed no reaction. She was in control again. She let three swings of the clock pendulum pass, and then she nodded calmly. "I see."

"You don't believe me." But instead of anger or disappointment, his expression was softened with something that was very close to sympathy. "I'm sorry to have troubled you."

"I didn't say I didn't believe you," Anne replied. "But I do have a question."

"I should imagine you have several."

She turned in her chair toward the bookcase that lined the wall behind her and bent down to the bottom shelf, where she kept the periodicals. The *New York Times* from two days ago was still there, glaring its lurid headlines about the crime of the century. She quickly flipped past the first section, with its violent black type and bleak, shattering photographs, until she found what she was looking for.

She folded the newspaper and held it up to him. The photograph in the center of the page was of the man who now sat before her. "It says here that you were making a speech at a People for the Environment benefit at the time the crime was committed. How could you have been seen in New York by five hundred witnesses and have committed a murder in Geneva at the same time?"

He smiled, gently. She noticed then what peculiar eyes he had: pale gray, almost silvery. Completely unreadable, as compelling as frosted glass. And how odd that at first she had thought they were green.

He said, "Magic."

Anne closed the newspaper, folded it on her desk, and returned it to the bottom shelf of the bookcase. During her internship and early clinical practice she had heard patients confess to the murder of space aliens, Elvis, and Abraham Lincoln, as well as a number of lesser personalities. Compulsive Confession Syndrome had become so common in this day of random violence and media reinforcement that it barely merited a few lines on a chart. But this was not a phenomenon she was accustomed to seeing in her current private practice. Certainly it did not seem likely in the case of a man like Randolph Sontime.

"Now I will ask you a question." Sontime spoke conversationally, in a pleasant, matter-of-fact tone. "Why did you agree to see me?"

The fingers that were laced atop the walking stick were beautifully manicured, the nails lightly buffed. Anne noticed that detail as she composed her reply. But he did not give her a chance to speak.

"I will tell you," he said. His tone was still pleasant, and mildly amused. "Because I'm rich and famous and powerful, and I asked you to. Perhaps you can get inside my brain and find something no one else has found. Perhaps you'll get a paper out of it. But whatever else, you will have my psyche to add to your trophy case. And that's what you do, isn't it? Collect trophies?"

Anne leaned back in her chair, her fingers straying toward the chain around her neck again. She stroked it once, as though for reassurance, and dropped her hand to her desk again. "You don't appear to have a very high opinion of me. Why, then, did you choose to confess your crime to me? Why not the police?"

He lifted one shoulder in a vague dismissal. "I have no interest in the police, and being arrested would be inconvenient."

Now the humor left his face, and the gaze he fixed on her was somber. "But it's important that you understand why it was necessary for me to do this thing."

"I see. May I record our conversation?"

"As you wish. But your machine won't pick up my voice."

"What makes you think so?"

"It's an electrochemical matter. The explanation would bore you."

Her smile faltered as she opened the drawer where her tape recorder was kept. There, in its usual place next to the recorder, was the remote control for the television set. She could not stop a quick glance toward the television, where the red "mute" display still glowed across the screen. She looked at him, and his expression was anticipatory and amused. She swallowed the question that hovered at the back of her throat. It was important that she maintain control of the interview. Important.

She assumed a pleasant tone as she pushed the button on the tape recorder inside. "This is a very expensive machine. I hope you're wrong."

He regarded her thoughtfully for a moment. "Such things are important to you, aren't they, Anne? Exclusive offices, expensive machines, celebrity patients with their pathetic little secrets. . . . Even Richard, your Park Avenue doctor-husband—all of it to remind you every day that you're no longer the little girl who spent her first six years in an orphanage in London and never even knew her parents' names."

Ah, he had gone to some lengths to make certain he had the advantage. This was not unpredictable behavior on his part. It was, in fact, almost reassuring. She was in familiar territory now. This she could handle.

"You've done your research, I see."

"I know everything about you." He spoke gently, but with confidence. "Everything."

"Of course. You broker power. And knowledge is power."

"It always has been."

His eyes reminded her of mirrors veiled in crepe, a peculiar image to say the least. Death and mourning, thunderheads moving across the sun. In fact it seemed almost as though the light in the room had changed, for now his eyes were dark, close to black.

Was it his manner, or his voice? For the first time Ann truly understood the meaning of the word *charismatic*. He had a personal energy that was almost palpable.

She glanced at the clock. And she looked again. There was no mistake: The hands of the clock clearly showed the time to be six-fifty. But how could that be? She could have sworn no more than ten minutes had passed since she walked in the door. Could she have misread the time when she started the session? How could she have lost over ninety minutes?

Her heart began to pound, and her throat felt dry. Nonetheless, she kept her voice even as she said, "My sessions are usually an hour in length. I've found it's best not to make exceptions."

"And tonight you have theater tickets." A quick glint of humor flashed in his eyes. "The world might be tumbling down around you, let there be rioting in the streets, but those tickets cost two hundred eighty dollars, and you have no intention of missing the curtain, am I right?"

She said nothing. The muscles in her face felt like stone.

"I am very sorry to disappoint you, but you will be missing the curtain tonight, Anne." His voice was as soothing as a caress, his eyes filled with sympathy. "And you mustn't worry about Richard. You've already called him to cancel."

"I assure you, I've done nothing of the kind."

He smiled. "It doesn't matter. He thinks you did. And perception is the only reality."

She could no longer tell the difference between the beat of her pulse—throbbing, throbbing, in her throat—and the swinging, stroking, beat of the clock. The faint hiss of the clock spring on the downbeat sounded like a whisper of breath. The room was alive with the rhythm. Or dying with it.

The effort to focus was greater than it should have been. Anne tightened her fingers around the pen she held as a prop, digging two fingernails into her palm. The sting of pain cleared her head. She said steadily, "Mr. Sontime, I want to help you. But my time is valuable and I'm not amused by your games. I have certain ground rules pertaining to my privacy, and if we are to establish a relationship, I don't think it's unreasonable for me to ask you to respect them."

"Well spoken. Perhaps I should even the odds by telling you a bit about myself."

She held his gaze steadily. She had been wrong, after all. His eyes were as green as a summer day. "That, I presume, is why we are here."

He sat back, crossed his legs at the knee, and balanced the walking stick across them. The clock ticked loudly. He bound her gaze in the quiet silvery gray light of his own, and he began to speak.

"My life began at the dawn of another millennium," he said, "when civilization was new and the veil between science and superstition could be rent with a breath. I have lived a hundred lifetimes. Over the centuries I have been known by many names—Rasputin, St. Germaine, Cagliostro, Merlin. Ah, you did not expect me to say that. I have surprised you."

"No." Her voice sounded hoarse, even to her own ears, and it hurt her throat coming out. "I didn't expect it."

The smile faded from his eyes and left the room chill. "I will surprise you many more times before the evening is done. For that I am sorry."

He said, "I wept with Nero when Rome burned, and I whispered in the ear of Caligula. I was there when St. Petersburg fell, and had my hand on the shoulder of the dictator who rose in its wake. I have seen heads roll, eyes wide with surprise and severed arteries still pumping, into baskets piled high with their like—minds that once listened to opera and read Molière, suddenly as still and silent as stone. There was no spark there. None at all."

His voice was thoughtful now, and his expression had turned inward, as though he was in fact examining the years as they rolled back through his mind. In the silence the blue light of the muted television flickered and danced, casting shadows on a face that could have been molded in bronze, and the pendulum of the clock swung loudly. Anne sat very still, waiting.

In a moment he resumed. "I have heard the screams of children who were raped in battle, and seen their small bodies floating and tumbling in the waters of a swollen river, where they were cast by weary parents who had too many to feed already. I sat at the right hand of a queen who ruled the world, and at the left of a cardinal who almost destroyed it. I have seen nations come and go, lovers live and die. Now I am merely . . . tired. It's time to put an end to it all."

Anne took a deep and even breath, pulling herself out of the spell of his voice much in the way a dreamer struggles against the web of a groggy night. "Tell me how you propose to do that, Mr. Sontime."

He smiled, but there was only sadness in his eyes. "You cannot hope to understand unless I start from the beginning. And . . ." His gaze seemed to turn inward, looking back, once again, over the years. He finished softly, "It's a very long story."

Anne simply looked at him, waiting. And in the slow descent of silence that settled over them like the night, she became aware that the clock, for the first time in centuries, had stopped ticking.

*Part One*

# THE AGE OF MYSTERY

## EGYPT BEFORE TIME

# *One*

Imagine if you will the days spinning backward: a millennium ends here, a century turns there, a year ends now, and another, and a thousand others, and finally there are so many days, so many years ending and beginning that you can no longer remember why it seemed important that you keep count of them at all. And yet I have counted them. I have counted every one, marking the beginning of each new year, of each new century, in my own quiet fashion: a glass of wine, perhaps, a silent toast. The world revolves, the view changes. Now I stand atop a castle turret, now upon the deck of a sailing ship. Here I gaze upon an ageless river, there a body-strewn battlefield; now I see the dancing lights of the Champs d'Elysée, now I see the smoldering fires of a fallen civilization. The years change, but the question does not. *Will this be it?* I ask myself. *Will this be the year I tell my story, the whole of it, from beginning to end, at last?*

And what a lovely entertainment it has been, all these thousands of turning years, to imagine the telling, the circumstances of the telling, and the reason for the telling. I have created the scenario and variations upon scenario over and over again in my mind. Where to begin? How best to glorify or debase myself in the telling, how to find the thread of truth that, in the end, must be the summation of any man's life—even if that life has been as long and as tangled as mine. So now the time has come, and the moment is—as so many greatly anticipated moments are—disappointing. For I realized some time ago that the whole story cannot be told, not today, perhaps not ever. Every man's life is simply a sum of parts, and these are the only parts I can tell you now.

But the beginning, where was that? I think sometimes it began with a lithe young girl of grand ambition and laughing eyes. At other times I am sure it all started with the wistful longings of a poet-priest I once called friend. Was it a woman's power, or a man's dreams? What dark god fashioned this unlikely tale and sent it spinning into space with a single smiling breath? And dare I think I ever, at any time, had any control over it at all?

It began with the magic, you see. And so, perforce, must I.

I had a name in that long-ago time, but I have forgotten it centuries since, so let me call myself as I was in those days: Han. Perhaps I had a mother, a father, and an early family life but I do not recall those either. Life began for me, as I remember it, in the House of Ra.

Much has been written in human history about this time in Egypt; entire lifetimes have been dedicated to piecing together the scattered bones of that long-ago life. As always, when what is shattered is reassembled with no model to follow, mistakes will be made in the reconstruction, great chunks, perhaps, will be missing and others will seem to have no place in the whole at all. The result is, more often than not, a monstrous grotesquerie.

So believe me when I tell you that, while historians have done a fair job of reassembling the past, so much of what they have learned is only what we wanted them to know, what was left for them to know. And nothing, I assure you, of what you know or what you think you know of that time can even begin to touch the truth of the House of Ra.

*Truth* is an interesting word. I cannot tell you now with absolute certainty whether the structure itself, the temple complex in which we lived and worked and ate and slept and studied was in fact composed of mortar and stone, or whether it was merely an illusion of the same—or, most likely, a combination of both. I will describe it therefore as I perceived it to be, remembering that in the end, in almost every instance, the difference between truth and illusion is so faint as to be almost inconsequential.

The House of Ra existed on a man-made oasis far from the banks of the Nile, in a part of the Egyptian desert that is today a particularly brutal and barren stretch of land in a place that is known for its inhospitable nature. Soaring sandstone cliffs surrounded the oasis which, from the sky, would be seen as an island of green in a sea of sand. Date and fig trees grew side by side with banana, papaya, and orange trees. Waterfalls tumbled from limestone boulders, formed deep pools and meandering streams. The ground was covered with a lush low carpet of a fragrant creeping herb that smelled like sweet lavender and felt like moss to the touch. Even after all these years, I can but think of the House of Ra and that fragrance will return to me. There is nothing like it growing in the world today.

The temple complex was enormous—larger, I think, than any of us imagined, for it seemed the more we discovered, the more there was to discover. There was a set of carved cypress doors at the entry to the temple, easily two stories high, which were closed only on ceremonial occasions. The door was inscribed with pictographs in the ancient language centered around the symbol of our craft—three interlocked globes in perfect balance that formed the points of a triangle. When the doors were open, the triangle was broken, leaving two globes joined and the one alone. Only when the doors were closed was the triangle complete.

The complex itself was laid out like a triangle, with long straight corridors containing classrooms, laboratories and sleeping areas, and large circular common rooms at each apex of the triangle. The whole was protected by a raised roof, so that indoor gardens and pools thrived in the artificial tropical rain-forest atmosphere that had been created by the designers. There were many levels, some labyrinthine, some so compact they were practically claustrophobic, each with its own internal environment—cool in the heat of the sun and warm when the cold winds blew across the desert.

Artificial light glowed from the walls and ceilings so that we might work or study at night, and could be discontinued when we wished it. Refrigeration was available, but rarely used, as our supply of fresh foods was abundant. Our clothing was manufactured so quickly and inexpensively that there was no need for laundering, and our food was cooked with a method that used no fuel and gave off no heat. We bathed in warm-water pools and used an internal, automated waste-disposal system. We had, in this ancient, long-forgotten desert temple, every modern convenience.

The House of Ra was a secret over two thousand years old even when I was there. Within those vaulted marble halls and sun-drenched galleries, magic met science, philosophy met truth, wonders and miracles were merely a matter of course. Years later a library would be built in Alexandria that would become known as the greatest in the world; it was only a shallow replica of the library contained in the vaults of the House of Ra. There were never more than thirteen initiates at a time; the best and the brightest of all of Egypt, hand-chosen by the Masters to live at the temple and study the truths.

And what truths were those? Ah, you could spend a lifetime and still not list them all. The nature of atomic particles and the nature of man, the composition of chemical alloys and the mysteries of the soul. The transmutation of matter, the source of all Power. To live in truth, and to practice deception. Magic. Medicine. Discipline. Mastery. Good and evil. Balance in all things.

We were chosen at a young age, male and female, for characteristics not even our parents could identify, and from that time until we gained adulthood we knew no life outside the House of Ra. It was, to the best of my recollection, a very ordinary life: we played, we studied, we ate and slept; we had childish spats with our classmates, we were impertinent to our teachers. We had moments of great joy and deep pain, of triumph and failure and enlightenment and humiliation. We grew, we learned, we loved. We formed loyal friendships and casual sexual liaisons. There was nothing special about us, at least in our own view. We lived in the same universe that you do today; we simply learned to operate that universe according to a different set of rules.

Yet I don't mean to minimize the grandeur of our time there;

the majesty of what we were becoming. Even now I have but to close my eyes and it will return to me with breathless, aching wonder, the first time I understood the workings of this world and the power I had over it. Let me speak the words, with proper tone and rhythm, choosing the syllables and the harmony they produce, let me hold the thought and say the spell, and what once was is no longer so. Watch me now as I pluck from the air the electricity that sparks from my fingers, for don't you know it was always there? And now with an outstretched arm I will lift that stone with the strength of my intent, and see how it floats like a feather in the air! Let me touch your hand and rewrite your memory. Let me bind you with my eyes, let me whisper your name and capture your will. We were dealers in magic, and magic ruled the world.

I have said *we*, but it is important to know that not all who studied at the House of Ra were of equal ability. Some would never do more than master the principles of physics and chemistry that would enable them to control the environment in which we must live; others might dip their fingers into the stream of the human unconscious and come away with a basic understanding of the arcane laws that govern existence here on earth. The study of the Art was intensely personal, and we competed against no one but ourselves.

But there were three of us who, from the beginning, excelled above the others at the Practice. We couldn't help noticing. And we couldn't stop, no matter how we disciplined our minds, the thread of ambition from snaking into our days. It was inevitable, I suppose, that that ambition should bring us into conflict. But even we would not have sought conflict within the mastery of one of the most dangerous and complex of all the mystic arts—nor could we have guessed how deeply, in the end, it would bind us together.

**It** is quite one thing to perform the mysteries on inanimate objects, to cause boulders to melt into lava, to dry up a stream with the force of one's breath, for it is well-known that all things exist in all forms at all times; it's merely a matter of learned skills to shift them from one state into another. But to transform *oneself*—that is the thing that will tempt and terrify every Practitioner, in one form or another, for as long as he lives. Many an adept, quite competent in all other areas, will never achieve the state of simple Oneness that is necessary to become another living being. But for the three of us, in that long-ago time in the House of Ra, the gift came easily. Perhaps too easily.

There has been much debate over the millennia as to whether this transformation was a literal, physical transmutation of matter, or an equally literal, but far less demonstrable, transfiguration of spirit. Did I become the frog, or did I merely cast my consciousness into the essence of frog-ness, and did I do it with such power and conviction as to cause others to see me as I saw myself—in the form of a frog? I tell you now it is one and the same. All magic is illusion, and all reality is only what one perceives it to be, and in the world in which we lived the line between these two planes of existence was so faint as to be almost invisible.

So if it will help your modern, Western-scientific mind to accept more easily the occurrences I describe, believe if you will that it was merely a function of the occult mind. That we imagined, and caused others to imagine, those things that seem impossible for you to believe. I'll not argue the point. Imagination can stop a heart, you know, or break a bone, or alter the face of time, and in the end it is all the same to those whose lives are affected.

Still, I should not wish you to think that it was a casual thing, this shedding of one form to become another, or that it might be summoned at random will. Quite the contrary. Most of us will never master anything more than simple animal forms—the frog, the fish, the bird or snake. Ah, but to attain transmutation to any form was a wonder almost too exquisite to bear; so intensely involving was it, so deeply, singularly pleasurable, that there was a real danger in giving oneself over to it so completely that one lost all desire to change back, and soon forgot how. Our history is rich with tales of such unfortunate occurrences: the prince trapped in the form of a frog, the lovers transformed into swans, the virgin who changed herself into a tree—and neglected to change back. Oh, believe me, I know the temptation. I know the pain of choice.

By the time I attempted to transform into a bird I had already mastered the sinuous silky lightning-quick form of the snake, with its incredibly enhanced olfactory senses that opened to me a hundred thousand scents and shades of scents I had never imagined before. I knew what it was to lie motionless on a branch in the form of a tree worm, surrounded by green, imbued with green, awash in the splendor of an infinity of green. I had breathed water through my lungs instead of air, I had seen colors in the muddy waters of the Nile that no one else knew were there. But to be a bird. To be lifted up by a breath of wind, to have all the world spread out beneath my wings . . . this I wanted beyond all things.

I practiced relentlessly, striving for the exact harmonic, the precise state of nothingness which would allow the molecules of my body to shift their composition that minute fraction that would allow my form to melt away and then, with exquisite timing and singular command of the universal laws, to synchronize my being into the form I held clear in my mind. Oh, I came close. I watched with a detached consciousness as my fingers stretched into feathers, and I felt in my body the tingling and prickling, the delightful whispering sensation as a breeze ruffled the pinfeathers on the underside of my barely formed wings. I felt my toes curl into claws, bony and strong, and deep in the core of me I felt consciousness begin to shift and dissolve. And then I heard the laughter.

My heart, which already had begun to shrink, molecule by molecule, into the tiny avian muscle required for what I was becoming, exploded to its full size with an abruptness that trapped blood in its gasping valves and sent a shocking stab of pain through my chest. Porous bones abruptly hardened, snapping several small ligaments in my toes as they straightened too suddenly into their human shape again. I screamed with pain, grabbing at my injured limb, hopping on one foot as I jerked around, seeking the source of the laughter. I fell in the sand, and she only laughed harder.

It was Nefar, one of only five female adepts in the House of Ra at that time. I had alternately adored her and resented her since the day I reached puberty.

Much has been written about the role of women in ancient rites and in the various mystic disciplines. They have been alternately portrayed as either purveyors of great power and superior skill, or as having been barred entirely from the pursuit of the arcane arts, objects of scorn and superstitious fear. I assure you that in the time and place of which I speak, under the great equalizer which was the discipline of the House of Ra, females were valued neither more nor less than males. It was one's adeptness in the craft that mattered. And Nefar was very adept.

I have said before that within the perfection of the Art one competes only against oneself. That would be the ideal. The truth is that any creature of pride will find himself seeking approval, even adulation, for his own accomplishments. In short, I enjoyed it when I was the only one, the first one, or the best one in the mastery of a study. I did not enjoy it when Nefar was. For all my time at the House of Ra there were only two who kept pace with my successes, and even, on occasion, surpassed them. Nefar was one.

"Are you mad?" I roared at her, clutching my twisted toes. "You could have killed me! Even a novice knows better than to interrupt a Practice. But to call you a novice would be a flattery. How dare you follow me! How dare you spy!"

The amusement was wiped from her face as she ran to me, but by the time she had dropped to her knees beside me it had been replaced with annoyance. "Now it's you who flatters himself," she said. "I didn't intend to disturb you. I didn't see you there. Stop writhing like a baby. Let me see."

I knocked her hand away as she tried to examine my foot, but the pain that shot up my leg almost shamed me with a cry. When she reached again for my foot I pressed my lips tightly together and did not resist.

The three middle toes of my right foot were randomly askew,

knotted and swollen and already beginning to turn blue. I felt a certain satisfaction at the look on her face when she saw what she had done, but it was short-lived and hardly worth the pain I was enduring.

The regret on her face was quickly disguised by indifference, and in an easy competent movement she passed her fingers over my toes from base to tip, swiftly straightening them. The sensation was like warm oil being massaged into the skin, the muscles, the sinew and bones; no, it was like a small sun being captured inside my bloodstream, spreading its radiant warmth in a cascading bright wave to the ends of my toes. The pain was not simply taken away. It was replaced by a localized euphoria that seemed to glow throughout my foot. The torn ligaments straightened and knitted, the blood and fluids that engorged my injured tissue gradually seeped away. My toes regained their healthy shape and color.

It was a simple energy transference, a natural healing. I would have done the same for her. But, still, it took my breath away.

"Was anything else damaged?" she inquired.

I shook my head, slowly flexing my toes. Now that she had removed her hands, some of the soreness was returning, as naturally it would, but full function was restored. "I think that was it," I admitted grudgingly.

Then I scowled at her. "What did you mean, you didn't see me? I'm the only one out here! What were you laughing at?"

She sat back on her knees, allowing her dark eyes to take on the glint of subtle amusement. "No, you're not," she said.

My impatience was showing. "I'm not what?"

"The only one out here."

A breeze blew a strand of dark hair across her face. She brushed it back with the fingers of one hand on her way to lifting those fingers to the sky. Her eyes turned silvery with the sun as her gaze followed her hand, and her face relaxed into a smile of pure pleasure.

I followed her gesture with a frown, and then I caught my breath. Silhouetted deep against a sky so bright it was almost white was the magnificent shape of a large falcon. Only it was not a falcon at all.

I let out my breath in a single word. "Akan."

"I wasn't laughing at you," she said softly beside me. "I was laughing because . . . it was just so beautiful."

The bird swept, it soared, it glided on a current of air; it turned lazily into the sun, it climbed swiftly and was in a moment only a dark speck upon the vast emptiness of the sky. And then in a rush of powerfully engineered wings he sped toward us, he dived for the ground, he drew so close that his shadow made my pupils dilate and I could hear the air that fluttered through his wings; I could almost count the feathers on his belly. And I hated him with a hot bitter envy that tasted like shame in my throat.

Akan. A quiet, studious boy who was generally disliked by his fellow students if for no other reason than that he kept so much to himself, and that he achieved—and often excelled in—almost every task assigned to him on the first attempt. He was the only other student—aside from Nefar—who could overshadow my own accomplishments. And now he was shadowing me literally, from the sky where I longed to be, a brutal mockery of my own pathetic attempts.

I couldn't watch anymore. Jealousy was making me ill, and the violence of my emotions had ensured no further Practice would be possible today. With a sharp breath I tore my gaze away from the hypnotic grace of the creature in the sky, and I prepared to lunge to my feet.

Her voice stopped me. "He reads the Dark Arcana, you know."

I stared at her. "Impossible. Not even the Masters—"

She shrugged. "The Masters don't know." Her eyes left the sky reluctantly and lost their silvery sheen as they came to focus on me. "I followed him one night to the upper library. It's not locked. Anyone can just go in and read what he likes."

"I doubt it's that simple." But despite the cynicism in my voice, I was intrigued.

"Perhaps not," she admitted. "I think the trick must be to understand what you're reading."

"Do you think he does?"

Again she shrugged. "I don't think it matters."

In that I supposed she was right. Whether his secret excursions were ever known or not, whether he himself ever learned enough to comprehend what he read, the very fact that he *tried* made him quite a different sort of boy than I had previously imagined. Oddly, I could not decide whether my new assessment of him was based on respect, or pity.

I looked at her, a little uneasy now. "Have you ever . . ." I gestured rather awkwardly toward the sky, though I could not bear to turn my head to see whether the bird still soared there.

She sighed. "No. Simple plant organisms are all I've been able to manage."

I was absurdly pleased. In that, at least, I had not been outshone.

"But Master says that once you demonstrate an ability to control the concepts, the bridge to animal life is really just a matter of realignment. And most animal forms are—"

"Merely imagined," I finished absently, by rote.

Reluctantly, I raised my eyes to the sky again. He sailed far away now, toward the banks of the river, wings dipped, riding the current. "Shouldn't he be getting tired?"

"He hasn't been up that long. And besides . . ." She flashed me a grin. "Who can say what is 'tired' to a bird?"

I stood abruptly. "Move away," I said.

She got to her feet in no great hurry, eyeing me with an odd mixture of amusement and wariness. "You don't mean to try a transformation now, do you? It's quite against the rules."

The rule she referred to concerned the necessity of undertaking advanced forms of the Practice in absolute privacy, which is why I had come to the edge of the desert to practice. A reminder of the danger of breaking that rule still throbbed in my sore toes as I tried to find my balance, stretching my muscles.

"Go then," I responded irritably. "Or stay. It makes no difference to me."

"Do you think you can?"

Ah, vanity. Even an adolescent Practitioner such as I should have known better than to succumb to its charms.

"Of course I can. I would have finished the thing before if you hadn't interrupted."

I thought she eyed me with new respect. "I think I'll stay, then."

Too late I realized that the admiration I had imagined in her face was in fact skepticism, and already I regretted the flash of temper that led me to make the claim.

I remembered snatches of overheard stories, whispered late at night, tales of such horror they must surely be apocryphal: the young adept who attempted to transform himself into a snake and baked to death beneath the merciless sun, having forgotten his skin. Another who died a slow and horrible death when his lungs reconstructed themselves on the outside of his body, and another who spent the remainder of his tortured days with the forequarters of a cat. Just stories, surely. But still, this was serious business, not to be undertaken lightly or for show. I couldn't believe I had let myself be goaded into such a position.

Nonetheless, I squared my feet, opened my palms, closed my eyes. I sought my center. And within moments I knew that nothing was going to happen today except my humiliation.

Such a complex transformation can take hours, even days, of concentrated effort, even for experienced Practitioners. It is not a matter of simple desire giving way to manifestation, even for the most advanced of us. There are a thousand steps, a hundred thousand tiny transformations that first must occur inside before an outward transformation can begin, and if even one of them is incomplete, the whole will collapse. Like all magic, it is a science as much as an art.

I was weary from my previous efforts, distracted by the presence of the girl, angry and annoyed, and my toes hurt. I couldn't even summon a quiet breath.

I was just about to turn on her, full of defeat and blame, when the most amazing thing happened. I felt her hand touch mine, and the tingle of energy transference that was much like what she had used to heal my toes. I was confused. The sensation was pleasant but pointless, mildly energizing but baffling. I hesitated just a moment before opening my eyes, and in that moment everything changed. Upon the white screen of my closed eyes I saw the shadow of a wing, I felt the kiss of a feather-borne breeze upon my cheek and heard the purring rustle of flight. Nefar gasped aloud. I opened my eyes.

Akan swept down, and captured me in his shadow. His wings brushed my face and ruffled through my hair and something sweet and pure and powerful passed from the essence of him into the essence of me. It was terrifying, it was consuming, it was the shock of a raging river tearing through my soul and suddenly I knew—as simply as that, I *knew*—the state of being a falcon. In effortless ecstasy I sank into the Oneness, on the wings of his shadow I was borne into the air. I was flying. I was feather and cartilage and air-filled bone; I was a bird.

The girl Nefar grew smaller and smaller beneath us, her eyes, wide with yearning as she followed our progress, and then I laughed, but the sound was wild and shrieking, a thrilling alien thing in my throat. I looked at my companion, my classmate, this creature I had never known, and I felt his surprise, which was as full as mine, I knew his excitement and, yes, his amazement. I let sound pour forth from my throat again, and he answered with a sound of his own, a joyous, piercing screech that flowed into my lungs like breath and buoyed me upward, spinning and turning, on currents of pure, unadulterated delight.

How beautiful he was, this powerful creature who soared beside me with the sunlight glinting like gold upon his wings, each feather ruffling with an individual rhythm as it manipulated the force of the air it encountered; and he was huge, the expanse of his wings seeming as broad as a barge there against the brilliant blank nothingness of the sky; huge but graceful, a master of grace so exquisite it could have brought tears to my human eyes. And how beautiful *I* was, a thing sculpted of fire and breath, master of all that lay below and all that swept beyond.

I was wonder, I was joy, I was the sound of every ecstatic cry that has ever been uttered and every laugh that has ever escaped a throat and every song that has ever been sung; I was rapture.

We glided and soared, climbing high and drifting low. The fertile valley of the Nile was a patchwork of color and random texture, now the tops of trees were barely distinguishable, and now so close that individual eggs could be discerned in their nests. We made a wide swooping circle, returning by accident or instinct to the place at the edge of the desert where we had left Nefar. She was so small beneath us, such a speck upon the vastness of the world that was unfolding before us and so irrelevant to our self-absorbed magnificence, that for a time we did not notice her. But there was, perhaps, still some impulse toward a recognition of our own kind, and gradually we circled toward her.

She came into sharper and sharper focus below us, a tiny clay doll, no bigger than a bead upon a necklace; now a carving on a tablet, now a girl, fully grown. She had assumed the posture of Transformation, her palms turned upward, her head thrown back, the power of her intent a palpable thing. It drew us like a sweet perfume, and we had no thought to resist.

We circled her, Akan and I, we performed a joyous dance in wing and dive; we soared high, we swooped low; from our simple, joyous, airborne state we teased and called and beckoned her. How did it occur, this magic we spun and gathered and set flaming between us? Even now I can't describe it. It was the product of what was within her multiplied by what was within us and augmented exponentially by what we all, together, became. It was impossible; it was undeniable as, in a single moment of consummate purity, she too was transformed. We were three.

I cannot say how long we soared in the ecstasy of a world newly discovered: hours, or mere minutes? When the breakdown came, it was abrupt, and it was terrifying. The first sign I had was a whirlwind of feathers, blowing into my face. I saw that they came from the rich mahogany form of Nefar, who had been flying above and before me, but who was now descending rapidly. Even before I understood that the cries she made were no longer joyful but filled with panic, I felt my own feathers begin to stiffen, and to crack. No longer the living, breathing bearers of light and air that had borne me aloft, they now were brittle and dead, falling from my body like leaves from a tree in a high wind. My bones began to lose their porosity, grew heavy and clumsy, causing me to lose my balance and my navigational instincts; I spun helplessly in the air, sky and earth, earth and sky, the former growing rapidly and alarmingly close with each turn.

Vaguely I saw Akan tumble past me, I heard my own panicked screams echoed in his. Dark fields roared toward me, sharp towers of trees, a flash of blue-green that I thought might be water. I tried to propel myself toward it with some thought of a water landing, but I overshot the mark and nothing but hard desert floor rushed at me with nauseating speed, flashes of gold and white and blue-streaked sky pulsed before my eyes. The merest vestiges of what was bird were left in me then, and though I summoned all the force of my will, I knew I would not be able to hold on to even those much longer.

When the ground was so close I could feel the heat of it blasting up to me, so close I could almost see the individual grains of sand, I invoked all the strength that was left in me into a single, focused manifestation. It was enough. I was able to maintain my form just long enough to slow my descent in those last few crucial seconds, and though I hit the ground hard, it was with no more force than if had I jumped from the branches of a middle-high olive tree.

The fall, and the abrupt transformation into boy again, left me gasping on empty lungs like a fish flopping on a dry bank. It was long painful moments before my head cleared, my breath returned, and my internal organs began to function properly again. Blood pumped, neurons sparked their rapid-fire delivery of information to the brain, glands secreted their life-balancing enzymes, digestive juices flowed. I saw, not far from me, the boy Akan slowly straightening from a slumped position in the sand, and beside him, Nefar. Both of them looked as stunned as I felt.

And then, slowly, a grin began to spread over Nefar's face, and Akan's, and then we were laughing, all of us, great whoops of incredulous, celebratory laughter that sounded, on that still bright day, not so different from the cry of wild birds. I crawled over to them, splashing through the sand as though it were water, and I threw my arms around them; I hugged their sweaty, gritty bodies to mine and they embraced me to them in the same motion, and we were for that moment united in wonder just as we had been in flight. I felt complete—yes, *complete,* in all the many complex and varied permutations of the word—for the first time in my life.

Our words tumbled over each other. "How—"

"Why—"

"Did you see? Did you see what we did?"

"What happened? How is it possible—"

And then Nefar said, "Don't you see? *That* is why it is forbidden to Practice in the presence of another!" Her face was dirty and streaked with sweat and tears, but her eyes were shining like coals aflame. "It was all of us together, *that's* what made the difference!"

I looked at Akan, my heart racing, my thoughts tumbling over each other. It made such perfect sense, I could not believe no one had thought of it before. "Did you know this?" I asked him breathlessly.

He shook his head slowly, his dark, heavily lashed eyes somber with awed consideration as he looked at Nefar. "It took me sixteen hours to achieve flight," he said, "and this after practicing the technique for over a year. I meant only to tease you when I swooped down, but then . . . it was as though I was caught in the net of your intent . . ."

I nodded eagerly even as I corrected, "Not mine. Ours." I glanced at Nefar. "She did a vitality transference—"

"I only wanted to see if it would help," Nefar interrupted, and her excitement was so intense I could feel it quivering in her skin and see it dancing in her eyes like illuminations on a night sky. "I didn't think, I never guessed—and then it was like lava, coming faster and hotter than it could be contained—"

"A sandstorm," I illuminated, "sweeping away everything in its path—"

"A stone tumbling down a cliff," said Akan thoughtfully, "gathering more and more stones as it falls faster and faster until, by the time it reaches the bottom it is large enough to bury a village. A single stone."

We were silent for a moment, contemplating the implications of this—or at least, contemplating in as much as we were able, given the high degree of our excitability and the dozens, perhaps hundreds of other possibilities that were leaping about in our heads. Finally, I could contain myself no longer. "Do you suppose—"

And almost at the same moment Nefar said, "Let's do it again!"

Akan said, "We should be methodical. We should try to manifest something else."

"No." Nefar got to her feet, reaching out her hands for both of us, and, shaking her hair away from her face, she drew in a deep, delighted breath. Her eyes were radiant. "I want to fly!"

And fly we did, rash, foolish youths that we were, again and again seeking the heights and diving low, riding the waves of air and our exuberance with equal confidence. Not once did we question what had caused the near disaster of our first midair failure, or if we did we did not dwell upon it for long. It never happened again, and there was so much for us to embrace and explore that we had no patience for dull and futile worries.

I look back and I can see us still, soaring high over the sun-baked deserts and fertile fields of long-ago Egypt, borne upon rising currents of warm air higher and higher and higher still until we tasted the cold of a sky unknown to us, with all the world spread out below us in a golden unending expanse, bound together in ecstasy and the thrill of discovery, gods of all we surveyed. And I know now that was the moment our destinies were sealed.

# Two

✣

After that day we were inseparable, Nefar and Akan and I. Akan the devout, whose thirst for knowledge was matched only by his hunger for truth, a good and generous soul whose quest for enlightenment was incomplete until he had shared its benefits with all those around him; Nefar, brilliant and beautiful, and as filled with wonder and glorious, untrammeled ambition as I was; myself, equal parts unsullied confidence and reckless appetite for adventure—we knew no boundaries, the three of us. We suffered no limitations to be put upon us. We were an entity unto ourselves, the most accomplished acolytes ever to learn the lessons of the House of Ra.

We were golden.

Much has been made of this business of turning lead into gold, of the philosopher's stone that could transmute materials from one state into another, that could produce powerful healing potions and grant its possessor uncanny knowledge. They call it alchemy. Child's play, all of it, the stuff of chemists and metallurgists. There is not one philosopher's stone but many, and we knew the secrets of them all. Could we make gold? Of course we could; how else should you imagine Egypt became the richest country in the history of the world? But why should we bother, when it was so much easier to make men *think* what they saw was gold?

The real alchemy is not in the physical world, you see, but in the world of spirit and will. The real magic is to take that which once lived only in imagination and cause it to live on earth. To transmute desires into reality. To control the elements and the ether, to know the terror and the thrill of balancing between this world and the next. To delve into the shadows and bring forth substance. To know the hearts of men. These were the secrets we learned. And more.

But there was a price for the knowledge, a payment for the power, and it was discipline. Just as we learned the laws of physics and metaphysics, we were steeped in the laws of our own Philosophy, immutable laws, an unbreachable Code. We must never use our powers to kill, or our knowledge to terrorize. We must not practice, nor attempt to practice, the Dark Arcana—those magical rites that dealt with conjuring human life, altering human life, transmuting ourselves into or transferring our consciousness into another human. That these things could be done were accepted without question. That we would never seek the power to do them was an oath we gave in blind innocence.

We must not reveal the secrets of our order, nor the truths behind our skills. We might observe and advise, but we must never, under any circumstances, control—whether it be a man, or a nation. We must at all times maintain the balance that is the natural state of all things. This was our charge, and our destiny. We were trained to rule the world, and sworn not to.

And before we were done, our little triumvirate would have broken every one of those laws.

But here is the truth that every human who ever gained wisdom must know: power, even when misused, even when in the hands of the young and inexperienced who drink its effects like a potent wine, is not in and of itself evil. It must be enjoyed, explored, reveled in; it must be inhaled, embraced, savored. Dip your hands deep into the well of forbidden power, let it drip from your fingers like fragrant oil. Bathe in it, dance in it, take it inside your body and roll it on your tongue. Know its every secret, its very shape and form, its smell and texture. Use it, and be used by it. Become it. Then, and only then, can you—can power itself—be transmuted.

So you see what we did was not evil. It was simply inevitable.

* * *

It was years, I cannot say how many, before we were found out—or I should say, before the Masters chose to let it be known that we were found out. What a delicately balanced world of wonder and naïveté we lived in, we three arrogant youths who held the secrets that controlled the universe in our hands but never imagined what secrets might lurk in the hearts of those who controlled *us*.

The first secret we learned was born of that long-ago day when we flew as birds: that our power, when combined among the three of us, greatly exceeded its source. We could feel it like molten lava rolling through our veins when we came together in like intent and concentrated will, a slow-swelling stream of energy that soon became a tidal wave that both thrilled and terrified us with its potential. The goblet we meant only to levitate exploded into dust in midair, the fox we had intended to enchant died horribly in our mental grasp. But from these early mistakes great lessons were learned and soon we were performing feats only the most accomplished of Practitioners dared try, and always we were looking for more.

No one actually ever told us that such a combining of power was forbidden; in our self-centered ignorance we imagined no one had ever thought of it before. Still we kept the extent of our accomplishment among ourselves, practicing always in private, making certain that the Masters saw in us no more than they expected to see. We weren't doing anything wrong. But we concealed it anyway.

The House of Ra was built deep in the heart of upper Egypt, a long and dangerous trek from any village or route of travel, a man-made paradise that ended abruptly in sun-baked desert on all sides. The others, Masters and students alike, rarely left the grounds. It was therefore to the desert that we three inevitably went. There, beneath the still pale shadow of the sandstone cliffs, we imagined we were alone.

On the day of which I speak, we undertook the challenge of the Invisible Bridge. Much has been written over the ages about this phenomenon: is it an illusion, a trick of mirrors, a spiritual concept alone? I will tell you now that to our immature minds it was none of those things. It was quite simply the difference between a safe passage across empty space and a precipitous plunge to the deadly stones a hundred meters or more below.

"We will fix in our minds," said Akan, whose idea such experiments often were, "a solid bridge that spans the length from this cliff to that one, beyond. There's nothing complete about it."

"It's an awfully long way," Nefar said doubtfully.

"Not so long as that," I felt compelled to argue, but the effort it took to conceal my uneasiness was considerable. The two sections of cliff were farther apart than I could see, and the distance to the ground was great. Of course such things mattered only in the material world. I, who had flown as a falcon, had no need to concern myself with such mendacities. Yet a hot dry wind combed through our hair and tugged at our clothes, and I could not help thinking about the difficulty in maintaining one's balance while crossing a bridge one could not see.

Akan said, "It is a simple manifestation. We've done them before."

"We've never done an invisibility manifestation before," she pointed out.

"That's what makes it a challenge," he said with a grin that was as unexpected as it was beautiful on his saturnine features. "Otherwise, we shouldn't need you at all, foolish girl."

"I'd like to see you try it without me," she retorted.

I picked up the challenge, teasing her. "Oh, we would build a magnificent bridge without you. You should only imagine the grandeur of the bridge Akan and I could build without your interference—"

"Using ropes and pulleys and a thousand slaves to do your bidding," she said, and we laughed.

We were each accomplished Practitioners in our own right; there was no doubt of that. Yet when we paired up—whether it be the two males, or either male in combination with Nefar—our magic was no greater than could be accomplished by either of us alone. Only between the three of us did the power escalate to the outrageous, emboldening and sometimes terrifying proportions we had come to revel in, even to crave. Akan thought it had something to do with the mathematic harmony created by the number three. I suspected there must be more to it than that, but had learned to trust Akan's opinion concerning intellectual matters and did not argue. Besides, I had no better explanation.

"Anyway," Nefar said with a sudden impatient gesture. "What purpose is there in a bridge that will take us from the top of one deserted cliff to the top of another? We'll still be nowhere!"

Akan and I were surprised. "Where would you prefer to be?"

She looked equally astonished at our question. "Don't you have any imagination? Do you plan to stay here forever?"

To be honest, I had never thought about it at all. I could tell by the impassioned look in Nefar's eyes that I should be embarrassed for that, and it made me defensive. "We could," I insisted. "We could stay and become Masters."

Nefar dismissed the consideration the way she would wave away an annoying insect. "Not me. There's far too much for me to see and do to spend my life confined on an oasis in the middle of the desert."

We did know something of the outside world, those of us at the House of Ra. Every third year we were taken, under close supervision, to a different town or village or settlement where we observed the life of ordinary people and participated in the workings of the ordinary world. We had seen Thebes with its grand temples and palatial estates on the banks of the Nile; we had roamed the alleyways of lesser settlements disguised as street urchins and tasted the life of the common man; we had seen the great barges and sailing ships lined up upon the azure crescent of the Mediterranean, bound for destinations unknown.

There was much to excite the mind in all of this, I suppose, and much to titillate the senses. But it seemed to me the world outside this protected oasis consisted greatly of malodorous alleyways and naked children with foamy diarrhea who squatted in the streets, of cutthroat camel drivers and brawling tradesmen in dusty taverns. The food had no taste, the brew no substance. The world outside was an interesting place to visit, observe, and speculate about. But I had truthfully never spent much time wishing to be there.

Akan said softly, "Just imagine what we could bring to the world, the three of us. Grain that grows in half a season and doesn't rot in the storage house. Water enough to turn this entire desert to green." His eyes shone with the cautious awe of an inveterate dreamer as he turned to us. "A potion that can cure disease with a single drop—and not just one disease, but all of them, and cause them to be gone forever. Camels that live to be a hundred and cattle that grow fat on half the normal ration. Even poor men should live in palaces and—"

"And we should be gods!" cried Nefar, flinging wide her arms and tossing back her head to catch the wind.

"But first," I said dryly, "we must learn to make the bridge."

"A simple matter for gods," replied Akan with another one of his rare glimpses of humor, and we laughed.

But in a moment Nefar grew serious again, and she caught us each in her gaze, first separately and then together. "We're old enough to take the Passage," she said.

In the silence we could almost hear each other's thoughts. The great sun blazed and the wind tossed little rivulets of sand across our bare feet. On a ledge below us a green lizard sunned. Above us a hawk glided in a wide lazy ellipse over the oasis. For a moment no one spoke.

Then Akan said, "It's not a matter of age. It's a question of skill." He had a tendency to be pedantic.

"Then we are overqualified."

The Passage was, in its simplest explanation, a conclusion ceremony by which acolytes left their apprenticeship and went out into the world as full Practitioners. But the ritual was so steeped in mystery and secrecy that very little was known about it at all. Only one or two of the students present at the House of Ra in any given year were chosen to take the Passage, and the ceremony itself was attended by only a select group of Masters. Once having completed the Passage, the newly anointed Practitioner left the House of Ra and never returned, so no one could say with certainty exactly what the ceremony entailed.

One might leave the House of Ra in other ways, of course—to earn one's living as a chemist or purveyor of minor magic, as a temple priest or a court magician. But only through the Passage could one achieve that rare greatness for which the House of Ra existed. Like all precious and mysterious things, such distinction was deeply coveted, and privately suspected.

I said with studied casualness, "I could grow to like the life of a High Priest well enough, I suppose. But I don't think they'll send the three of us to the same temple, do you?"

That was, of course, the underlying concern that each of us shared about the future. We would be separated.

Akan lowered his eyes. We were silent for a moment.

Nefar looked at me. And then she said, rather quietly, "What makes you think the Passage will lead to a position as a High Priest?"

I was confused. "What else could it be? Only the most elite—"

Akan said, "What if it's something better? Something more important, more valuable even than a position as a High Priest that the Passage qualifies you for?"

I laughed. "Like what? Pharaoh?"

Nefar scowled her exasperation. "Don't be absurd, silly boy. Pharoah would bow quaking before us, and so would any High Priest you care to name. *No one* can outshine us, don't you understand that? No one!"

I considered that for a moment, but had no argument. I grinned slowly. "I wouldn't have said it myself, but I think you may be right." It was a glorious feeling.

Akan opened his mouth as though to say more, and then seemed to change his mind in mid-breath. "Come," he said, extending his hands to us. "A bridge."

Why did we wish to do such a thing? you may well ask. There was no point, no reward, no accolades to be gained from our unknowing peers for our accomplishment. But why, then, does reckless youth ever set its headlong course on any untried path? Because the thing is there to be done, that is all. And so we set out to do it.

The sun had begun to shoot ragged streaks of magenta and boiled gold low upon the horizon as we three set the potency to spinning between us, rooted it in the ground far below, let it rise up strong and steady before us. Our fingers were linked, our breaths still, our intention set. We would walk the bridge together, in a single line, hands held. As it happened, when we turned to face the edge of the cliff, I was the first in line.

I could feel the vitality pulsing through me, a strange harmonic that altered the state of my being on a level that went beyond the visceral, that seemed to go into the very particles of being that even *thought* about being me. I was not the boy Han. I was not a set of eyes and ears and lungs to breathe and fingers to grasp and tongue to speak and legs to stand as I had been only moments previously. I was something now entirely different, an entity subservient to, bound by and yet in complete mastery of a power it had itself created. I was no longer *I* but *we*, and the plane of existence upon which I breathed and moved and thought bore very little resemblance to that which nurtured more ordinary beings.

Still, with the thrum of their vitality coursing through me and the certainty of my own will strengthening me, it was a terrifying thing to face the vast emptiness between earth below and the clifftop on which we stood, to place one foot into the air and feel nothing but air, to edge the other foot slowly, timidly, toward the edge of the cliff and listen to the sickening hollow clatter of pebbles as they tumbled so far to the ground below and landed at last with a dull and tiny sound, inconsequential in the hugeness of the space they had traversed. Nefar's fingers were in mine, hot, alive, singing with power. I focused my eyes on the opposite cliff. I stepped out into nothingness. And I did not fall.

I took a step, and another. I felt nothing against the bottoms of my feet but the breeze, only air streamed past my ankles. Behind me, I heard Nefar's laugh, the music of sheer delight, and I knew she too had stepped onto the invisible bridge. I looked down at my feet—and beyond them into the chasm below. I laughed out loud too. I turned to see that Akan had stepped into the air as well, and his hands were raised high in triumph, his eyes alight with joy. *Look at us, creatures below and creatures above. Look at three magnificent youths who stand astride your world and scoff at the rules you must obey. Look at us, young and alive and alight with the potential we have harnessed. Look at us, and call us gods.*

Our eyes met, and then our voices, in a shout of triumph. Akan leapt forward and embraced us both. Nefar danced around us in midair. Wildly emboldened, I propelled myself over her in a somersault. We laughed, we raced, we challenged the fates and our own improbable magic. We were more than halfway across the expanse between the two cliffs when, without warning, it happened.

Nefar was slightly more than an arm's length ahead of me. I recall how the wind sent the length of her night-black hair streaming about her body in playful floating wreaths and strands, and how it snatched and snapped the folds of her garment as it might sails upon a ship. Simply watching her, dancing upon an invisible balancing board of air, struck me with wonder at the magnificence, the simple profound beauty of what we had done, and my appreciation of it was so great that my breath actually caught in my chest for a moment.

I called out to her, "You are a funny-looking bird!"

She spun around, balancing on one foot, to stick out her tongue at me, and then the most awful look of terror came over her face. She teetered, flailing her arms wildly, as though on the edge of a support—which of course was absurd because there *was* no edge to our support. She cried out and lunged toward me; I leapt to meet her, grabbing for her hand, but already she was falling, and my fingernails raked her flesh but grasped nothing.

I screamed, "Nefar!" And her own shrill scream, fading too fast, was all that floated back to me.

I felt something crumbling beneath my feet, balance escaped me, I plunged forward, falling as had Nefar into thin hot air. Then there was a jerk on my arm so fierce as to almost cause it to leave its socket and Akan pulled me against him. *"Run!"* he shouted hoarsely in my ear, and I spared but a single glance backward toward the place Nefar had been before I once again felt something crumbling with the breeze beneath my feet and I ran, I leapt, I threw myself with Akan toward the cliff we had abandoned.

"Nefar!" I gasped. On my belly in the dirt I swung my body around to peer over the edge of the cliff.

Akan clutched my shoulder. "Don't," he said in a choked voice. "Don't look. . . ."

I flung him away. I had to look. My thoughts were racing down the dry desperate corridors of imagination in search of some magic, some enchantment or manifestation or potion we could use to save her, because only moments ago we had been gods and this could not happen to a god. I looked, and magic was what I saw.

"Nefar," I whispered.

She was still falling. She should have been nothing more than a crumpled shape upon the rocks below, but in fact she was airborne some distance above us, a limp tangle of hair and clothing, still falling but falling at a miraculously slowed rate. Beneath her, visible only in glimpses of its shadow upon the rocks, a hawk glided. And as we watched, the hawk began to draw in its wings, to gather itself, stretching and lengthening and transforming itself into the shape of a white-robed man. It caught Nefar in its arms and floated safely the remaining short distance to the ground.

I heard Akan's harsh breathing beside me. I turned and saw his face, ash-gray and streaked with dust, and his eyes dark with shock. My heart was shuddering with such power that my whole body quaked and it was hard to draw a breath. Nonetheless, I somehow managed to get to my feet and, without a word being exchanged between us, Akan and I scrambled down the cliff.

Nefar had recovered from her swoon by the time we reached her. She was sitting against a boulder looking shamefaced and uneasy as she tried to scrub away what were undoubtably the traces of tears on her face with the palm of her hand. Lounging with one shoulder braced against the cliff face and his arms and ankles crossed, waiting for us, was the Master Darius.

It occurs to me that I have said little about the routine matters of education at the House of Ra, and that the temptation might be to imagine orderly classrooms wherein wise and learned teachers strode up and down rows of attentive young students, imparting to us the essentials of science, philosophy, and magic. In truth, there were some subjects we undertook in what was later to be known as the Socratic style, and there were Teachers whose sole duty it was to counsel us in such subjects as mathematics and physics, and to oversee our experiments in chemistry and metallurgy. But the vast majority of our education was undertaken on our own initiative, and conducted at our own pace.

We developed our understanding of the arcane arts by reading and copying the ancient texts, by learning to understand them, and by allowing our own innate skills to unfold. For this part of our education and development, the Masters were solely responsible. They were not our teachers; in fact "to teach" was a verb that seemed to have been left deliberately out of their vocabulary. A closer description of what they were might be "counselor" or "sage," but even that is hardly accurate. Their job was not to teach us but to test us; not to impart wisdom to us, but to make certain we discovered the flaws in our own powers of reasoning; not to encourage us but to torment us. They were at times our most vigilant protectors and at others our most dangerous enemies and our challenge was to know the difference—and, eventually, to understand that there was no difference at all.

Darius was as he appeared to us in those times a starkly handsome youth with loosely styled shoulder-length hair and a strong, muscular form that was somehow shown to advantage even in the loose linen robes he wore. Young women fell in love with him with boring regularity, and so, upon occasion, did young men. He had an interesting, expressive face with lips that were at their best when curved in sardonic humor, and eyes that hardly ever flared with temper. His eyes, on this occasion, reflected little more than lazy amusement, but this we knew meant nothing. The most distinguishing and consistent characteristic of a Master was that at no time was anything he thought or felt discernible in his countenance.

We stumbled to a stop a few feet before them, gasping and streaked with sweat and dirt, and Darius declared mildly, "There they are, my dear, your cohorts in crime." And he sent her spinning toward us with a shove of his fingertip upon her shoulder. "What have you to say for yourselves, young lords?"

Akan caught Nefar against him, inquiring breathlessly, "Are you all right?"

She nodded, still gulping and trying, I could see, not to cry. "It collapsed. It simply—I don't know what happened, it simply . . . wasn't there anymore. I didn't fall, it just—"

"Collapsed, yes, yes," said Darius in a bored tone, with a dismissive twist of his wrist. "As you've said perhaps a dozen times now. Your magic was flawed, of course it wouldn't hold." And his eyes took on a glint that was perhaps not so pleasant as it once had been. "In the same way it was flawed the first time you tried to fly. Fortunately, the consequences of that error were less serious than this one. A few scattered wing feathers hardly compare to a broken girl, do they?"

I looked at Akan. Akan looked at Nefar. I was the first to find my voice.

"How was our magic flawed?" I demanded boldly. "What did we do wrong?"

The silence rang for an instant across the desert floor. He was motionless, only the white of his robes and the hard glitter in his eyes a testament to his presence in the deepening lavender twilight beneath the cliff. I felt pinned by those eyes, pierced by them. My throat went dry, and I knew I could not speak again had my life, and the lives of both my friends, depended upon it.

He burst into laughter. It was a hearty, carefree, young man's laugh that rang upon the canyon walls and scattered across the sands like music. I felt myself relax. Then, as abruptly as it had begun the laughter stopped, and with the grace of a jackal he leapt away from the rock face and landed before me with his arm outstretched. I tried not to gasp or flinch away. In the tips of his fingers he held a living, dancing flame.

For an instant the flame cast colorful, twisting shadows upon the planes of his face, and I could feel the warmth of its glow on my skin even from where I stood. He parted his lips in a grin, light glinted on white teeth. He swept the flame toward Akan and Nefar, startling them, then thrust it at me. I refused to blink. He chuckled, gave a conciliatory little shrug, and made as though to turn away.

Without warning he drew back his arm and flung the flame with a flash of blinding white light and a percussive explosion that shook the ground on which we stood. A blaze erupted to the left of us, crackling and burning on naked sand, consuming nothing but giving forth shimmering waves of heat that scorched my face and made me squint my eyes as I backed away. He spun and drew back his arm again, and another blaze exploded on our right, sucking the nourishment out of the air with the intensity of its heat. Nefar and Akan and I sprang apart, forming a loose semicircle between the two flames like wary herd animals trapped in a blind.

Darius turned to us, smiling. "So now, clever children, tell me. Which is the real fire, and which is the illusion?"

We looked at each other. I could feel the glow of the one blaze on my arm, uncomfortably warm, and I could see the shadows cast by the other jumping and dancing on Nefar's shift. Akan said, "Both are magic. Both are real."

The smile deepened slightly at one corner. "Yet one possesses a significant quality the other does not. So tell me, little bird." He looked at Nefar, his voice soft and pleasant. "If I should take that lovely length of hair of yours in both my hands and hold it over a flame, which one do you suppose would cause it to catch, and burn? The one on my left. . . ." He walked toward her, his hand upturned toward the left. "Or the one on my right?" He opened his hand toward the right.

Nefar did not back down. "Neither," she said, meeting his gaze. "Both are illusion."

He lifted an eyebrow. "Ah. Very clever indeed. An inventive solution to the unsolvable problem. Unfortunately . . ." He closed the distance between them in a single stride and grasped her long hair roughly at the nape of the neck. "It is incorrect. Which one, little bird?"

Nefar made no sound but her nostrils were flared and her eyes wide with fear. I said loudly, "This one." I flung out an arm to my left. "This is the flame that consumes."

He looked at me, his expression still pleasant and implacable. "You're certain?"

I swallowed hard. "Yes."

"Certain enough to risk your pretty friend's lovely head of hair? If you are correct, and I take her here, to the flame nearest me, she will be unharmed. But if you are wrong, alas . . ."

I couldn't look at Nefar. And I couldn't say anything at all.

"Well then, let us see if you've chosen rightly."

I cried out a protest and Akan sprang toward Nefar, but Darius was too swift for both of us. He released Nefar with a suddenness that caused her to stumble and whirled instead toward me, snatching loose the belt that held up my kilt. While my kilt fluttered down around my ankles he sent my belt spinning into the fire to the right of me, the one I had believed to be the illusion. I watched in dry-mouthed horror as it snaked and writhed in the living flame, glowed to ash, crackled to cinders, and was gone.

Darius said, "*That* is why your magic is flawed."

He clapped his hands, and both fires were gone.

I knelt quickly and gathered up my kilt, wrapping it around my waist and holding it there with one hand. My face was hotter now than it had been when the illusory fire had blazed near it, hot with humiliation and anger and defensiveness born of fear.

Darius laughed. "Well, well, my friend. It would appear you have a problem even magic can't fix."

He took the hem of his own shift in his hands, made a tear in the linen, and ripped from it a long strip of cloth. His eyes danced in an easy, friendly fashion as he handed the length of cloth to me. "Sometimes," he advised, "the simplest solution is the best."

I swallowed the lump of embarrassment and indignation in my throat, and tied the sash around my kilt. Darius clapped me on the shoulder, and held out his arm to the others. "Come now, little ones, I'll see you safe to your couches. We can't have such valuable Practitioners wandering about in the desert after dark with the beasts and the snakes, now can we?"

Even in the rapidly gathering gloaming I could see the set of Akan's jaw, and the lift of Nefar's chin. I walked away from the Master's touch, and Nefar and Akan were quick to join me. Darius kept pace with us, exactly as though we were toddling children who could not be trusted to find their way home in the dark. Worse, he kept murmuring lines from some obscure bit of poetry, "Ah, if I but had wings to soar aloft and leave behind this frail shell that binds me . . ." with such deliberate mockery in his tone that I felt my muscles knot.

Akan interrupted him harshly, "How long have you known about us? About what we can do?"

Darius replied without hesitation, "Why, since the day you were born, of course."

We shared a stunned look, and I almost missed a step. Akan drew in a sharp breath, and he said, "You lie."

"Quite frequently."

My thoughts were reeling with the implications of this. All these years we had practiced in such desperate secrecy, thinking we had discovered a rare and unknown talent, while all the while . . . "That would mean that we were *chosen* because of it. Because of what we could do together—"

"Everyone who comes to the House of Ra is chosen for a specific gift. To think yours is greater than any other would be a mistake."

"How could you know that?" demanded Akan. "How could you possibly know that one day we would stumble upon each other, the three of us, and take it into our heads to combine our efforts into one?"

"Dear boy, don't vex me with foolish questions. I will make you a riddle: one of you has something the others do not, and two of you have something the one will forever lack."

Nefar had been observing the interchange thoughtfully, and now she spoke up. "Why? Why did you want us here, together?"

He was so silent as he moved beside us that I had to glance over to make certain he was still there. When he spoke it was not to answer Nefar's question, of course. The Masters rarely, if ever, answered a question that was put directly to them.

"What do you imagine will be your charge when you leave this lovely place in the middle of the desert?" His tone was as of one musing aloud. "Shall you spend the rest of your splendid days in the luxury of a temple, writing your philosophies and perfecting your magic, dining with pharaohs and adorning yourself with jeweled raiment?"

I shot a quick glance at Nefar as I remembered, as I knew she was, our earlier conversation. I began to wonder if we had ever been alone at all.

"Shall you go to court, perhaps, and impress the crowd there with your magnificence, counseling kings and assassins alike, or wander among the common people, dispensing potions and brews? Or perhaps you will travel abroad to exotic lands, and there you will be worshiped as gods. I tell you, you will do all of this. But you will do more."

With a flutter of garments and a move so swift I did not see it, he stood before us, blocking our path. He looked down upon us, and though his face was in shadow, there was in his eyes a look that was as somber as any I had ever seen on any man. He spoke very quietly. "Who do you imagine raises the waters of the Nile and causes them to fall back again? Who will induce an army to rise up against another, or strengthen the arm of a pharaoh or bring issue to the womb of his queen? Who will fill this ship with barrels of precious oil, and cause this one to be dashed against the rocks?

"Shall a hundred people die so that a thousand might live? Shall this village be swept away in the floods so that all of Egypt might fill its storehouses with grain? No, you say? Then how are you to stop the drought that will soon sweep down upon the land, and the pestilence that will follow, and the bodies that will rot in the street and fill the air with poison?" He drew a breath, eyes like polished onyx in the darkness, their glint like the point of the blade. "*That* is why you were brought here. That is your destiny."

We were silent, almost breathless in the dark, staring at him, willing him to say more, for never had a Master or a Teacher spoken to us so clearly about our nature, about our future. Our very imaginations stuttered at the possibilities he had invoked.

He stepped back, and his shoulders seemed to loosen, and the intensity of his expression relaxed into a careless smile. "Then again, as your friend has so wisely pointed out, I have been known to lie.

"Come." He gestured toward the lights that filtered through the palms of our oasis, casting waving shadows upon the distant sand. "You will miss your suppers. But first, little bird . . ." he turned to Nefar, and took her face in his hand, upturning it slightly in an oddly tender gesture. "I will answer your question. No, not the one you spoke. The one you think. You were wondering if you might bed me, and if I drove my power into you, would you come away with a measure of it for your own? Would you steal my vitality as you steal my seed? Perhaps, my dear. Perhaps I shall come to you, and we will see. Perhaps I will slither onto your couch as a snake while you sleep, or float through your draperies as a shadow, or swoop down upon your dreams as a bird of prey. Or perhaps . . ." He dropped his hand, grinning. "I will come to you as a giant cat, little bird, and eat you up!"

He laughed, and stepped back into a pool of shadow. His laughter was still echoing long after he was gone.

We closed the remaining distance to the lights of our temple compound in silence, each of us consumed, I supposed, with our own brooding thoughts. But as we stepped beneath the cooling rustle of the palms once again and heard the familiar music of trickling waterfalls and splashing pools, I shot a curious glance to Nefar. "Is it true what he said of you? Is that what you were thinking?"

She returned nothing but a scowl, and I could see, in the reflected glow of the torches that guarded the entrance to the temple, that her cheeks were flushed. I suppressed a grin.

Akan said thoughtfully, "I think he caused the bridge to fail."

My amusement faded, leaving a kind of hollowness in its wake that went all the way to the pit of my stomach. I said in a moment, without looking at him and in voice that was low and smothered with uneasiness, "Yes. I think so too."

"We might have died."

I said nothing.

We entered the House of Ra with a sense of foreboding I had never experienced before.

# Three

✣

If one stills one's thoughts and quietens one's breath and makes one's heartbeat slow to the merest of whispers; if one softens one's skin and stops the blinking of the eyes and if even the fine hairs upon the arms and legs cease their slow unfurling, one might sink effortlessly into one's surroundings and become, for all intents and purposes, invisible. Witness the cat crouched flat upon the rock while the dog snuffles by mere steps from its prey—yet seeing, smelling, and hearing nothing. For a determined adept, it is not so difficult to master the art of shrouding oneself in this same quiet shield of invisibility while moving through a crowd. But only the boldest of Practitioners would try to maintain invisibility in the presence of others of their kind.

A lack of daring had never been one of Nefar's failings. She glided like a phantom through the late-night corridors of the House, blending into the giant pillars that cast their angled shadows across the marble floors, becoming the breeze that stirred the low-burning torches high on the wall; whispering past a lone stroller, circling a dozing leopard—which may or may not have been a leopard at all but which did not so much as twitch a whisker at her passage. Like liquid she flowed. Like a shadow she floated, until she reached the Chamber of the Masters.

Unlike many of the temples of the time, which were designed in clusters of buildings so elaborate the complex might easily be taken as a small city, the House of Ra was sheltered under a single roof.

Upon initial survey, it was deceptively well contained: an impressive structure whose soaring columns of polished stone supported a roof so high that colorful birds nested in the rafters and the sound of waterfalls tumbling from the heights was at times a roar. There were common rooms decorated with gilded statues and silk-cushioned couches for dining and lounging, there were study areas whose walls were lined with orderly rows of parchment or whose stone tables were scattered with mortars and pestles, balances, tightly sealed jars of oils and dusts and essences and acids. There were recreational pools and indoor hanging gardens, and quiet areas for contemplation or solitary Practice. These common areas were separated from one another and from the private chambers of the students by diaphanous curtains of sheerest silk and finely woven linen, and by the artful arrangement of half walls and blind corners. It was, upon casual survey, a luxurious, but not particularly spacious structure.

Yet what was visible to perfunctory observation represented only a fraction of the chambers and corridors of the House of Ra. A sliding panel here, a hidden staircase there, a revolving niche in another place—it was rumored that no one, during his tenure at the House of Ra, had ever explored them all. But Nefar liked to think she had come closer to mapping all the secrets of the House than most others who had tried.

The corridor that led to the Masters' chambers was accessed by means of wall that was carved with the story of the creation of the earth: an exploding sun in the center from which spun off a number of orbs. When one pressed the center of the exploding sun and at the same time the third orb from that center, the panel pivoted open on a silent hinge. No one had ever specifically forbidden access to these chambers, but very often in the House of Ra one did not discover what was forbidden until one had already suffered the consequences of breaking the rule. Nefar therefore thought it was wisest to do as much as possible to prevent her presence from being detected, until she herself was ready to reveal it.

She had so far been somewhat disappointed in what her explorations had revealed, for the private chambers of the Masters were not so different from those of the students—comfortable couches and silk curtains, bathing chambers and herb-scented toilet facilities. The corridors were not so well lit, perhaps, and the shadows seemed deeper. The smoky fragrance of incense and herbs seemed to be woven into the air of these compartments in the way that oxygen and nitrogen were infused into the air of more ordinary places, making it taste richer and heavier; making the act of breathing a sensual experience. The gauzy fabric that draped the walls seemed in constant, subtle motion, as though stirred by a breeze that was indiscernible to the skin. The rippling motion was slightly disorienting and made it difficult to tell where a wall ended and a private chamber began. She met no one as she moved, silent and invisible, from the fold of a curtain to the curve of a pillar, her feet barely touching the floor, her breath stirring not so much as the hairs in her own nostrils.

And then she heard the murmur of voices, muted by distance, and she stole forward as swiftly as she dared, until the words were intelligible. "Sopdet will rise at dawn two days hence, and on the night that precedes it the moon will be full. I would like to have the ceremony then, if it can be done."

The next voice was familiar in its careless undertone of amusement. "You will find superstition a burdensome baggage for a Practitioner, young lord, useful only when it can be turned against those you wish to impress."

"Your pardon, my lord, my references were chosen only as a matter of sentiment, not superstition." Nefar found this voice, younger, anxious, and quicker in tone, familiar as well, though she could not place the face.

And now a third speaker, his tone deeper and graver than either of the previous two. "No one can force this Passage on you, and if you fail you will not get another chance. If you have any doubts about your readiness—"

"Sir, I have none!" Too loud, too eager. The voice quickly calmed itself. "I most humbly beg that I be allowed to pursue the right that is mine as a full Practitioner who has come into his time."

Now Nefar was able to put a face with the voice, and it both puzzled and excited her. It was a young man by the name of Mirisu, who was close to her own age yet far from approaching her degree of accomplishment. He had once expressed a sexual interest in her and she had laughed and sent him away. He had shrugged off the rejection with ease, and had found another, more receptive, girl within a matter of days—which had annoyed Nefar only slightly. Now he had just been given permission to take the Passage. There was no mistake. If *he* was considered a proper candidate for the Passage, how much more easily might she achieve it?

Darius drawled, "It is unbecoming to beg," while the other Master said, a bit brusquely, "We will honor your request for the ceremony two nights hence. You have been given instructions concerning how to prepare yourself."

Nefar moved closer, trying to position herself for a view of the speakers, who appeared to be gathered in a chamber just beyond a sweep of rose-and-violet drapery. She was growing weak from the effort to maintain her invisibility shield while fighting the curiosity that tugged her deeper and deeper into the world of what was solid and visible. She glided to the edge of the drapery, she melted into its folds. She was rose-and-violet silk sighing in the breeze, she was gossamer and translucent tint; she was little more than nothing at all. She peered into the chamber.

She saw a room not unlike others she had passed—a polished stone floor, a sleeping couch piled with cushions and fine weavings, a table upon which was a jug of wine and some goblets. It was empty.

"Where have you been, little bird? You keep me waiting."

The voice came from behind her, and Nefar whirled, forgetting her shield, abandoning her composure. Darius stood so close she should have felt his breath upon her hair, his warmth upon her skin; not a feather or a leaf could have passed between them he was so close. The familiar amusement sparked in his eyes and his smile was lazy. He gestured toward the chamber. "Do come in. It's impolite to lurk in corridors."

Nefar did not blink. "Did you cast an invisibility shield over the room? Or did you draw the voices from another place—or even another time?"

A corner of his smile deepened. "What voices?"

"If it was an illusion," she continued blandly, "it was a clever one. I would like to learn how it was done."

Without warning or even so much as a previous thought, Nefar flung herself through the drapery and into the room. There she saw, as she had expected, Mirisu and the Master Hay, a tall thin man with an impressive wig and a saturnine demeanor. Neither of them looked around when she appeared, or seemed to notice her at all.

Beside them, lifting his goblet in a salute to the young man, stood Darius.

"I drink to your very good fortune, young Mirisu," said Darius, "and to a decision I hope none of us will come to regret."

Nefar snapped her head around. Darius stood beside her, smiling. She looked back at the three men in the room.

Mirisu raised his own goblet a little uncertainly. "Master, I thank you."

Master Hay drained his goblet and placed it on the table. Mirisu quickly put down his goblet as well, understanding the gesture of dismissal.

"You are cautioned against boasting of your upcoming ceremony," said Master Hay, "and you understand that you will be sent from this house in disgrace should the rite of secrecy be broken."

"I do."

"Then be off with you, and return to us in two days' time."

Mirisu hurried from the room, passing so close that the breeze created by his movement rustled against Nefar's shift. He never even glanced in her direction. Nefar stared once again at Darius, who remained by her side, watching his other self with critical interest.

Said Master Hay, "I have my doubts about this one."

Darius gazed into his goblet. He no longer seemed amused. "It is not for us to judge. The boy himself will do that."

"They always do," agreed Hay.

A silence between the two men. Nefar could hear Darius breathing at her shoulder and feel the light brush of his linen sleeve against her bare arm.

Master Hay glanced at his goblet, saw it was empty, and said, "Well, then. I'm to bed."

He moved toward the door, looked directly at Nefar, and added, "You will mind your manners, I trust?"

Beside her, Darius chuckled. Nefar jerked her head around at him, but he was no longer there. She turned quickly back toward the other Darius, but he was gone too. Master Hay left the room as though nothing were amiss.

Nefar said, with what she imagined to be an extraordinary display of calm, "It was a reflection enchantment, wasn't it?"

"No."

Darius lounged on the couch where no one had been an instant ago, holding out a goblet to her. "Will you have some wine?"

"No." Nefar moved cautiously into the room, trying not to allow her gaze to dart too obviously about her. There was a peculiar quality to the air here, as though the potency that spun around this man had a life of its own, flavoring the air with a hot, dry charge and the taste of molten metal. The quality of the light was different too, sharpening colors and penetrating corners, seeming to illuminate the very air itself so that it shimmered slightly when she blinked her eyes. It was disorienting, and a little terrifying. She knew, even as she moved deeper into it, that what she was experiencing—what she saw and breathed and tasted and took into her very pores—was power in its purest, rawest form.

"Then it must have been a time distortion," she said. Even her voice sounded different in this place, as though she were speaking into a hollow tube. It was with a great deal of effort that she kept her composure, refused to betray her excitement. "I would like to learn how you did it."

"No," he said, and he smiled at her. "Do you still think you're ready for your Passage, little bird?"

Nefar tried to moisten her lips with her tongue, but her mouth was too dry. There was a tingling on her face and neck and in her armpits, and she realized the sensation was caused by her pores, desperately trying to release a cooling mist of perspiration. But the moisture was sucked into nothingness by the arid air before it even reached her skin.

"None of us will ever learn all there is to learn," she said when she was relatively certain of her ability to control her voice. "I believe it was you who said that."

She passed a high stone table and let her fingers rest lightly on its surface for a moment, reassuring herself of its solidity. She felt every bump and scratch, every smooth indentation and every rough scar on the tabletop; she felt the mark of the craftsman's tool and the irregularities of the grinding wheel, she felt a hundred variations of heat and cold and light and dark within the living stone. It was the most *real* sensation she had ever experienced, and it caused her to jerk her hand away as though stung, her breath quickened and her head reeling.

Darius leaned back on one elbow, his ankles crossed, and sipped his wine. "You know it is forbidden for you to be in these apartments."

Nefar swallowed hard. She had the oddest sensation that he could hear her heart pounding, as though it were a drum broadcasting her fear throughout all the House of Ra. The room pulsed with it. "Mirisu was here."

"He was invited. I wonder how many other rules you have broken—or have yet to break."

Nefar focused her gaze on the length of golden dark leg that was exposed by the open fold of his robe to avoid meeting his eyes—and his thoughts, and the power of his magic which, until today, she had thought to have understood. It was so very hot in the room, hotter than the sun at midday but without the sun's power to burn and to weaken. This was an elemental heat, the heat of the earth's molten crust, the heat of lightning as it is formed, the heat of a thought just before it explodes into reality. It crawled through her skin and dried the viscous fluid that protected her eyes and parched her lungs with every breath. Yet it also excited her, emboldened her, and made her feel more intensely alive than she had ever been before.

She squared her shoulders. She met his eyes without a flinch. She said, "Is it I who has the thing the other two lack?"

He laughed. "Is that what you came here to find out? My dear, vanity is a virtue, but I fear you take it to extremes."

She raised her chin, and her gaze did not waver. "Then tell me this. If it had been Akan or Han who had fallen from the bridge, would you have saved them as well?"

"Perhaps a better question would be, what if no one had been there to save you at all?"

Nefar drew in a deep breath. The sparkling air seared her lungs like hot cinders, but oh how sweet it tasted, how heady. "Someone is always there," she said, tossing her head a little. "We are the chosen ones, the acolytes of the House of Ra, you would not waste us so carelessly. Someone is always there."

He looked at her steadily. "Have you learned anything at all in your time here, Nefar?"

"Perhaps more than you think." Another breath. Power, possibilities. She could feel it glowing on her skin, blazing from her skull. "Because I think you would have let them fall."

For a moment he did not react at all. And then he burst into laughter. "Why have you come here, foolish girl? What do you want of me?"

She studied him for a moment. It was difficult to focus through the burning, aching of her dry eye sockets and the dancing quality of the light that wavered like a veil in the breeze between them. "I will tell you that, if you don't know it already, when you answer me a question." How brave she felt, how reckless.

"Only one?" He sipped his wine.

"Has it ever happened before, that three came together with such talent and learned to combine their force to achieve what we have done?"

He held the goblet just beneath his nostrils, as though savoring the aroma of the wine. Above the rim his gaze was unwavering, expressionless. "What do you think?"

The heat in the room had escalated without her noticing, and the tingling sensation in the air pricked like a thousand tiny daggers at her skin. Her nasal passages burned with every breath, and there was a high-pitched ringing in her ears. Still she savored it, she was drunk with it. "I think no; otherwise, we would not have been chosen. I think we are special, and you are afraid of us."

Ah, his eyes. Suddenly she could not move her own gaze away from them, suddenly they were the only thing of import in all the world. They were ablaze, a dark inferno that sucked every cool breath of air from the room and spewed it out again as crackling dry heat. But his face, and his voice, were very calm, almost disinterested. "Why afraid?"

She parted her lips for breath. It was harder than it had been before. Drawing in the air was like inhaling dry steam, and her lungs ached and burned with the effort. Her voice was hoarse, and her throat contracted and wanted to cough. But she held firm. "Because of our power."

Now a faint smile. Lights began to dance in the distant corners of the room, magic bursting to break free.

"Might there be another reason?"

Nefar said, "No." Struggling not to gasp now, trying to calm the frantic pace of a heart that was starved for oxygen.

In the blink of an eye he was beside her, too swiftly to have moved by ordinary means, and he grasped her face between his hot dry hands and he held it hard. Sparks crackled from the swirling tips of his hair and exploded in the air like tiny dry bubbles. His eyes were a slow boiling vortex of churning ice and melted stone, a simmering kinesis of thoughts and possibilities, of violent potential and erupting actuality, of all the power that had ever been. When he spoke she heard his voice not just with her ears but with her skin and her muscles and the viscera that held her together. It seized her spine with hot-cold fingers and spread outward like a thousand pincer-footed spiders and she was paralyzed in its grip.

He said very softly, "You understand that I could crush your skull like a grape between my fingers."

She tried to speak. No sound came. Her heart was like a ripe fruit in her breast, squeezed to the point of bursting. She felt a moisture on her upper lip and welcomed the cooling perspiration, then she tasted iron as the fluid seeped into her mouth and she realized it was blood.

"I could twist your head from your neck and toss it aside, or I could send my thoughts into your brain and cause you to see such things, and know such things, as would make you beg for death, to scream for death."

Her larynx strained but no sound came. She could not feel her fingertips, or her feet. Only the drip of blood from her nostrils, and the taste of iron.

"You are," he said, "completely in my power."

Slowly, by fractions, he relaxed the pressure of his fingers upon her face. A tingling sensation returned to her extremities, her heart beat with a loud irregular thumping, and slow clean breath trickled into her lungs. She brought the back of her hand to her nose, and blotted the blood. The flow had stopped.

She whispered, "Yes."

He smiled. He moved his hand from her face to her hair, where he lightly threaded his fingers through the strands in the affectionate way one might caress a child. He stood so close to her that his breath was her breath and his shadow consumed her. "Think of this, little bird," he said softly. "The one thing you have learned here. Nature will seek its balance. And in the end there must be only two."

He stepped away from her, his manner at once easy and detached. "Now answer my question, if you will. I have answered yours."

Nefar could feel her heart shaking her body, but she strengthened her legs, forced herself to stand her ground. She drew her hand across her nose and her mouth once more, removing the last traces of dried blood. She looked at him. "What I want from you," she said steadily, "is what you have already guessed—your magic. But I don't have to steal it. I have it inside me already, and I think you know that. *That* is why you're afraid. Because I am the one who has the thing the other two lack."

Not a blink of an eye nor a twitch of a muscle. Deep violet shimmers danced against the far walls of the room, like waves of reflected light cast up from the desert floor. The high-pitched ringing decelerated to a hum, and the air seemed not quite so thick as before, not quite so dangerously charged.

The Master said, very quietly, "Go away from me, young one, while you are still able. And never come to this place again."

Nefar turned and left the room. As soon as she was past its threshold, she began to run. She did not stop until she was far from that place, burrowed deep in the safety of her own bed, and there she lay awake shivering with the thrill and the terror until the sun rose to meet the House of Ra.

# Four

That then, was how we came to break our final, and most important rule at the House of Ra.

I think we knew there were parts of her encounter with the Master that Nefar did not tell us, but we did not care. What she had told us was all that mattered. A Passage ceremony would be held with the rising of the next moon. And we would be the first acolytes at the House of Ra to witness it. The idea was as impossible for us to resist as it would have been for any schoolboy who is presented with a foolproof opportunity to cheat on his exams. The Passage, when we took it, would be the most important examination of our lives. It was a matter of practicality, not morality, for us to do whatever we could to gain inside information.

That was what we said aloud to each other. What we did not say, but was equally true, was that the secret of the Passage was, to our young and limited minds, the last great secret of the House of Ra. It was not simply our right, but our duty, to uncover it.

We looked at each other in respectful silence once the decision was made, contemplating in our own small ways the import of it.

And then Nefar said practically, "How?"

We had abandoned the desert as our playground once we realized that nothing we had ever done there had gone unobserved. We sat now beneath a canopy of stars and the rustle of palms, screened from observation by an invisibility shield that the Masters might notice but could not penetrate, our whispered voices lost in the tumble and rush of the waterfall near which we sat. The Masters might be the most powerful Practitioners in the world, but they still were only human and their ears were no sharper than those of any other man or woman who walked the earth. We had learned our lesson well: oftentimes the simplest solution was the best.

Nefar went on, "It's true we may be the first to have foreknowledge of the *time* of a Passage ceremony, but it does us no good if we don't know *where*."

I feigned surprise. "How can it be that there is something you don't know? Do you mean there is one place among all the twists and turns of the corridors of the House of Ra that your secret wanderings have not taken you?"

In truth, I was a little put out that she had undertaken her most recent adventure without us, and I could tell Akan was too. She thought we were jealous, and perhaps we were. But for reasons she could not yet imagine, and even we did not fully understand.

She scowled at me in an absent and dismissive fashion that only irritated me further, and then Akan said, very quietly, "I know where."

The surprise with which we received his words rippled through our joined consciousness with such an effect that our shield wavered, making the world outside appear to my eyes for a fraction of a second like a reflection in a wavy pool. Instantly we righted ourselves, and Nefar and I stared at Akan.

The very faintest ghost of a smile touched his lips, but his eyes looked far away. "I've told you before, there are no secrets in the House of Ra. It's all written down for anyone to see. One has only to learn how to read it."

I said, only barely a breath, "So it's true then? You do read the Dark Arcana?"

He lifted his shoulders in a small shrug. "I read all the Arcana. We're taught to seek balance, aren't we? How can we maintain balance unless we know *all* there is to know—the hidden and the obvious, the dark and light?"

Nefar interrupted him a little impatiently, "But do you understand it? Do you understand what you read?"

He considered the question studiously for a moment. "That's the magic of it, isn't it? Some I understand, some I don't, some I think I understand but am really only supposing . . ." He shrugged again. "It's all a matter of interpretation."

My cautious excitement was replaced by disappointment. "Then what good are you?"

"Maybe none. Maybe . . ." A slow, deep cornered, lopsided grin spread across his face. "All we need. I may not understand everything I read, it's true, but I always remember it." He tapped his head. "It's like a drawing, locked here in my brain, everything I've ever seen. All I have to do is think about it to reproduce it exactly. Especially . . ." And he paused for dramatic effect, for not even Akan, as earnest as he was, could resist trying to impress us whenever he could. "Maps."

We *were* impressed. We stared at him, hardly daring to believe our good fortune. Nefar's voice was a mixture of accusation and wonder as she said, "There's a *map* of the House of Ra? And you've seen it?"

"Portions of it, yes," he admitted. "Enough to get us to the ceremonial chamber, at least. We won't be able to get inside," he cautioned, "as it's a completely sealed room at the center of a maze. But there is a corridor that will lead us down into its center, then open on a ledge above the room. From there we should be able to see everything."

We looked from one to the other, and smiled. No discussion was ever given to the question of whether or not we should. We simply knew that we would.

Ah, what children we were. What simple, fragile, rash, and hopelessly doomed children.

**A**nd so we crept, trembling with excitement of a dark and forbidden adventure, past the prohibited quarters of the Masters, through a turning wall, down a staircase that had been so long unused that the air within was barely breathable; it caused us to choke silently, and then to wheeze and grow dizzy as we moved deeper and deeper into the bowels of the earth. Akan carried a small perpetually illuminated torch that cast a circle of light before us and revealed nothing but more dusty, downward-spiraling stairs. When it seemed we had sucked the place dry of oxygen, when our heads were throbbing and our eyes were burning and the next breath we drew would cause us to fall to the floor, clawing desperately at our throats and weeping dry tears of agony, the stairway abruptly ended in a sandy embankment.

I recall how my heart pounded, how furiously I fought back panic. Had Akan's map been wrong? Had the ancient corridor collapsed years ago, or had it all been a cruel trick to confuse the enemies of the House of Ra?

I looked at Nefar and saw the tight lines of desperation forming around her eyes and her lips, for we dared not waste breath with words. Her fingers sought mine and squeezed hard.

Akan was sweeping his torch over the sand embankment, looking for we knew not what. I knew we didn't have enough air to retrace our steps, but I felt an irrational impulse to turn and run back the way we had come.

There was a solid stone block on my chest and spots danced before my eyes. Akan brushed his hand over the sand, back and forth, and his movements seemed jumpy and unsure, and extraordinarily slow. I felt Nefar's fingers slip from mine and saw her sag against the wall. I knew I too was about to lose consciousness.

When I saw Akan's hand pass through the sand embankment I could not be certain whether it was a hallucination. But then I felt the taste of air, a rushing breeze of cool clean air on my face and in my mouth, and I saw that Akan had merely parted the sands of illusion. On the other side was a tunnel, and we hastily crawled through, drinking in the air like draughts of water. At the end of the tunnel we could see an orangish light, and smell the acrid scent of superheated stone. Voices, deep and powerful in ritual chant, floated back to us and we hurried, our hearts pounding with excitement. Akan had been right. Nefar had been right. We were about to be the first to witness the ritual of the Passage.

We exited the tunnel on our bellies, emerging onto a narrow stone ledge which, as Akan had predicted, overlooked a circular chamber composed of stone and forged metal. We crept to the edge and looked down. The room was filled with a sulfuric glow and a bitter smell. There was a muted roar that seemed to come from underground, and it filled the air with distant thunder. Waves of heat rose upward toward us.

The four Masters, draped in white hooded robes, formed a loose circle in the center of the room, surrounding Mirisu. He was naked, as was only proper for a ceremony of this significance, and his feet and hands were bound, and he was blindfolded. One of the Masters was speaking words in a loud, authoritative voice, but the words were unfamiliar to me. He lifted his arm as though in benediction, and lowered it slowly.

Now it was Darius who spoke, in words that we all could understand, and in a voice powerful enough to be clearly heard over the thrumming background roar that filled the room. "Mirisu, son of Ki and of Obisis, do you undertake this Passage of your own free and joyful will?"

Mirisu's reply, strong and clear, "I do so undertake."

"Walk, then, into your future."

I was aware of Nefar on one side and Akan on the other, the three of us with breaths suspended and heartbeats stilled with the thrill, the awe of what we were witnessing. And then I was aware of our collective horror, rolling like a wave toward us and over us and through us as the floor opened up in the center of the room, revealing a roiling pit of molten flames whose thunderous roar filled the room with choking, gaseous heat. Mirisu walked toward it.

I couldn't scream or move, or do anything but watch as Mirisu's foot went over the edge. He fought horribly for balance for an instant then plunged into the flames. From our vantage point we saw it all. His hair exploded, his skin began to pucker and crisp, and his face—his face contorted in the most intense screams of agony, silent screams that were consumed by the roaring fury of the blaze just as he was, but screams that would nonetheless echo in my mind forever. Before our eyes Mirisu died a screaming, writhing, agonizing death, consumed to the bone by the flames.

Somehow we reached the tunnel; I do not recall how. I remember crawling with such frantic, uncoordinated terror that I lost my balance and splayed flat on my face like a baby, and I remember the taste of sand mixing with the salt of tears in my mouth. I remember Akan dropped his torch and how we fumbled for endless, soul-numbing moments to recover it. And then we were back in the safety of the airless stairway, and the sound that filled my ears was of sobs—my own, and the others.

"They—they *sacrificed* him!" It was Nefar's voice, the sound of a strangulated animal, garbled and toneless with terror. "It was—it is—a blood ritual!"

And Akan kept saying over and over again on a single note like a breath or a talisman, "No no no no no. . . ." Without pause or intonation, just "No no no no no . . ."

I collapsed to my knees and retched, splattering vomit on my clothes and my hands and on Nefar's bare feet, and she didn't notice or try to move away. I retched again and again, and even when my stomach was empty and my breath was gone I couldn't stop it. I couldn't get the taste of burning flesh out of the back of my throat.

The world had simply ended for us that night, in the nightmare chamber of fire and dust. They had killed Mirisu. All we believed to be true about the sacred House of Ra was illusion. The Masters were murderers, the priesthood a lie, and the great House of Ra was nothing but a device to disguise human sacrifice.

Nefar grasped my shoulder, fingers digging like talons into my flesh. "We have to—we have to get out of here!" she gasped.

Even in the yellow light from Akan's shuddering torch I could see her face was ashen, streaked with oily soot and white dust and the channels of tears. I could not help wondering whether the soot upon her face contained the ashes of what once had been Mirisu's flesh, and my stomach heaved again. I gagged unproductively, and she shook me hard.

"We have to get out before they—before they—"

"Yes," said Akan, hoarsely. His voice was shaking, jumping, broken from high to low pitches, and beneath it was the raw panic, the paralysis of loss, that I felt. "A lie. It was all a lie. We have to run. We can't stay here . . ."

*Stay here.* No. We couldn't stay here in this house of horror, we had to warn the others, we had to leave, we had to save ourselves. We had to run.

And so we did, up the long airless staircase, tripping, falling, tugging at one another and pushing past one another, our chests bursting, our throats collapsing, we ran, we stumbled, we crawled until at last we pushed, all abreast, through the turning wall and into the safety of the Masters' corridor.

Only the corridor was not there.

We stumbled through the turning wall into the pit of hell, and there the Masters waited for us. Our desperate flight back through the airless staircase had taken us in a complete circle, and now we were back where we had started . . . except we were no longer looking down upon the stone chamber with its central fiery pit, we were within it.

The roar of the fire was even louder there, and though the flames themselves were below ground, the air shimmered with heat like a curtain waving in the breeze. My lungs burned with every inhalation, the room was so hot, and perspiration soaked my body within seconds.

The Masters simply stood there, virtually unaffected by the heat, looking composed and calm, as though they had been waiting for us. Which of course they had.

Darius came forward. "So," he said, and he looked sad, or perhaps merely tired. "It's time."

I was the first to turn, frantically searching for the latch that would make the wall turn again, and Nefar joined me, running her hands up and over the stone, pressing her weight against it, to no avail. Only Akan stood still and quiet, resigned perhaps, or simply understanding that there was no escape. There never had been.

We were young and foolish, and we forgot we were dealing with the most powerful magicians who had ever lived. There were no secrets in the House of Ra, and the greatest illusion of all was the illusion we had created for ourselves, in thinking we were safe.

Nefar pressed herself flat against the wall as Darius approached. I could hear her panting breath, and I could taste her fear as sharply as I could my own. Yet she kept her head high and her gaze strong as she demanded, "Another one of your grand illusions, Master?"

The very faintest ghost of a smile softened the edges of Darius's mouth, although the great sadness in his eyes only deepened. He extended his hand to her. "Come, little bird," he said softly. "Let us see."

In a movement as swift as a cat's he seized her wrist and spun her toward the pit. It was all over in an instant, less than that, yet each detail was as clear and as sharp as though every portion of the scene occupied its own place in time. The sound of Nefar's scream, its ragged edges slicing through the air like broken glass, occupied a world. A universe collapsed as my own scream joined hers, as I lurched toward her, and then Akan. A star exploded as we saw the heat from the flaming pit billowing her hair and her garments and turning her skin to scarlet, and a wild terror of the soul filling her eyes. All in an instant, yet all so slowly that it spanned a million years.

We rushed forward as one, Akan and I, and wrestled her free.

It happened in a breath. I flung Nefar to safety as Akan tackled Darius. I recall the surprise in Darius's eyes, and the sudden startled movement of the other Masters toward us. They had not expected this. I thought we had won. I thought we might be free. A heartbeat—no, half—and in a motion as fluid as a dance Darius whirled around to break Akan's grip, spinning him toward the pit. I cried out reached for Akan, grasped his wrist, but it was too late. His balance was broken, and we both went over, screaming, into the pit.

The agony of Hell, it has been said, is to burn but not be consumed.

Oh, but first you must be tossed about by currents of searing air, you must see your garments burst into flame from nothing more than the sheer heat of their surroundings, you must struggle to scream and draw flaming ashes into your lungs. I begged to die as my flesh began to crackle and to peel, then exploded in charred strips across my body. Why didn't I die? My guts began to boil, superheated blood burst from my ears and was vomited out my mouth. My eyes melted in their sockets, flesh suppurated and boiled, muscles crisped in their surrounding layer of fat. I felt every exquisite moment of anguish, every agonizing detail with lungs that were too scorched to breathe and a throat too burned to scream. *Oh, let me die. Why can't I die?*

And then there was the most amazing thing. I felt a hand, yes, a hand, grasping the slippery raw flesh of my arm, pulling me up. Slowly my blind eyes began to focus again, and I saw that it was Akan, climbing through the flames with his charred flesh hanging in strips, his hair and lips burned away, his hands consumed to the bone. Yet, impossibly, he had found a foothold on the wall of the pit, and step by step, he guided me up and out.

There were no nerves left in my feet or legs as I pulled myself up and over the edge of the pit; I felt no pain from the slick trail of melted flesh my hands left upon the stone where I grasped, nor from my legs as I dragged them, fraction by fraction, over the coarse floor. My tongue was a shriveled slip of charred flesh pressed against my palate, blocking my breath, and I gagged and coughed, trying to free it.

I became aware of Akan, collapsing next to me on the floor, and I looked at him—yes, I looked, with eyes that once had been cooked in their sockets. He was alive, choking and gagging as was I, but alive. Not only alive, but—*restored.* Glistening scarlet flesh covered his cheeks where once there had been bone. There was a nose where once there had been an empty socket crisscrossed with shrunken cartilage, and lips that had been melted away were now smooth and plump and pomegranate red. I had seen the blackened bones of his fingers and felt their grip upon my arm. Now I saw skin and fingernails.

I became aware that my breath was moving more easily through my lungs, my tongue seemed to be loosening in my mouth. Hesitantly, I looked down at my own naked body. Pink and tender skin covered my wounds. My hands could grip again; the muscles of my legs could flex.

I looked again at Akan. His gaze moved slowly from his outspread hands to my face. I saw in his eyes the same wonder that was in mine. From the flames, we had been reborn.

The room was filled with a reverence so complete that it seemed to muffle even the thunderous roar of the fiery pit. I was aware of the Masters standing over us, paralyzed with awe, and of Nefar, half-crouched upon the floor where I had flung her. Her eyes were wide and still and her fingers were pressed tightly to her lips, as though with their strength she could push back a scream. Did she see monsters when she looked at us, or miracles?

A gurgling sound came from my throat, and I made a furtive, half-completed movement toward her. The stillness was broken at once. Darius moved toward me then—I shall never know why, perhaps merely to help me to my feet, perhaps to fling me again into the pit—and an instinct for self-protection like nothing I had ever known leapt forth in my mind. Without thinking, without plotting, without willing, it simply appeared: a thought of pure force that leapt from the core of me and into Darius's chest, knocking him backward through the air.

There should have been surprise, or hesitance, or even remorse. There was only terror, and hate, and the taste of the flame that was too fresh in my throat. I sensed a rush of movement among the other Masters, and I heard Nefar scream, *"No!"* and I felt her rage join mine, and Akan's horror link with both of us, and without planning it or thinking of it we turned our joined wills onto the fiery pit.

The tongue of flame that leapt forth seemed to hold all our fear, all our outraged betrayal, our only defense. It fed upon itself and exploded outward, it nourished our power even as we sustained it and all at once the pit began to regurgitate its flames, a great volcanic upheaval of fury and fear and desperate self-preservation. We couldn't have stopped it if we had wanted to. It fed upon itself, it exploded outward from itself, a mad wild thing that raged forth from us in a furious bid for freedom.

Akan and I scrambled toward Nefar, shielding our newly healed and desperately tender flesh from the shower of fire, screaming when the cinders brushed us, until we reached the shelter of the overhanging ledge. Almost before we could dive for safety the entire room was blazing and the Masters, our teachers, those great and powerful magicians, were after all only human.

I saw Darius stumble to his knees, tearing at his flaming clothing. His hands caught fire and he flung himself to the ground, rolling, screaming, choking on the smoke of his own consumed flesh. I was mesmerized in horror as his face, his beautiful face, turned toward me, a mute grotesquerie of swollen broiled flesh with slits for eyes, his hair burned away, his mouth open to scream but his vocal cords burned away. A wall of fire leapt up between us, and he was consumed.

One by one they fell, those Masters of all knowledge, those great and powerful Practitioners. They tried to run, but their robes gushed upward in whooshing columns of fire, then their hair, and at last the flames drove them to their knees with screams of the same kind of agony Akan and I had experienced only moments ago, and was I sorry for them? Did I feel remorse for what I had caused? Ah, no. I watched them burn, and I exulted in my own power.

The fire spilled forth from the pit like water, a tide spreading and undulating, a fountain spewing, and a new and terrible panic shot through me as I saw the bodies of the Masters consumed, their charred and twisted forms tossed about like flotsam upon the great encroaching river. I could not face the fire again, I could not bear the pain. I grabbed Nefar's arm, I shouted, "Stop it!" into her face, and I shook her, but her eyes were bright and glazed, focused upon the horror that was unfolding around us like a lioness might focus on a bloody feast.

Akan grabbed me, and pointed. The illusion the Masters had used to hide the turning wall had dissolved, and the latch was clearly visible. We burst through only steps before the roaring wall of flame. We forced the door closed behind us but it was instantly too hot to touch. We jumped backward from the grinding, splitting noise of baking stone.

"Did you see?" Nefar cried. Her voice was shrill and her face wild with triumph. "Did you see what we did?"

"Dead!" gasped Akan, white-faced. "They're all dead! We killed—"

"Run!" I shouted, and grabbed his arm, pushing Nefar ahead of us.

We were no more than a dozen running steps away when the door burst outward and the roaring tide of fire spilled through. The blast knocked us off our feet and propelled us through the air. Superheated fragments of stone rained down around us like soot as we scrambled to our feet and stumbled toward the staircase. We were sobbing for breath and slapping away the flaming stones as we raced up the staircase and we felt the hot air rising even faster than we did, the heat of the flames pushing at our backs.

Once Nefar stopped and looked back. "It's burning the stone!" she cried. Her soot-streaked face was stiff with disbelief. *"It's burning the stone!"*

I pushed her hard and she started running up the stairs again.

We reached the Corridor of the Masters, deserted now, yet strangely alive. Coils of smoke writhed along the ceiling, a dancing orange glow tossed sinuous shadows back and forth along the walls. Somewhere a small explosion. A drapery burst into flames and was consumed, and another.

Akan looked around in desperate disbelief. "We have to stop it! We can't—the others, we have to warn them! The writings, the artifacts—"

"We can't!" I shouted. Pillars began to tumble, draperies to fall. The fire burst through wooden doors and began to race down side corridors. Smoke billowed toward us, black and thick. "We can't stop it!"

And so we ran, shouting as we ran, hoping to wake the others, knowing even as we tried it was hopeless. What we had begun, if indeed we had begun it, was far beyond us now.

We fled the building, dragging Akan when he turned back, and into the desert.

We ran through the desert until we could run no farther, pulling Nefar along when she stumbled, or sometimes being pulled by her. We stopped when our legs would not take us another step and our lungs could not pump oxygen through our bodies fast enough, and even though we were so far away that we could no longer see the temple compound, the light of its consumption turned the night to day and cast long shadows on the desert floor. We stood there, drawing in harsh gasping breaths, and looked back helplessly toward the place it used to be.

Explosions shook the night as the chemicals inside the temple ignited and fed the blaze, and the entire House of Ra collapsed in upon itself. Teachers, Masters, acolytes, laboratories, books, the arcane knowledge of the world—all were destroyed.

In the light of the flames of the death of an era, Akan fell to his knees, and wept for what was lost.

I looked at Nefar, suddenly filled to choking with the horror and the wonder of what we had learned this night, of what we had done . . . of what we had lost. But Nefar's eyes were not on the horizon. They were on me, and her face was filled with awe.

"You should have died," she said softly. "You and Akan . . . Mirisu was consumed, but the two of you walked through the flames, and were born again."

She lifted my hand, and stretched out my arm in the reddish dancing light. She touched my face, and my chest. My skin was as new and perfect as that of a baby. I looked at Akan, weeping in the light of the destroyed temple. He had not a scar on his body.

We were immortal. And we were only seventeen years old.

# *Five*

And now let me tell if I can how it was between us in that time after we fled the ruins of the temple: the isolation, the fear, the inner chaos that tormented us day and night. We were immune to death, but not to pain. We were filled with power but afraid to use it, we had the knowledge but not the wisdom. We were, as far as we knew, the last of our kind. We clung to each other desperately for courage and for comfort, for the only dreams any one of us dared dream lived in the hearts of the other two.

We lived as fugitives in the land of plenty, exiled by our own shame and by our fear of the priesthood, who would surely be seeking revenge on the destroyers of the House of Ra. The priests in that time were second in power only to the pharaoh; in some cases even more powerful. There were the priests of high order, who had been trained at or by a student of the House of Ra, and who possessed genuine expertise in the Practice, an understanding of and a responsibility for its use. Then there were the lower priests, who were by far the majority—political appointees whose magic was weak or nonexistent but whose power in the world of kings and gold was strong. They were constrained by no morality but their own, concerned with no consequence except their own advancement. They were, for obvious reasons, greatly to be feared.

We had another fear, as well, one we dared not speak aloud or even acknowledge, but one that was so deeply embedded it ruled our every waking moment and haunted the bleak landscape of our dreams. We, the grand gods of our own estimation, Practitioners of our own secret Art, had in one mad ungoverned moment of raw passion unleashed a force like none we had ever known. Stone had burned because of us. Innocents had been consumed in their beds because of us. Because of us the most powerful Practitioners in all of Egypt had toppled and burned, and the knowledge of all eternity had been lost. What might happen should we ever join our forces again? Perhaps the next time the destructive force we generated so effortlessly would consume us as well. Perhaps it would destroy something we loved even more.

We lived a life that was penurious in comparison to the one we had left, not only because of our newborn fear of our own power, but equally because of a much more pragmatic handicap—a simple lack of the basic ingredients necessary to perform the more advanced magic.

There were two levels of magic in which we were trained: the one involved manipulating reality through the use of our inner wills and our personal vitality; the other *altered* reality by combining our personal vitality with the elements of nature much as one might combine oxblood and resin to make ink, or distill willow bark to make aspirin. A certain herb, for example, dried and concocted with calcinated salt and then sublimated with sal ammoniac will produce the vapor necessary to transmute wood into stone, if the intent is correct and the will is disciplined. Without the requisite elements, however, even our strongest intent could do no more than cause wood to appear to be stone; the object so transformed would still feel like wood, break like wood, and burn like wood, because it essentially *was* wood.

We had become accustomed to outrageous luxury in the House of Ra, where even the rarest of materials was available in abundance. But deep in the desert, lacking even the mortar, pestles, and flasks that were basic to our vocation, we were greatly limited as to what we could create. And when even the most fundamental conjuring spell or the mixing of the most common alchemical formula was haunted by the taste of ashes and the screams of the dying, we dared not try for more. I think perhaps if it had not been a question of survival we would not have used magic at all, ever again. Any of us.

There were worse things than death, as we had discovered in the pit of flames, and we knew we would face all of them if we were captured. At first we hid in caves and masked our fires, we crept through the cities and moved our camp every day. But we were young, and fear is a difficult state of mind for youth to maintain. Eventually we found a place for ourselves deep in the desert, safe from the priests, and we made a more permanent camp.

I cannot say how much time passed before we began to emerge, separately and together, from the hard cocoon of shock and terror we had wrapped around ourselves. Time had no meaning for us there in the desert so far from the rise and fall of the Nile, and even if we had cared to track it we would not have done so. In youth, the time of a single life span is incomprehensible. How much more so was eternity. There was no time to us. There was only breathing in and breathing out, lying down to rest and awakening to eat. There was only the endless dull wordless rhythm of our thoughts.

**A** mirage can be nothing more than the peculiar refraction of light across the shimmering desert sands that causes faraway objects to appear much closer than they are. Or it can be an optical illusion, encouraged by the desperate yearnings of a man half-dead of thirst or starving for some relief from the unrelenting desolation, causing him to see what he wishes to see. Or, occasionally, it can be magic.

It was perhaps our fifth day of living by our wits on the parsimonious benevolence of the desert, of huddling together for warmth at night and following the predators to water in the early dawn. Nefar had torn strips from her own charred and stained tunic to provide loincloths for Akan and me; otherwise, we would have gone naked. None of us had shoes. We were hungry, filthy, thirsty, and frightened. We were desperate enough to see a mirage, and we were desperate enough to believe it.

In the heat of late morning we huddled in the shadow of a shallow cliff, our energy so thin that even our argument lacked passion.

"We can make water from sand," Nefar said. Her eyes were half-closed with weariness, and the strands of dusty hair that trailed down her cheeks made her face look gaunt and ashen. "We have seen it done a thousand times."

"We would require a glass beaker," I put forth.

"Glass can be made from sand," Akan said.

I looked at him, letting my eyes convey what I had not the strength to force into my voice. "All it would require is a powerful fire. We are quite expert at that, aren't we?"

He shifted his gaze away, but not before I saw within it a hurt that stabbed at my own heart and made me sorry I had spoken.

Nefar said softly, "Or we could simply walk a few hundred steps in that direction."

I glanced at her without much interest, for my own thought processes were dull and slow to work. Her face had an odd sharpness to it, her eyes the alert and hungry quality of an animal on the hunt, and she was sitting up a little straighter. I followed the direction of her gaze, and so did Akan.

What we saw was, just beyond a slight undulation of the desert floor, a stand of green palm trees lining a pool big enough to bathe in and surrounded by a carpet of colorful desert plants. Behind the pool were the pastel silk panels of a tent, and a man in turban and shift watered his camel from a leather bucket.

I said, "Impossible." Could my senses have been so confused that I failed to notice so remarkable a sight until this moment? I did not think so.

"It could be a day or more away." This from Akan, as cautious as I.

"I can see the flies on the camel," replied Nefar scornfully, and got to her feet. "It's not more than a few steps!"

"It could be illusion," cautioned Akan again.

Nefar cast him an impatient look. "We are not in the House of Ra," she retorted. "There is no more illusion."

I said, "Can you smell that?"

Akan looked at me. "Roast lamb," he said.

Both Akan and I got to our feet, slowly, and when Nefar took off across the desert, we did not hesitate to follow.

The old man waited patiently for our approach, his eyes as sharp as faceted stone beneath the folds of weathered wrinkles. His shoulders were stooped and his bones were thin, and when he parted his lips in a smile of welcome, he revealed teeth that were broken and brown. He said, before we asked, "You look in need of water. There's plenty to share."

Almost before he finished speaking, Nefar was on her belly on the ground, her face buried in the pool and her hands splashing water over her head and her arms. Akan and I attempted to exercise restraint, but it was a short-lived effort. Within moments I had dropped to my knees beside her and was lapping up the cool sweet liquid like an animal at the trough.

The old man invited us to his fire, where we pulled hot flesh of lamb off the skewer with our fingers and ate until our bellies were distended. We told him we had been set upon by bandits, all we possessed had been seized, and we had barely escaped into the desert with our lives. He told us he was from Thebes, traveling to visit his daughter who had married a man near Giza. He said he expected to die there. He complained about the price of grain and about the tariff charged by the temple priests for an offering to Amun. And then he said, around a mouthful of lamb, "You've heard the news I suppose?"

At our blank looks he expounded, "Why, the temple, the great House of Ra—it is no more. Destroyed, they say, by a bolt of lightning from above, a judgment against the corruption of priests everywhere."

Akan began to cough and choke, and while Nefar pounded him on the back I struggled to swallow the suddenly dry lump of meat in my own mouth. The old man looked at us oddly, and Nefar said, "Forgive my brother. He once studied at the House of Ra. This is a great shock."

The man passed him a skin of wine, his eyes still narrowed suspiciously. "You don't look like a priest," he said.

Akan drew from the skin, his eyes watering, and managed to reply hoarsely, "My studies were—interrupted."

I said, trying to distract him, "Surely you don't mean everything was destroyed."

He nodded solemnly. "Charred to the ground. Not even bones were left. A judgment against wickedness." He retrieved the skin from Akan and took a long draw himself, then added casually, "Of course, they'll just build another temple and start again."

A quick, shocked look flashed between Akan and Nefar and me, and though I knew the wise thing to do would be to let it pass I could not stop myself from speaking. "Who will build again? How?"

And Akan insisted, his words tangling with mine, "Everything was destroyed, all the magic lost—"

The old man chuckled. "Magic is never lost. It wouldn't be magic if it were."

"But all the writings, the knowledge of all time—"

He shrugged. "Just words. And what can be written down can be copied."

I could almost feel Akan's face go white, and the intensity of his focus was like a shimmer in the air. "Copied?" he said. His voice was very still, kinetic with what he hardly dared believe. "There are copies of the writings? Everything that was lost?"

The old man tore another strip of flesh off the bone with his jagged front teeth. "Of course. It has been the job of priests and acolytes for generations to copy the writings; that is how they learn. Didn't you do so when you were there?"

We three were silent, but our eyes were wide with things we wanted to say to each other. We had assumed our copies were for no purpose other than our own enlightenment, and that they had been destroyed along with everything else in the House of Ra. But if they had been taken away before the fire, if other copies had been taken away . . .

Akan said hoarsely, "Where? Where are the copies?"

Again the old man shrugged. "The temple at Karnak I should imagine. Isn't that where all the priests' treasures are kept?"

A strange uneasiness was beginning to creep over me that I couldn't quite define. I glanced at Nefar to see if she felt it too, but her attention was focused on Akan. I knew she was trying to signal Akan to say no more, for already he had revealed too much. I opened my mouth to change the subject, but was too late,

Akan said softly, barely on a breath, "And the Dark Arcana? Would those writings have been copied too?"

The old man met his gaze. "Why shouldn't they have been? If it was written once, it was written again."

I said harshly, "What do you know of the Dark Arcana? What do you know of any of this?"

He smiled. It was a very strange smile indeed, making him seem at the same time much younger than I first had thought, and much older than he now appeared. He said, "Do you think you are the only students ever to leave the House of Ra? There are many of us throughout the land. Be careful you do not find their magic less benevolent than mine has been."

He arose then, in a single graceful movement from a cross-legged position, and we scrambled to our own feet only a moment behind him. The green oasis was gone. The cold pond from which we had drunk was only a shimmering pool of sand. The tent was a low dune and the camel the skeleton of some long-ago beast whose scattered bones made it difficult to determine what it once had been in life. Only the fire remained, and the sticky bones of lamb in our fingers.

He said, "You will not survive until the rising of the next moon without your magic. Nature has filled this desert with all you need to create abundance. There is no crime in using it."

I looked at Nefar, and I saw in her eyes the same guilty, terrified questions that were racing through my mind. Who was this man, and how much did he know of us? Was he a temple priest himself? What lies had he told us? What would he do with us now?

And when we looked again, he was gone.

The fire burned low at our feet, and went out. I couldn't find my voice, and even if I had, I was not sure I would have given words to the terrible dreads that were congealing inside me. Slowly, I brought my fingers to my face, sniffed them, tasted the grease on them. That much, at least was real.

I looked again at Nefar, and we both looked at Akan. But his face was focused upon the place the old man had been, and his eyes deep with the fever of an idea. "The writings," he said, "they weren't destroyed. They are at Thebes!"

**B**ut Thebes was the one place even Akan was too afraid to go. Perhaps the old man was a harmless magician, a Practitioner living out his last days, and perhaps he had told us the truth. Or perhaps he was a temple priest sent to spy on us, and even now had returned with news of our whereabouts. We could no longer afford the tottering, tortured steps toward survival we once had attempted. Safety was an urgent issue. And oddly enough, it was the old man who gave us the courage to use what we needed to survive.

We began in small ways. We used our magic to draw the animals to us that we might slaughter for food, to build the fires that cooked their flesh, to locate the water that would keep us alive. For the longest time we lacked both the will and the imagination to do more. But as night turned to day and the moon swelled and ebbed and the frost came and then the heat, healing began. Life, we discovered, had a force of its own, whether or not we wished it.

We grew in confidence and an unspoken understanding of the past that must be left behind. We established a routine of sorts that gradually expanded to include activities beyond those necessary for survival. We searched for salt deposits, and for sulfur, and scraped limestone into the bowl we had made from the skull of a dead animal. Slowly, experimentally, we assembled some of the basic materials necessary to our craft, and we began to flex our muscles within the Practice.

One by one, with a hesitance that spoke at first of uncertainty, then almost of embarrassment, we provided ourselves with the creature comforts—a multiroomed tent made of silk, fountains of fresh water that poured from a stone, exotic fruits bargained from a trader who thought we gave him gold. These were simple matters that required nothing more than our ordinary skill and the common elements of the desert. We dared not explore the larger, more difficult conjurations, even if we had possessed the materials; nor did we even consider coming together as we once had done to master the impossible . . . except, perhaps, in our deepest and most secret yearnings.

Akan, who never stopped mourning the volumes that were lost in the temple, set himself to trying to re-create from memory the knowledge that had been contained within. And Nefar and I, because he was the brother of our spirits and we shared his pain, helped him.

I should explain that the Arcana—those great volumes of secret knowledge that delineate the methodology of science and magic—were then as now cryptic and coded, relying as much on the intuitive discovery of the reader as on literal formulae. It would take dozens upon dozens of years to record what we had learned in our study at the House of Ra. As for what we had not learned—what we had only read, or half-remembered, or heard might be discovered—it could not be written until it was first learned. The task that stretched before us seemed beyond achievement. But then, we had an eternity in which to master it.

Centuries later I would come to observe that immortality consists largely of boredom. I had been immortal less than a year and I think already I had begun to suspect the truth of that.

I cannot say how long we might have held to our restraint and our dull penitent vocation, exiled priests who looked into the future and saw nothing but an eternity of atonement awaiting them. Our intentions were noble, but our spirits were weak. Time and distance dulled the pain of memory and we missed the excitement we once had known, the discovery, the adventure. The power. This I know. I could see it in Nefar's eyes, and hear it in Akan's voice, and feel it in my own heart. But we were strong, and we were determined. We might have continued on our self-prescribed path of retribution and denial for decades or even more, and in so doing we might have built a foundation of character and wisdom that would enable us to ignore temptation. But we were never to know.

Some might say Chance conspired against us. Others observe that we make our own chances. I only know that when I emerged from the tent after a cramped and tedious afternoon of inscribing and saw the small caravan silhouetted against the indigo-and-scarlet sky, my heart leapt in my chest. It was excitement, not fear, that sharpened my voice as I called to the others.

In the time we had been in this camp—a long string of waning and waxing moons, perhaps even years—only two other travelers had happened by, both of them lost and near death with delirium of the sun. We had given them water and traded for what meager comforts of civilization they might supply. Never had anything so grand as a caravan approached before, so filled with the promise of news and commodities of the world outside. We watched from the shelter of our canopy as the string of riders and pack animals grew larger upon the horizon, and we hardly dared speak, as though even a whisper might break the spell that had brought them to us.

We had by this time created a small oasis of green living things in the vast white sea of sand and death—a ring of palm trees, a pool surrounded by ferns, a small garden of fast-growing fruits. Our tent was brightly colored and well lit, a beacon by day or night for any who might pass within sight—and in the desert, sight can be a very long distance indeed.

Now Akan, perhaps paying some token tribute to the concerns that had driven us into hiding in the first place, murmured, "Perhaps we should extinguish the lamps."

"It's too late," I said. "They've seen us, and the moon will be bright enough to light their way in only a few moments."

Nefar said, in a voice hungry and low, "I wonder if they carry spices."

"Or news from Thebes," said Akan.

"They could have come from Thebes," I agreed, perhaps too eagerly. "Their course is true. They might have been there only months ago."

"Perhaps they are traders in silk and fine jewels," speculated Nefar.

"Spices would be more welcome," I said.

And so for the sake of spices, and silk, and news from a world we could barely imagine, we stood, giddy with anticipation, and waited for their approach.

There were a dozen men and half again as many pack animals, tearing at the turf of our small oasis and filling the air with sand and hot, foul breath. The camels were burdened with bulky loads wrapped in coarse cloth; the men wore rough clothing and carried sharp weapons. Their manner was boisterous but their eyes were hard. Within moments they swarmed over us, their quick harsh movements and their loud voices making their numbers seem greater than they were. They plunged unbidden through our tent, helping themselves to the roasted meat and flat bread that were the remnants of our supper, plucking dates from our tree, splashing in our pool. And we stood there, the magicians who had brought down the House of Ra, helpless to prevent them.

One man, broad-shouldered and bearded, was obviously the leader. He watched the misbehavior of his troops with a tolerant grin, and approached us at leisure. "Well now, I heard it but didn't believe it. A paradise in the middle of the desert, and three whelplings alone to defend it."

I said, "Hardly a paradise, sir. A humble tent, a few meager belongings."

The man's eyes were on Nefar, and his grin showed two missing teeth. "Any man who possesses a beauty such as this can hardly call his belongings 'meager.' "

Nefar said sharply, "I am the possession of no man, camel-driver. You will do well to remember that."

The gap-toothed man laughed.

From the pool came a shrill screech of abandon as a man trampled to the center with his filthy robes swirling around him and upturned a skin of wine—ours, obtained at great risk to ourselves from a traveler many turns of the moon past. Spilled wine and gritty sand discolored our only source of drinking and bathing water.

We had brought a fountain to the desert, we had caused fruit to grow from a single seed, but we could not, at that moment, think how to stop these renegades from destroying it all.

Akan's face was tight, and I knew his heart must be pounding in his chest as mine was, his stomach must be tight with knots. Yet he made his voice casual, as though we were overrun by ill-mannered travelers every night of the week and were quite accustomed to dealing with it. He nodded toward the camels. "What is your cargo?"

The man's gaze shifted from Nefar to Akan, and narrowed cannily. "What do you need?"

"Very little." Akan glanced askance at the man in the pool, who had now been joined by two companions. "A skin or two of wine, perhaps."

"You've got gold?"

"We have no gold. But we have other things to trade."

"I hear you have gold." The man took a step toward us.

Nefar suddenly swept forward, across his path, and to the nearest camel. "What is this? Wool? Not a very good quality I fear. I hope you didn't pay too highly for it."

Across one of the camels, lashed between lumpy stacks of wool blankets, was a long, canvas-wrapped bundle. Its size and shape were unmistakable, as was the faint stench that even the dry wind and baking heat could not completely prevent. Nefar, pretending ignorance, jerked at one of the lashings, then gave a little scream as the canvas fell away, revealing the hard gray features of a corpse several days old.

It was the body of a young man, tossed so carelessly across the camel that his face and torso, frozen with rigor mortis, were twisted toward us and all too easy to see. Strings of dark hair fell forward over eyes that were bulging from their sockets. Yellow teeth, crooked and malformed, were framed by the horrible rictus grin of death. I felt my stomach lurch and I thought that Nefar's scream of horror was not entirely faked. Visions of melting flesh and gaping eye sockets washed through my memory like a wave and left weakness in its wake.

A hush rippled over the ruffians as one by one their attention was attracted to what Nefar had done. They shuffled toward us, splashing out of the pool, ripping doorways through the tent with their knives. A roar of rage swelled from the back of the crowd like thunder rolling across the desert. "Whore! You defile the body of my brother!"

Red-faced, his lips flecked with spittle and wine, the man lunged forward Nefar with his knife drawn, and in the same instant, almost more quickly than it can be told, the gap-toothed man lunged. A grinning red mouth appeared across the assailant's throat and he staggered, stunned, falling to one knee as his head wobbled unsteadily upon the spurting stump of his neck, then came to rest for an odd little moment upon his left shoulder before he pitched forward and spilled a fountain of blood into the sand. His head rolled a few inches away, and was still.

Nefar stepped back from the river of blood that was flowing her way, picking up the hem of her robe. The gap-toothed leader closed in on her, grinning, and folded his grimy fist around a length of her hair. "No manners, that one," he said. "You'll find me more to your liking, I promise."

Nefar drew back and spat in his face.

The bandit laughed and wiped spittle from his chin. "You'll do with some taming before you're fit company for our journey, I see. I think maybe I'll let my men break you in while I take my pleasure with your two boys. And in between times, I'll make certain the men bring you over to watch."

At some point I had lunged for Nefar, but was caught by the hair in a vicious grip that jerked my head back and almost wrenched a cry from me. A blade appeared at my throat. From the corner of my eye I saw Akan in a similar circumstance.

I might have called forth a burst of superhuman strength and flung my captive across the desert floor. I might have melted the blade of the knife with my eyes, I might have flung a bolt of lightning from my fingertips; I might have summoned the sound of a predatory cat or the shape of a monstrous viper to send the brigands fleeing into the night. I might have had my choice of a dozen ways in which to assure our safety and in truth most of them raced through my head at that moment, roiling and tumbling and tangling with each other even as a choking sensation gripped my throat and magic—the very magic that was as natural to me as lying down in the evening or rising in the morning—eluded me. I could not find the focus, I could not remember the magic, and every time I tried a wave of panic consumed me that grew larger wider and deeper with each failure. The smell of burned flesh filled my nostrils, the screams of the dying echoed against the thunder of my heartbeat, and I couldn't breathe. I thought I would burst with the terror that was swelling inside me.

They couldn't kill me. But the torment of this moment alone was worth a thousand deaths.

I cut my eyes wildly to Akan, who was being restrained by two of the ruffians with his arms twisted at a severe angle behind his back. Several perfectly round drops of blood were visible on his robe from the sharp point of the knife that was now pressed against his ribs. Yet the expression on his face was still, oddly arrested, and his gaze was on Nefar.

The gap-toothed man had her by the throat in a one-handed grip that forced burgundy color into her face and pressed her chin upward at an odd angle. Nefar did not struggle, and her eyes were fixed upon the headless corpse on the ground in what to the ordinary observer might appear to be a state of fixed shock, or abject terror. It was neither.

My own eyes moved toward the body of the headless man, sprawled forward on the ground with his hands outstretched, as though reaching for the knife that had fallen a few inches away. As I watched, the fingers began to twitch, and the knee moved slightly, leaving a shallow path in the sand. The other leg moved, the arm stretched out. The dead and headless thing was crawling.

A shock of instinctive repulsion went through me even as I filled my lungs with a breath of pure exhilaration. I watched as lifeless fingers closed around the hilt of the knife, as the headless corpse staggered to a kneeling position and with jerky, uncoordinated movements, swayed to its feet.

I released my breath in a laugh of triumph that was lost in the screams and shouts and scramblings of terror that welled up around me. The captor who held my hair twisted in his fist let go with a jerk and stumbled backward, his mouth gaping and his eyes wild. The knife he held flew from his fingers and into my own at my command and I heard a gurgling sound from deep within his throat, a pathetic effort to scream through the terror that paralyzed him, as I spun the knife by its sharp tip on my outstretched finger then flung it in a single dramatic motion into the night sky, where it disappeared.

Ah, the thrill of it, the surge of precious empowerment, the joy; the simple intoxicating joy.

I spun around and spied the canvas-wrapped corpse that was mounted upon the camel. With a twist of my wrist and a spark of intention I loosened the last of the lashings and the dead man slid to the ground, breaking several of his brittle bones with the impact. While Nefar's headless monstrosity lurched and danced in an ever-widening circle I brought my fellow to his feet on the invisible thread of my will and walked him forward, broken bones protruding at odd angles, swollen tongue pushing through the grin of his crooked teeth. The air smelled strong of camel urine and human bowels abruptly loosened, and the stillness of terror was broken only by a whispered curse, a broken sob as the ruffians stood frozen in disbelief and paralyzed with their own panic.

It was the gap-toothed man who recovered himself first. With a howl of rage, he charged toward my reanimated corpse, his knife raised high. Startled by the unexpected revolt, my will wavered, and so did Nefar's and our corpses dropped like puppets upon severed strings to the ground. But almost before the breath of our own surprise could be drawn, there was another sound, a sound like the rushing of the wind or the thunder of the sea, a roar that rose up into the night like a pillar of flame. It was Akan, and the power of his intent drew us in, Nefar and me; almost without our knowing it we gave him the force of our will, the glory of our magnificent magic, unleashed and magnified.

He grew tall, and taller, with windswept robes and eerily illuminated features he loomed above them, and they began to scream, for his features were no longer those of Akan but of the dead man with the stringy black hair and the yellow-toothed grin; he had transformed himself into the corpse and we—the three of us together—made it a thing of great and grand proportions, a living horror that would never be forgotten by any who told the tale. He cast a shadow from the moon that stretched halfway to the horizon and when he roared the earth shook.

The bandits trampled each other in their haste to flee, the camels they could not catch and mount ran off bleating into the desert and we found the trail of their abandoned cargo—stolen goods no doubt—scattered across the desert in all directions for days afterward. We released the illusion only when the last sounds of their flight faded from the night air, yet the dread and the awe in their eyes when they had looked back at us assured us they would never return to this place.

We collapsed to the ground amid the remnants of our trampled oasis, the two dead men all that remained of the invasion of the outside world. For the longest time we simply looked at each other, breathing hard with the effort of our exertion and with the simple wonder of what we had done. We had performed the magic in a grand and glorious way; we had brought our vitality together and we had called forth a magnificent illusion; we had saved ourselves, and *we had harmed no one.* No great wrath had been visited upon us, the world had not erupted in flame, the tombs of the pharaohs had not opened up to devour us. We had contained the power. We had done this thing, we had performed this great wonder, and we had done it with perfection. We were in control.

I said in a breath, "Did you see it? Did you see what we did?" at the same time Akan whispered, "We were magnificent! Could you feel it? Can't you feel it still?" and Nefar gasped, "We did it! We were better than before, stronger than before! We did it!"

And then we all laughed together, words and exclamations tumbling over each other as we reached for each other, grasping hands and shoulders and fingers while the sparks of our excitement danced between us like starlight and fragments of leftover magic tasted like burned honey in the air. I said, holding tight to Akan's hand and to Nefar's, "Do you know what this means?"

Nefar's eyes were filled with faraway moonlight as she said, "We don't have to hide anymore!"

And Akan, in a voice that was soft with wonder, added, "We don't have to be afraid anymore. We can go where we will, be *who* we will. We can protect each other, even from the priests. We'll have to be careful of course, but—"

"But we can leave this place!" cried Nefar, and she flung one arm around my neck and the other around Akan's, drawing us close to her. We laughed at her silliness as she cried again, lifting her voice to the desert sky, "We're free!"

"We're magic!" I echoed.

"We're invincible!" cried Akan.

I threw my arms around them and the magic of sheer joy bubbled through us and out of us like molten oil in a cauldron, spilling over into the night and charging every particle of it with our exhilaration. I kissed Nefar hard on the mouth, and then Akan, and we tasted the laughter upon one another's tongues, we inhaled the delirium of one another's breaths. What began to happen then between us was, I suppose, as inevitable as the rising of the sun or the setting of the moon, yet it was filled with such wonder, such simple, overwhelming astonishment, that we were not so much a part of it as captured by it, swept along on the swelling tide of our own expanding vitality like flotsam in a storm.

I suppose we had always known on some level that it was sexual energy that fueled our power, the kinetic balance of two male portions and the life-giving force of the female. To take that energy and turn it outward was the basis of our great magic, the seed of life itself; the tiny particle around which all energy revolved that, when introduced to precisely the right elements in precisely the right atmosphere with precisely the right timing, resulted in an explosion of power, the limits of which even we did not yet fully understand. Yet to take that energy and turn it inward, to taste it in the breath of the others and feel it in the touch, to revel in it and bathe in it and let it wash over us in ripples and waves and tidal floods of pleasured sensation . . . ah, this was a thing so sweet, so exquisite and pure, that even the imagining of it would have been impossible for us before this night.

It was beyond sensuality, yet it was the most intensely sensual thing I have ever known. It was every dream I had ever had of making love to Nefar, and it was empowered by the energy of Akan. It *was* Nefar, the adored one, my beloved, the essence of female power . . . and it was Akan.

I tasted them in every pore of my body, the sweet-sharp Nefar, the honeyed musk of Akan; I felt them, blended and absorbed into every cell, I *heard* them, their thoughts, their breaths, their muted whispers of wondered pleasure, swirling inside my head like zephyr's caresses, I *was* them, and they were me, and this was a union so perfect, so astonishing and inevitable that the mere word *pleasure* had no meaning here. I understood at once why men and women are compelled to join together in sexual congress, desperately and repeatedly seeking to ease the ache of emptiness with which they are born—for the ache was for this moment, the emptiness was for this completion. Ah, how could we not have guessed it before?

Nefar. Nefar. She was the conduit, and the focus. She joined us together, she opened us to this marvel. We were the background notes, Akan and I, she was the symphony. She filled me, heart and mind and soul. And because I had known this moment, no part of me would ever be complete without her again.

No physical mating could approach the power of what we generated between us; what we offered to each other and drank from each other in delirious, greedy gulps. No man and no woman, at the peak of their most perfect union, could have known even a glimpse of what we shared. But between us it was transcendentally sexual. It was sensation beyond the physical, beyond even the psychical; pleasure that increased exponentially until it burst the bonds of mere pleasure. We melted into one another, male and female, male and male, in a white-hot wave of surprised possibility, we fed on one another, we dissolved into one another, and in the process we Became something new. The tail of the serpent pierces the mouth; the divine penetrates the mortal. I wept to think of the small shallow unions with women I had known until then; I weep now recalling how it was when we, perfect in our innocence, were transmuted into one.

And in all of this, we never touched more than our fingertips together.

I think I must have known on some level that what she caused me to feel, this hopeless and unconditional adoration, this wondrous unquestioning joy, Akan must have felt also. But I never thought of it. Truly I did not.

And even when the energy that was required to maintain the union began to fail us and we slowly, reluctantly, drifted back into our separate consciousnesses, there was no sorrow, there was no loss. We three, born of separate mothers, would never be separate again. There was a part of each of them inside of me, and the best of what was me was inside of them. We fell asleep wrapped in each other, and dreamed each other's dreams, and we arose filled with the joy that was the strength of each other, and fearing nothing in the world.

# Six

Sometimes it seems my memory of our time in Thebes must be nothing more than our collective imaginations, wishing it into being. Surely nothing so blissful, so completely unblemished, could ever have existed on earth. Or perhaps the sheer perfection of it was Great Nature's compensation, in however small measure, for the afterlife paradise we would never know.

We took a grand house in the prosperous market center near Luxor, with a lush courtyard in which we kept trained monkeys and a tame giraffe. There were sparkling pools inlaid with lapis and fountains scented with exotic perfumes. Our house was three stories high, like many of the finer structures of the day, and was furnished with marble floors and carved ebony couches draped in silk and animal furs. We kept several dozen servants, not because we needed them but because it was an obligation, more or less, to provide shelter and employment for those less fortunate than ourselves.

We obtained the necessary raw materials with which to transform more common metals into gold and we produced a sufficient quantity, but this was a tedious and time-consuming process in which we were not tempted to overindulge. We used the advanced ventilating and air-cooling techniques that were common at the House of Ra to maintain a cool, even temperature throughout the summer and reversed the techniques to keep the house warm and draft-free when the icy winds blew; we combined dung and cow's blood and a few other common materials to cause the melons in our garden to grow to the size of boulders in a matter of weeks, and our servants were impressed by our magic. In fact, we performed very little actual magic during our time in Thebes. We were far too busy reveling in each other, in our newfound freedom, and in the life we had created for ourselves—a life we had not even dreamed about during our years at the House of Ra.

Simply going to the marketplace was a magical adventure for us. Watching the barges on the Nile like mammoth monsters from the deep, laden with exotic cargo and sun-darkened, harsh-tongued slaves, or the delicately carved barques of the wealthy, painted in gold and inset with turquoise, their silken curtains wafted by the breeze; sampling and discarding the wares of loud and eager vendors on the street, scattering coins to dirty children, filling our senses with the dust and the sweat and the dung of the streets—we saw it all, experienced it all, through the wonder of our new enhanced unity, and it was magical to us.

I should not wish to paint too grand a picture of Thebes during our time there, for the truth is that although there were memorable, even lovely aspects to this grand city on the banks of the Nile, and certainly we lived a more privileged life than most, I was not in general much more impressed with life in the city than I had ever been. I liked our garden, and the great cool marble halls of our house, and the feasts we gave with dancing girls and boy acrobats and ribald pantomimes. I did not like the sounds of quarreling and violence that drifted through our curtains like dust on summer evenings, nor the beggars who sat outside our gate, nor the maimed and starving children who hovered about the marketplace with big solemn eyes. I didn't like the smell of rot that drifted upward from the streets nor the cry of an abused slave nor the scream of a donkey, beaten to death for refusing to carry too heavy a burden.

But for the most part we managed to shut out the world that displeased us and create our own paradise within our gates—and within our hearts.

Occasionally we brought home a nubile girl with flashing eyes or a handsome, lithe-framed boy to dine and drink and dance and have sex with, and this too was magical in its simple lack of complexity, in the delight of needs felt and needs met. We were hedonists, in our way, but even our profligate self-indulgence had the taste of innocence to it, of wonder.

I wish I had the words to explain the power, the miracle, of this union between us, for nothing I can say can begin to do more than suggest a shallow image of its magnificence. Imagine that deepest loneliest core of the human heart uncovered and made to ache, to throb and bleed in yearning for the part of itself that was incomplete, and imagine the pieces of its completion sliding into place like slices of a magnet long separated yet inexorably drawn together to form a whole again. And imagine the wash of joy, the flood of radiant wonder, the explosion of power that might burst from that aching heart, once more made entire.

So you see even as I try to describe it my words fall into the mundane hyperbole of lovers everywhere, and yes, we were deeply, madly in love with one another. But we were not lovers. Sex was a delightful recreation in which we all indulged freely—but never with each other.

And if I tell you now that my deepest most secret soul did not yearn for a union that, in the flesh, duplicated what we knew outside of it, I would be the worst kind of liar. I was a young man, full of lust and the glory of my own power. I was delirious with the joy of life, the eternal miracle we three had discovered in one another. I was in many ways a youth as youths have always been, and I was madly in love with one girl.

I cannot say when it began. Perhaps as long ago as the day she first reached out her will to mine and doubled my strength; perhaps as recently as the night I lunged to save her from the fire and plunged into the pit myself, counting my life well lost if it spared her pain. I only know that by the time we discovered the ecstasy the three of us could share in spiritual union, I was greedy enough to want more.

My shame was that in the deepest most secret part of my soul I wanted there to be two of us, not three.

Yet in the peculiar way of shame and guilt, the very process of keeping my secret intensified my desire, causing my longing to grow, until the secret itself felt like a brilliant scarlet stain upon my face for all to read. Every woman that I lay with had the face of Nefar. Every dream that played across my night-quiet mind shuddered with the need for her. And the struggle to subdue my intemperate longings was a battle I could never win.

There were days that were better than others, and for the most part, to all outward appearances, everything was as it should be between us. Nefar made me laugh and she made me irritable as she always had done; Akan drew from me puzzlement and impatience and awed admiration as he had always done, and the two of them turned to me for decision and moderation and practical leadership as, in so many ways, they had always done. But we lived for the time we would come together in that secret way, the touch of fingers, the caress of breaths, the sweet warm floodtide of blending essences filling the empty parts of each other, bursting through our veins and arteries and corpuscles and cells and neurons, filling us with power, with wonder, with the glorious, dizzying certainty that we, together, might touch the face of the Universe. And yet even in the throes of that joint ecstasy, even in the aftermath of wonder that accompanied it, there was that small dark thread of selfish greed that snaked through me, a place within me, secret and protected, that remained untouched by what we three shared and hungered for what only two could know. I wanted her to myself. I wanted the magnificence and the rapture to explode between us alone, I wanted to own and possess and revel in the possession. It is the nature of men and women, and has been so since the beginning of time.

Still, my love for Akan and my fear of losing everything we shared strengthened my resolve to subdue my instincts. And I think I might have succeeded—I truly do—had not Nefar come to me.

We were often alone in the house. Akan was obsessed with the temple at Karnak and with finding the copied writings the old man had told us were hidden there. He devoted his days to devising disguises and personae that might enable him to engage the confidences of the priests; he stole into secret rooms of the temple concealed behind an invisibility shield, he devised truth potions and worked enchantments and occasionally he unearthed some small bit of knowledge that led him to believe the writings did exist, and that he was close to finding them. For a while Nefar and I had assisted him in his efforts, and there had been a certain adventure in penetrating the great fortress of Karnak, in proving our own magic greater than that of the priests who ruled the land. But the futility of the search soon grew boring, and I was not certain I had ever believed the words of the peculiar old magician in the desert.

So Akan went alone almost daily to the temple, and Nefar and I amused ourselves with idle pursuits. She was interested in devising a formula to increase the production of hybrid fruits in our garden; I was interested in watching her. And I was resolved to do whatever was necessary to avoid indulging my fantasies about her.

She came upon me in a small alcove garden where I dozed in the shadows of the late afternoon, listening to the splash of the central tiled fountain and the drone of bees. A serving girl massaged oil into my feet, and two others waved pond fronds over my head. With a clap of her hands Nefar dismissed them all, and I sat up with a scowl of annoyance, wishing she had found me in a more industrious pursuit.

"There's no need to be rude," I told her irritably. "What has happened to put you in such a prickly state?"

She sat upon the raised edge of the fountain pool, dipping her fingers into the water. She wore a pale light gown that was artfully tied to accent her breasts and her full round hips, and when she sat, its graceful folds parted at her crossed knees. Did she know how beautiful she was? Could she have any idea what a pleasure it was simply to gaze at her?

She said, "Don't you ever wonder what our purpose is?"

I was more embarrassed than ever to have been caught dozing in the shade, and my tone was abrupt as I replied, "No."

She gave an impatient wave of her hand. "Oh, I don't mean how you occupy your time today, or tomorrow. I don't mean growing fruit or transmuting metals or even like Akan, who is so fixed on finding those books."

"A foolish pursuit," I pointed out, easing a little as I realized her criticism was not directed at me. "Since even if the books did exist, what use can they be to him? The priests are hardly likely to let him walk out with the only existing copies of ancient texts under his arm. Besides, what need do we have of textbooks when we can do more magic together, the three of us, than was ever written down?"

Her grimace was both indulgent and remonstrative. "There, you see? That's exactly what I mean. You have no ambition."

There are things in this world more wounding than to be accused of a lack of ambition by the woman whose admiration you seek above all else, but at that moment I could think of none of them. I said, in a voice as stiff and heavy as the weight of my thoughts, "I have ambitions. You have touched my inner heart and you know them as well as I do. My ambition is to carry out the charge we were given at the House of Ra. To grow in magic and use my knowledge to keep the balance."

"To counsel kings and walk with pharaohs," she said softly, smiling. "You are a good man, aren't you, Han?"

Ah, what a quiet and indescribable thrill that was, to hear myself described as a *man* from her lips. I said, "For the most part, I think. I try to be."

A sudden urgency came into her eyes. "But to be merely good—whether a good Practitioner or a good student or even a good person—that is for ordinary people, Han. Don't you ever wonder—doesn't it torment you at night—what purpose we three are intended for? That we have been given this gift cannot have been an accident. That we came together this way—there must have been a reason."

I said, "Perhaps we are living the reason. Perhaps simply finding each other, and being together, was enough." And though I knew she spoke of the three of us, when I responded, my thoughts were only of her and me.

She shook her head, though it seemed to me the gesture was regretful. "Even the most ordinary person comes to life with a purpose—even if that purpose is only to meet another ordinary person, marry, and make progeny. For us there must be more."

I came to her, though I was hardly aware of moving, and sat beside her and took her hand. I said huskily, "Why? Why cannot loving, and marrying, and having children be enough for us?"

She looked into my eyes and I saw understanding there, and no surprise. A lovely softening, a sweet tenderness. My heart soared and pounded and leapt in my chest as she lifted her fingers and stroked my face. An eternity of wordless communication passed between us, everything I wanted to tell her but could not; everything I wanted to hear from her but dared not.

"Han," she whispered at last. Her fingers trailed across my lips, and I kissed them lightly. "If only you had said these words to me sooner."

"We were children then."

"And I have adored you since we were children. Didn't you know that?"

I could only shake my head. The enormity of my foolishness made me weak.

Her eyes were filled with so many things, dancing lights and darks, hope and shadow, most of them welcome, some of them not. I could barely look into them for the power of emotion they evoked in me. I kissed her eyelids, and felt her sigh go through me. I kissed her throat, and her breasts, soft warm mounds dressed in silk. "Let me be your lover," I whispered.

She stroked her fingers through my hair. She was like liquid in my arms, flowing into me. She kissed my neck, and pressed her lips against my temple. "He said that in the end there would be only two," she murmured.

"Who?" I asked, not really caring.

She took my face between both her palms, gently, and she made me look into her eyes. She said, "But not now."

I felt my breath die in my chest.

"Han, listen to me." Her fingertips tightened against my skull, as though to restrain me from slipping away into the abyss of disappointment and loss. "The three of us, together, have a power like none the world has ever known. Would you destroy what we have before we even know what it might become?"

I dropped my eyes, and every muscle in my body grew heavy with the truth I had always known. "We cannot betray Akan," I said, and to me it was that simple.

She kissed my cheek, her lips lingering like the last breath of a dying benediction. "Ah, Han. Beloved. It is not a betrayal when it is destined."

I raised my gaze to her slowly, and her own eyes were filled with radiant tenderness, and certainty. "We were meant to be together. Our time will come. But now the time is for the three of us, and the things we were meant to do. The destiny we were meant to build. There is a reason. There is a purpose. And we're going to find it. Soon."

"Yes," I said, and my heart was swollen with joy, with promise, because the only words I heard were *we were meant to be together.*

She smiled, and brushed my lips with a kiss, and then I heard footsteps behind us.

There was no reason to feel guilty. It was as common for Nefar and I to embrace as it was for Akan and I to do so, but I saw in his eyes that he knew, just as we did, that this embrace was different. He tried to hide his expression, just as we tried to hide our embarrassment with a pretense of casualness as we moved apart.

I said, "How goes the search, then?"

Akan crossed to the flagon of fruit nectar that was set on a table beneath the shade of a palm, and he poured himself a cup. "The books," he said, "are not there. They have been moved."

Nefar rose with an expression of genuine concern, and went over to him. I, too, felt my spirits sink in sympathy for my friend.

"Are you sure?"

"I used the truth enchantment on one who has seen them." Akan did not meet our eyes as he spoke.

"Perhaps the temple at Luxor," I suggested.

"We'll help you look," Nefar promised.

Akan passed a quick look from me to Nefar, and I saw question there, and hurt, and uncertainty, and I had no more doubt that he had seen, or sensed, more than we wanted him to. The remorse I felt was bitter in my throat.

Then Akan smiled, and sipped from the cup. "Yes," he said. "Perhaps Luxor."

And it seemed for the moment everything would be all right. Or at least that was what I wanted to believe.

# Seven

In the weeks that followed, our life together did, in many ways, grow easier and more free than it had been since we had come to Thebes. My passion for Nefar, though it did not diminish, was easier to bear now that the secret was broken, and I lived on the promise of her whispered words, *our time will come. . . .* I looked into Akan's eyes and I saw no accusation there, and I began to imagine that he suspected nothing, and that, even if he did, he bore us no ill will. It seemed as though we might continue our lives together in a pattern of uninterrupted contentment and turn our attention to grander things.

Akan came home from the temple at Luxor angry and impatient and full of impassioned speeches about the ignorance of the priests who, presented with the opportunity to enlighten and advance, instead controlled the populace with ignorant tales of stone gods who demanded gifts of food and gold and fine-spun cloth—to which the priests, of course, helped themselves. I considered it a rather clever scheme, supporting, as it did, the economic base of entire cities whose laborers and artisans were kept busy crafting the icons which embodied the ka of nonexistent gods, weaving the cloth that clothed them, fashioning the jewelry that decorated them, growing the grain that fed them—and that, of course, supported an entire population of priests who had dedicated their lives to seeing to the needs of these gods who lived only in the imaginations of a superstitious public. The flagrant disregard of the principles of harmony and balance we had learned at the House of Ra did not enrage me as it did Akan, although I did wonder with him why the High Priests felt it necessary to concoct such elaborate fictions when a display of genuine magic would have served them even better. Nefar was concerned only that Akan spent too much time at the temples, for even though we now were confident we could defend ourselves against the priests if need be, we were not anxious to provoke a confrontation.

And therein was perhaps the most peculiar thing of all. The longer we stayed in Thebes the more we grew convinced that no one sought us, no one knew of our crimes; no one seemed to know, in fact, that the House of Ra had fallen at all. When finally we grew brave enough to say the words out loud, to imply, however obliquely, that once we had heard of a great temple in the desert called the House of Ra where powerful priests and magicians went to take their training, we received nothing but blank stares even from the most learned of our acquaintances. Slowly we began to understand: the House of Ra was a secret even more protected than we had imagined. And if no one knew of its existence, no one could possibly know of its destruction.

This, of course, made the encounter with the magician in the desert even more troubling. And though we did not speak of it, we didn't forget it either. And because of it—because we knew that somewhere there was at least one man who knew of the destruction of the House of Ra and whose intentions toward us were not entirely clear—we were never to feel completely safe.

Akan found no sign of the missing books at the Luxor temple, nor anyone who knew of them. The more specific inquiries we made, the more we began to suspect that no one would ever admit to knowledge of the House of Ra.

Was it possible that a memory enchantment had been unleashed when the House of Ra was destroyed? We had heard of such things, but had never witnessed it. Or wasn't it more likely that the High Priests and magicians who claimed such power in the nation had not, in fact, been trained at the House of Ra at all? Were they all pretenders, imposters, ignorant to a man of the full scope of the Practice? How, then, had they gained such power—power, it was said, even over Pharaoh himself? The questions, and their potential answers, haunted us for weeks. And then, in a single moment, all that we had learned and all that we had become since leaving the House of Ra came together to form a picture of startling clarity and shining simplicity, and we saw reflected within it nothing more than our inevitable destiny.

In the thirty-eighth year of his reign the old Pharaoh passed into the next world, leaving the guardianship of the Two Kingdoms of Egypt to his son Amunhotep IV. Our love for the pageantry and festival that had been so denied us in the House of Ra drew us down into the streets with the masses to view the coronation parade, a grand spectacle of gilded chariots and exotic animals and scantily clad dancers performing impossible acrobatics with flaming torches and jeweled swords. We laughed and cheered with the rest of the crowd, and we even got a glimpse of the new Pharaoh, a weakling youth wearing a heavily ornamented gold turban that looked too big for him, yet making quite an impression on the crowd by standing at the head of his own chariot and controlling the horses himself.

Preparing the way for the appearance of Egypt's newest deity marched a procession of priests from each temple, escorting the lesser gods—or a reasonable likeness of each—dressed in elaborate garments and adorned with sacred jewels. The gods themselves were either carried on litters or rode in high chariots with their priest-guards, and occasionally someone from the crowd would dart forth to beg a favor of the gods, to make an offering, or to ask a question of urgent import.

We were standing at the front of the crowd, having secured that position by the fineness of our garments and the aggressiveness of our servants, who kept back the unclean masses with raised voices and raised fists. Unlike other aristocrats, we had not set out chaises and tables of food to see our party through the long day of festivities, for we intended to stay only an hour or two. Our interest in the proceedings had begun to wane as the procession bearing the god Amun approached, and we turned to go, when suddenly a child bolted past us from the back of the crowd and into the street.

He was scrawny and naked, like so many of the peasant children in Thebes, and I noticed as he scrambled past that he had but one eye. In his hands he held a string of blue beads, no doubt an offering to the god, and he cried out something in a high thin voice that I was not attentive enough to hear. I was in fact laughing with Nefar over some dry comment one of us had made about the new king when we heard the child's screams, the shouts of horror and confusion from the crowd.

Akan, who had turned to glance back at the parade, saw it first. His face went white and he rushed toward the street. Nefar and I followed, already half-suspecting what we would find.

The elaborately decorated wagon that carried the god Amun had stopped in the street. The priests were in disarray, some of them driving back the crowd while others struggled with the suddenly skittish horses, whose silver and gold plumes danced in the sunlight as they shook their heads and snorted. One of the priests was trying to get the wagon to move back, another jerked on the bridles of the horses, urging them forward. Trapped beneath the front wheel of the wagon by his leg was the screaming child. Dark blood had already begun to stain the earth beneath the wheel, and a string of broken blue beads were scattered beneath the hooves of the horses.

A woman ran forward, screaming, and flung herself upon the writhing child. Someone shouted, "Get on there, get on!" and someone else, "You dare to halt the progress of the god!" Two of the priests surged forward, cursing the woman. One of them dragged her to her feet and when she tried to break away, wildly struggling for her child, the other flailed at her with a whip. The wagon lurched forward and the priest jerked the child free, tossing him out of the way like a broken doll. The child collapsed in a heap, his skin ashen and his sobs reduced to shuddering whimpers. His foot was connected to his leg by a few strands of rubbery, soil-encrusted flesh, and the stump pumped blood.

The mother gathered the child in her arms, wailing loudly, while the procession marched on and the bystanders began to shift their gazes away from the uncomfortable scene, moving back from the mother and child. I confess when I saw the pathetic bundle with the chewed remains of its leg and its life ebbing out in puddles of blood my stomach lurched and I turned away. Akan, who was always most deeply affected by the small tragedies of life, whipped around to follow the progress of the god's wagon, his face twisted with rage and horror. I touched Nefar's hand, urging her to come away, but instead she broke through the crowd and sank to her knees beside the grieving mother.

Many times during the centuries to come I would revisit that scene in my mind, and I would remember: it was Nefar who ran to the child. Akan saw only the cause, and I saw only the hopelessness, but Nefar saw the child.

Nefar shouted for water, snatching off her linen belt to bind the leg and reduce the loss of blood. I looked around until I saw someone with a traveling skin filled with water, and a wrestled it from him, rushing to Nefar.

"Quickly," she said, and I splashed water over the wound to cleanse it. The child was limp, unconscious from the pain and loss of blood, and his skin was cold. The mother began rocking him back and forth, her wails wearing on my ears like the screech of wild birds. Akan dropped down beside us and began scooping up the blood-soaked earth. I added water until it formed a firm mud.

"Have you sulfur?" he asked Nefar.

She dug into her pouch until she found a small quantity wrapped in a bladder. I produced shaved flint from my box of fire starter and scattered it into the mix. A few spectators had gathered around, watching and muttering curiously among themselves, but when Nefar began to pack the blood and mud mixture into the stump of the leg the mother shrieked her protest and tried to pull the boy away from us. "Leave him alone, go away from us! My baby, my son, you've killed him, you've killed him!"

The crowd began to stir uneasily, looking for someone on whom to vent their anger and their fear. Nefar and Akan and I made easy targets. I moved quickly to the woman, close to her tear-streaked face. I touched her forehead with one muddy finger, and her mind with my thoughts. "It's all right, Mother," I said softly. "Nothing to fear. So happy you're feeling better."

Her face smoothed, her eyes calmed, her tears dried. She cradled her son's head against her breast and watched calmly as Nefar continued to mold the broken pieces of flesh together with mud. When at last the foot was reshaped to the leg and encased in a mud cast, Nefar reached for my fingers with one hand and for Akan's with the other. Our eyes met. I know she saw the doubt in mine, as I saw the uncertainty in Akan's. But she whispered, "We can do this."

Alone, neither of us could have managed a healing of such proportions on one so far gone. But as our vitality slid into one another, as our intent meshed and locked and our strength doubled and redoubled upon itself, currents of energy flooded toward the wound and into the broken child, positive flowing into negative, the vacuum of need sucking life into emptiness. I could feel the rush of heat, like a fever, spreading from our joined fingers throughout my body in a wave and then draining from it with equal rapidity, leaving me cold and nauseous. There was a ringing in my ears, a momentary blurring of my vision, and the air tasted dry and bitter, tingling on my tongue. Slowly, the residual energy dissipated and I felt my strength returning. I blinked my eyes to clear my vision. My hands slid away from Nefar's and Akan's.

The mud cast on the boy's leg had dried and begun to crack. As I watched, it fell away in chunks, revealing a wholly joined foot and ankle where once there had been mangled flesh and crushed bone. The boy stirred and moaned.

I looked at Akan and Nefar and saw my jubilation reflected in their eyes. From the crowd came awed murmurs of "Magic!" and "The gods walk among us!" They began to back away, forming a wide respectful circle around us.

We might have taken our leave quietly then, or perhaps made a bow or two and gone contentedly on our way to let them admire us as they would. But the gold-trimmed white robes of a priest caught my eye, pushing his way into the circle, and a voice bellowed, "Back there, back I say!"

He stopped before us with his hand on his purse, scowling down at the boy who was whimpering sleepily and crawling into his mother's lap. "What's this?" he demanded. "I was told there was a dead child, and I've come to compensate the family. It wouldn't do for the ascension of the Pharaoh to be marred by such a thing, the gods would be displeased."

Akan leapt to his feet, his cheeks flushed dark. I tried to stop him, but it was too late. "And how much is the life of a child worth to the great Amun these days? How many children can you kill for the sake of the gold in your purse?"

The priest jerked his gaze from Akan to the mother. His eyes were filled with scorn. "What is this trickery? There is no injury here. Do you think to cheat the temple?"

"No!" gasped the mother, holding her child close. "He has been healed—he was dying, his poor foot torn from his leg, his blood pumping into the dirt—but look, he has been made whole!"

And someone else cried, "It's true! They're powerful magicians, great healers!"

Cried another, "The gods have come among us, they've visited us with their favor!"

The crowd began to press close, jostling us, trying to touch us. Some fell to their knees, others stretched out their hands toward us in obeisance. The priest narrowed his eyes on Akan, and swept his gaze toward Nefar and me. We got slowly to our feet.

"What is this?" he demanded. "Are you healers? Why aren't you in proper raiment, serving the temple? What are your names?"

I said, bowing my head as humbly as I was able, "We are no one worthy of notice."

But from the crowd came the cries again, "Gods! With my own eyes I saw it! The child was torn asunder and they made him whole again! His flesh mended in an instant, while we watched, there was no trickery!"

The babble of voices grew louder and more energetic. The mother put the child on the ground, and he began to hobble around experimentally on his newly healed limb while she pointed excitedly. The priest looked at us with renewed interest. "One can't help but wonder how three such talented healers could have been overlooked by the Pharaoh's court. Perhaps you'd best come with me to the temple, and make yourselves known."

I cast a quick frantic glance at Akan, silently begging him to remain silent. "Please," I said to the priest. "Do not allow us to squander your time." I took a step forward and fastened my gaze on his. My heart was pounding in my chest. "After all you have so many more pressing matters to attend to. There's nothing to interest you here."

A momentary confusion blurred his gaze. "The child . . ." And he seemed to forget what he had intended to say.

"Yes," I offered helpfully. "How fortunate for all that the child was uninjured."

"Yes," he agreed. "Fortunate." But he scowled as he glanced around at the excited, protesting crowd.

I felt the touch of Akan's energy tingling through my brain, and the locking thread of Nefar's. I raised my voice and opened my hand toward the crowd. "The gods do smile upon us on this great day," I said. "The child could have been seriously hurt, but he jumped out of the way just in time. How kind of you to return to make sure he was unharmed. But there is nothing to interest you here."

"Nothing," he repeated.

The murmurs of the crowd were growing more subdued.

"Nothing to interest anyone here," I said, loudly.

Frowning impatiently, the priest turned and walked away. The mother picked up her child, scolding him for his disobedience, and carried him away. The throng of admirers began to disperse, looking confused and uneasy as they arose from their knees, glancing around as though for reassurance, or in search of something they had lost. No one's notice fell upon us now at all.

I drew in a deep breath and released it. I looked at Akan and Nefar, and without a word we began to edge our way through the crowd. We did not speak until we reached home. We didn't have to. Everything we were thinking was reflected in our eyes.

# Eight

We took our supper on the rooftop that evening. In the distance the sounds of continuing revelry still reached us, and the city was illumined with flickering torchlight and dancing bonfires. We could smell the smoky flavors of roasting goat and succulent fowl, and hear snatches of music from at least half a dozen different sources amidst the drunken laughter and raucous voices. Across the river, the royal palace was ablaze with celebration as the worthy came to pay their respects to the newest living god.

Our own bowls of fruit and crusty bread remained largely untouched, although we did justice to the wine. For a time Nefar and I joined hands and danced to the music that drifted up from the streets, laughing and tossing back our heads, and the incident in the street was forgotten. But when we opened our circle and invited Akan to join us, he scowled and waved us away. The joy was gone from our dance after that, and we soon abandoned the effort.

Akan paced back and forth, scowling, while Nefar and I lounged on cushions near the fountain, thinking our own unhappy thoughts and nibbling at the fruit in a desultory fashion.

"They are useless," declared Akan for perhaps the fourth time, "all of them. They know nothing of the ways of the House of Ra, or if they ever did, they have now forgotten. They set themselves up as servants to ridiculous lumps of stone and deceive the people into worshiping what does not exist."

"If they did not," pointed out Nefar, "they would all soon starve."

I tasted a fig, and tossed it away. "I think we should leave the city," I said.

Nefar looked interested. "Where would we go?"

"I don't know." But I sat up a little straighter, considering it. "To Africa, perhaps. Or perhaps I'd take a ship to some even more distant land."

"And what would you do there?" demanded Akan.

I shrugged. "What are we doing here?"

"Exactly!"

He stopped his pacing and came to us, dropping to his knees on the cushions beside us. His face was filled with an urgency I had not seen in him before. "Do you think we survived the fire for no purpose? Do you think we owe the world nothing for—" a small catch in his voice here, and he made a backward gesture with his hand that was all too easy to understand. "For what we did? You are my brother, Han, and my sister, Nefar, and I know your thoughts as I know my own. You suffer as I do with the memories of what we lost, but don't you understand if we don't do something to help the lives of those who have been forever deprived of the knowledge of the House of Ra, we are no better than the murdering deceivers who died there . . . no better than the false priests who are parading their wealth in the streets while children are being trampled underfoot!"

His passion made me uncomfortable, as though a challenge had been thrown down that I was unable to meet. I said, "There has always been cruelty, Akan, and injustice and tragedy, and there always will be. We can't change the world."

He sat back on his heels, his eyes luminous in the twilight. He demanded softly, "If not we, then who?"

Nefar stirred beside me. Her tone was defensive, even a little dismissive, but I sensed her curiosity had been piqued. "What would you have us do, Akan? Heal every cripple and feed every mouth that comes by our door? Touch the minds of every citizen of Thebes and turn them against the priests? We soon would have time for nothing else!"

He said stubbornly, "It would be a start. Look at what we did today!" Excitement returned to his voice. "The child's leg was severed! We had never applied our strength to healing before, yet it was effortless! And then, in an instant, to rewrite the memory of everyone who witnessed the event—do you realize what we could accomplish with that enchantment alone? But even that is nothing—less than nothing—when compared with what we might eventually do."

He stood again and resumed his pacing. "The Nile overflows and seeds the soil with the nutrients to feed a nation, but also with disease and black flies and swamplands that can destroy a family or a village in a single season. The great sun that ripens our fields of grain also causes men and beasts to stagger and die beneath it, and the grain that stands between prosperity and starvation for an entire nation can be destroyed in a matter of days by the touch of blight that begins as an organism too small to see. Pharaoh alone can afford to maintain a herd, so Pharaoh alone dines on beef. We must trade with faraway lands for that which we cannot grow, and journeys of months or even years are required to obtain such things—meanwhile the wealth of Egypt is being used to maintain foreign armies that may one day rise against us."

He turned and faced us with eyes glowing so intensely in the dark that they seemed like coals aglow in his narrow face. "We could change all that, don't you see? *We could change it.*"

It was a moment before I could recover from my astonishment to speak. "Are you serious? Change the flow of the Nile—"

"The strength of the sun—" chimed in Nefar incredulously, "the nature of disease, the growth of grain—"

"We are not gods, Akan!" I said, laughing.

His eyes glittered in the dark. "Aren't we?"

In a catlike movement he lunged toward us and snatched the fruit knife from the table where the remnants of our supper were scattered. Before either of us could stop him or even guess what he was about, he plunged the knife into his neck where the blood of life pulses most fully. His face twisted in pain and a font of blood spurted forth from the wound as he twisted the knife free. An instinctive cry of protest was wrenched from me, as it was from Nefar, and I sprang to my feet. As I did so, Akan took the knife and plunged it deep into my belly.

I felt it going in, hot-cold, a dull ache at first that surprised a grunt from me, and I felt my gut twist, a slow writhing ripple of torn intestine and shocked muscle, as it was pulled out. I stared at Akan in astonishment, my hands gripping the wet wound, and then an icy wave of pain exploded through me that caused pinpricks of darkness to dance before my eyes and left me dizzy and nauseous.

Nefar cried, "Akan, you fool!" and wrested the knife from him. She threw it off the roof with an angry gesture and rushed to me.

But already the healing had begun. The blood was sticky on my fingers, but no longer pulsing. I thrust my fingers beneath my tunic and felt the smooth thin scar that had formed over the gash in my stomach. I said hoarsely, shakily, "Damn you, Akan."

He came to me and laid his forehead against mine. His shoulder was black with blood, but the source of that enormous spill was no longer visible. "I'm sorry to cause you pain," he whispered. "I'm sorry."

And I felt him brushing through my mind, and Nefar, a whispered caress that shivered through my soul, smooth warm honey flowing through my veins, these two whom I loved. I felt them, tasted them, smelled them, was filled with them in every pore of my body for one brief, buoying moment. Then, like a kiss that was over too soon, we parted.

For a moment we were all three silent, together yet apart, comforting each other as we adjusted once again to our aloneness. Then Nefar said softly, "He is right, you know. If we cannot use what we are to change the world in which we live, then why are we here? And if not us, then who?"

I knew she was right, and yet a frisson of superstitious uneasiness ran through me. I remembered a night in the desert when we had walked with the Master Darius, and the words he had spoken to us then. . . . I could not recall them all, nor even their general purpose, but the face of the Master would not leave my mind. I said, "We made a vow not to use our knowledge or our magic to change the destiny of nations, or of civilizations."

A flicker of distaste was revealed on Nefar's face and I knew her words before she spoke them. "And to whom did we make that vow? To men who cast young boys, blindfolded and bound, into a pit of flame to be consumed and bought their own magic with human sacrifice!"

I had no argument, nor did I wish to make one. Nothing we had learned regarding the morality or responsibility of our station could now be counted as truth. We were alone now, and must make our own rules.

I searched Akan's face, though I could not say entirely what I was looking for. "It's no small thing, what you suggest." Yet even as I said it, I was aware of a coil of excitement beginning to unfold within me. "To do even half of what you wish would require more magic than we know."

Nefar said slowly, "Perhaps not. Perhaps only one or two conjurations would serve, if they were the right ones. If we had control over the resources of Egypt, managing the rest would be simple."

I said, "Only Pharaoh has control over the resources of Egypt." But even as I spoke I felt the understanding unfold within me, and I accepted it with more wonder than surprise. I looked at Nefar, and she was smiling.

*Our time will come.* I could almost hear her thoughts in my ears.

Akan was watching us, and had I the presence of mind to notice, I would have seen something disturbing in his eyes. When he spoke it was with a watchful, almost challenging tone.

"It would require a blood sacrifice," he said. "You would have to consume the flesh of the Pharaoh in order to assume his form."

*Blood sacrifice.* The screams of dying innocents echoed in my ears, and faded when I looked at Nefar. Hadn't I always known—wasn't every man born knowing—that the old must die to make way for the new?

I said, "I am not afraid."

And for the sake of the wonder and pride in Nefar's eyes at that moment, I would have slain armies.

The silence was long and heavy. To our ears, even the sounds of revelry in the distance faded, and became dull. There was only the sound of our breaths, our heartbeats, our thoughts.

Then Nefar said, very softly, "To become another human being. The Forbidden Art."

The words hung in the air for a moment, experimentally, even tenuously. Then she looked at Akan. "Can we do it?"

A dozen emotions raced across his eyes, but already he was far away from us, plotting, exploring, discovering. "If we had the books . . . there's so much I can be sure of . . . but I recall reading . . ."

He took a breath. "Yes," he answered, "I think we can."

Once the words were spoken, there was no turning back, I see that now. A thing, having been determined to be possible, virtually demands to be done—or so it seems when you're young, and idealistic and possessed of unlimited imagination—and unlimited power. The discussions in the days that followed were passionate and intense, but they concerned only how we should execute our plan, not whether or not we should try.

Egypt would have a new Pharaoh, one whose powers over the forces of the Universe were real and not imagined. One who was benevolent, wise, visionary, and capable. And Pharaoh would have a queen. *Our time will come.* I saw the promise dance in Nefar's eyes, I felt it sing in my heart.

Our time had come.

The months that followed were consumed, day and night, with detailed plans of the government we wished to build, the improvements we wished to accomplish, the miracles of science and technology—though it was in those days more often called magic—that we wished to introduce to civilization. After much debate it was agreed that the simplest course of action would be to start from scratch and build our own royal city some distance from Thebes, to move the royal court there, and to let the corrupt and useless priesthood die a natural death. And oh, what a utopia we designed!

The streets would be paved in hard brick to eliminate the dust, and cleaned four times a day. Every night they would be washed with a swift flood of water released from a nearby storage pool, and dried sparkling clean by morning. Cooling fountains of elaborately designed statuary would spray and play at every intersection. Each home would be a palace, and even the lesser classes would dwell in well-maintained apartment houses with slate roofs and brick floors, cooled by thick walls and turning cedar fan blades in the summer and warmed by generous fireplaces in the winter.

We would bring battery-powered light into every home, and refrigeration to those who could afford the price of the materials necessary, and electronic conveyance that would take its fuel from the sun and cut in half—no, in quarters—the time it took to trade for goods, or to travel to other parts of the land to oversee one's holdings or businesses. In due time we would build bigger and faster ships—perhaps even flying ships!—that would bring the world to Egypt, rather than forcing Egypt to conquer the world.

We would engineer cattle that could grow fat on one-tenth the ground they now required, and that would grow twice as big in half the time. We would design more efficient beasts of burden, larger, lusher gardens, faster-growing, disease-impervious grains and fruits that could thrive on small plots with little water. We would impregnate these fruits and grains with modified bacteria which would impart immunity from all common diseases to those who consumed them.

Akan insisted passionately that we would make the knowledge of the House of Ra available to all who wished to learn it, not just to a privileged few. We would expose the false gods and teach the people the truth of the One Power, that single universal circle of infinite energy whose symbol is the ever-burning sun, benevolent King of Egypt. We would impart our own exalted morality upon the people, condemning adultery and the taking of more than one wife, the desertion of children, the abuse of lesser animals. In a matter of years we would advance the course of human civilization millennia. We would create paradise on earth.

Ah, we were brilliant, we were farsighted, we were indomitable. No detail was overlooked, no possible need for our self-determined utopia was unanticipated. Never in all of history had anyone been more qualified to rule the world than we three, or so we firmly believed. In many ways we were right.

We decided on a conjunctive enchantment, in which all the elements required for the various bits of magic we intended would be distilled into a single substance, empowered by our joined wills, and activated at once in a chain reaction. This was no simple matter. Thousands of different concoctions, diffusions, distillations, and contrivances were required, each with its own enchantment and empowering of wills, and a single misstep at any point along the way would have caused the entire chain to collapse. Months were required to assemble the materials, both common and dear, the base elements, the rare metals, the precious and semiprecious stones; the herbs, spices, and fluids that would capture and enable our various enchantments. We set up our laboratory in a low windowless room of our house and we worked day and night, often without sleep, and our servants began to gossip about us nervously, as did our neighbors. We barely noticed. We had embarked upon the greatest undertaking in the history of mankind. Nothing would deter us from its completion.

Very close to a year from the time the plan had first been conceived, the talisman was completed, distilled into a few ounces of black powder, and concealed inside a circlet of gold with a tiny hinged lock that Nefar would wear upon a chain around her neck. A few ounces of powder, shaken loose from its container and activated with the right words and intonation, compounded by a single final surge of our joined vitality, and a work of magic like none that had ever been known would begin to unfold, unstoppable, upon the world. Gazing upon the small gold circlet nestled between Nefar's breasts, we were still with reverence, and with awe for what we dared to undertake.

Into the silence Akan spoke. "We will use an invisibility spell to make our way past the guards and into the Pharaoh's sleeping quarters. Should anyone be lying with him, or should a servant be present, we must immediately control that mind and cause him to see only what we wish him to see."

Nefar and I nodded soberly. Already built into the conjunctive spell was an enchantment that would allow us to rewrite the memories of all those in the palace after we had taken our new places, but we had to plan for all contingencies that might occur before the spell was activated.

Akan went on, "As soon as it is done, the distillate must be poured upon the Pharaoh's beating heart. It is the hot blood that will activate it and cause it to be absorbed into the flesh." I saw him swallow, and his eyes were steady upon mine, yet gentled with a question. "Can you do this thing, Han?"

The thing. The one thing with which neither of them could help me. The murder. We had never discussed who would do the actual deed, there never had been any question. Akan was the dreamer, I was the one who put those dreams into action. I was the strongest. I could be counted on to do what was necessary.

I was to be Nefar's husband.

Of course the old Pharaoh must die before the new one could assume his likeness. A young man, full of confidence and raw unfettered strength, emboldened by the nobility of his cause and certain of his own immortality, does not think long about the need to kill, nor his ability to do so when required. It is for this reason that young men go so cheerfully and thoughtlessly off to war; have done so for centuries uncounted and will continue to do so to the end of time. I did not want to kill. But for the sake of this magic, for the sake of Nefar, I could do it.

I nodded.

He said, "The flesh of the heart must be consumed while the heart is still beating. There will only be a few moments, and we'll need every one of them. If you hesitate, all that we've worked for will be gone. The Pharaoh will be dead and we will have nothing."

I felt my throat constrict. I was strong, and I was young, and my knife was sharp. I believed I could carve the heart from the sleeping

Pharaoh's chest without a qualm. But the thought of putting the thing in my mouth, bloody and writhing, or biting down on it with my teeth and forcing it down my throat—what if I couldn't swallow? What if, having swallowed, I regurgitated the whole mess immediately? These concerns and others had caused me more than one sleepless night as I lay going over the plan in my mind.

I glanced at Nefar, and then at Akan. I was the strongest, both physically and mentally. There really was no choice. I was meant to be Pharaoh, and Nefar was destined to be my queen. I said, "I can do it."

Akan nodded. "The transformation should begin immediately, and should take no more than a few moments. If it doesn't—then we'll know we've failed."

"We won't fail," Nefar said.

"I will be Pharaoh," I said, my voice now soft with wonder. Ruler of all Egypt, which was, in effect, all the world. A god, worshiped and adored, bringer of peace and prosperity to all of his people. "Pharaoh," I said again, trying to become accustomed to the title. It was less difficult than one might imagine.

Nefar slipped her hand through my arm, squeezing it a little. "And I shall be your queen. And Akan High Priest."

It seemed Akan hesitated a fraction, and then he smiled. "Don't be uneasy, Han. You won't be alone."

That was true, nor would I have wished to attempt this magnificent venture without them. But in the end, it all depended on me. For all the centuries to come, humankind would look back on this era and remember my name, my face.

Only of course it would not be my face.

The sense of history, of import, pressed down heavily upon us, thickening the air. In an attempt to lighten it, though with a genuine underlying anxiety I had not fully admitted before, I said, "I'm not certain how I feel about carrying around the features of that ugly weakling for all of eternity. Are you certain the enchantment can be reversed?"

"Nothing in nature is irreversible."

That was, of course, no answer at all, but instead of pressing for details, I said, "Good. Because I've grown rather attached to my own handsome face."

Nefar kissed my mouth, her eyes sparkling. The thrill of it sang in my soul. "As have we all."

Akan took a breath. "Then we are ready. When shall it be done?"

We looked at each other for a moment, solemnity descending. After all this time, to have no more work to do, to have our goal within reach . . . we had to pause, and absorb it all.

Then Nefar said simply, "Tomorrow?"

Barely a heartbeat passed before the two of us nodded. "Tomorrow."

# Nine

And so the plan that was born of a hundred feverish midnights unfolded into the world of stone walls and creaking gates, of torchlit corridors and armed guards. On several occasions previous Nefar, who was the best of all of us at maintaining invisibility, had stolen into the palace proper and mapped the way to the Pharaoh's sleeping chamber, exploring hidden hazards. We followed her lead with hearts pounding and breaths stilled, using all our inner discipline to sublimate our anxiety into that quiet center that transformed what was seen into what was little more than a whisper in the night, a ripple of a shadow glimpsed from the corner of an eye.

We slipped unseen past the guards and into the Pharaoh's chamber. Somewhat to my surprise, it was not so much more luxurious than my own bedchamber at home: layers of pale silk that sighed and stirred in the breeze draped the doors, the sleeping couch was painted in gold and turquoise, bottles of colorful oils and ungents stood upon the rim of the bathing pool. A servant girl stood over the sleeping figure on the couch, waving a palm frond slowly back and forth. Without dropping the invisibility shield, I tossed a handful of sleeping powder into her face. She sneezed, coughed softly, and staggered a step or two back. Then, as the powder dissolved into her pores and sent its essence into the nerve centers of her brain, she closed her eyes and dropped into an ungraceful heap on the floor. Nefar dragged her out of the way.

We released the invisibility shield that was consuming so much of our energy and approached the couch. There the young Pharaoh slept, naked and sweaty, with his mouth open and his lower jaw slimy with a trickle of saliva. The rumble of a breathy snore came from his throat and, as we watched, a black fly landed on the corner of his mouth. I had to restrain my hand from reaching out to brush it away.

In silence we stood, and for that moment we shared a single, paralyzing thought: *He is just a boy!* An ugly, cave-chested boy with thin strands of sweaty hair plastered to his skull and foul-smelling breath. Not an immortal ruler, not the most powerful man on earth, not our enemy, but a boy like Akan, like me. The ivory handle of the knife I had tucked into my belt was slippery in my hand, and I felt my courage ebbing away.

My eyes met Akan's, and there was a moment . . . a moment when everything almost changed. Then Nefar's fingers pressed hard into my arm. "For Egypt!" she whispered urgently. "For all of mankind!" Then, even more softly, but with a passion that reverberated in my soul, "For *us*!"

Ah, immortal words that ring unchanged down through the ages: *for country, for civilization, for the love of a woman!* Weaker men than I have charged into battle for the sake of that anthem, greater crimes than mine have been discharged. The press of a woman's fingers, the passion in her eyes, and debate is ended; swords are unsheathed. So it has always been. So it was at that moment.

My knife was in my hand, cool and steady and familiarly weighted. My eyes focused on the snoring Pharaoh's chest. Early in our education we had been extensively indoctrinated in anatomy, physiology, and surgical techniques. It crossed my mind to wonder whether such education had been for purposes just such as this as I tightened my muscles and swung the blade downward with precise expertise, cracking open three ribs and severing the greater vena cava in a single motion. The fountain of gushing blood surprised me and made me drop the knife; it spattered into my face and hair and even my eyes. Akan gasped, "Hurry, hurry!" and I saw that he and Nefar were both streaked with blood, big-eyed, gasping as though they themselves had performed the assault. I thrust my hands into the cavity, fingers slipping through hot glistening tissue and snagging on broken bones. I could hear my own breath now, irregular and roaring, as I grasped the ribs with both hands. They made a sucking, cracking sound as I pulled them aside. The heart was still quivering in its bath of blood. I plucked it free with both hands, and Nefar spilled the measure of black powder over the wet, weakly convulsing muscle. I watched with fixed gaze as the powder dissolved and was absorbed into the flesh.

There was a moment, though it was no longer than the space of an indrawn breath, when all of time seemed to stop. Nefar had fallen to her knees, the empty circlet of gold clutched in her hands. Akan had staggered back against the couch and clung to it for support. Both gazed at me with eyes ablaze in passion and triumph, trembling with the magnificence of our ambition and the anticipation of its fulfillment. I trembled too. I felt the adoration that surged from them, and it buoyed me, emboldened me, washed through me like a potion. This was my destiny, this was my glory. For the woman I loved, for the greatness of Egypt, for the sake of all mankind, I was born for this thing.

I held the heart before my lips, this living thing filled with the magic of all our futures, and without another moment's hesitation brought it to my mouth. And then, without warning, Akan lunged forward and snatched the quivering muscle from my hands, thrust it to his lips, and sank his teeth into it.

I must have cried out in protest and in shock, but it was too late. Already the magic was begun. The spell was cast, the Fates called forth, the elements surged to our command. Oh, how the earth quaked beneath our power. The winds of flame roared through our minds. The stars bowed down before us, we three in the blind innocence of passionate conviction, joined in ecstasy to change the world.

I heard the roar of it sweep through the room, sucking the air of oxygen. I felt the concussion of a silent explosion and was buffeted by the aftermath, blinded by the colors, turned inside out by the vitality that rushed from me, was pulled from me, was *seared* through me like a foundry iron bursting through the top of my head. When the storm was passed, I was on the floor, clinging to Nefar, and the room was filled with the smell of burned blood.

On the floor a few feet away from us, Akan writhed in the throes of violent convulsions. Bloody foam spewed from his mouth and his clothes were drenched with sweat and urine. I wanted to rush to him but I was frozen with horror. I could hear his bones snap as violent muscular contractions flung him against the marble floor again and again. Choked, gurgling sounds came from his throat. The skin of his face began to ripple, as though some small animal were crawling on tiny fast feet just beneath the surface of it. His fingers contracted and lengthened with a jerk; I could see the fingernails growing and reshaping themselves. It was then that I realized the harsh sobbing breaths that filled my ears were not Nefar's, but my own.

I lurched toward Akan, but Nefar clutched my arm with both hands, her nails digging into my flesh. "He's dying!" I cried, and tried to pull free.

"No," she said. She was breathing hard, but her eyes were like glass, bright and still and reflecting in their depths the flashes of light and dark of the violence that was taking place before us. "No."

Akan vomited forth a great stream of brown foul-smelling liquid, and it seemed to me then his entire face seemed to convulse; muscles contracting and small bones dislocating, skin stretching and beginning to crack. Fine fissures opened and bled around his mouth, nose, eyes, and cheekbones. Clumps of hair, matted with blood, were left on the floor when he rolled his head in agony, and though his mouth was twisted in an anguished scream, no sound came out.

It lasted an eternity, this I know. But I also know that in real time only moments had passed from the time we slipped past the sleepy guards and into the Pharaoh's chamber. Perhaps there came a time when I could no longer watch my friend's death throes, perhaps I turned my head away. Perhaps I stared, fixed in horror and bursting with helplessness, through the entire transformation. I know only that at last he lay still, surrounded by the smeared film of blood and waste on the marble floor, and, to my astonishment, he was still breathing.

I whispered his name. He did not reply. Nefar's fingers were still squeezing my arm, pressing so hard that I could feel the shape of them on my bones.

Akan got up on all fours, head bowed and shoulders hunched; then, shakily, he rose to his feet. Without looking at us, he staggered to the pool. There was a difference in him, the shape of his body, the length of his stride. He seemed smaller, his shoulders rounder, his legs oddly shaped. He reached the edge of the pool and slipped off his stained clothing. My breath caught in my throat.

It was not Akan's body that descended into the water, not Akan's head that ducked beneath the rippling pool, not Akan's face that emerged a moment later, not his hands that slicked the water away from his features, and not his eyes that looked into mine. I turned my own gaze toward the bloody form on the couch, the face vacant and still, robbed of life. I looked at Akan and saw that face again, animated, living.

Nefar went weak with relief, her fingers drifting away from my arm. I had to hold on to the wall as I got to my feet.

There must have been a hundred, a thousand, thoughts and impressions and emotions cascading through my mind, all of them fighting each other for attention: astonishment, shock, disbelief, horror; the triumph of success, the amazement of what we had dreamed and schemed and planned and toiled toward made manifest at last in the world of reality . . . all of this and more crowded up my mind with their thousand separate clamoring voices. But what I said was, hoarsely, "Why?"

The brief sharp silence, had I but listened, spoke volumes. The way Akan, Akan who was no longer Akan, shifted his gaze from mine, the way Nefar stood slowly beside me, the way she touched my fingers with a hesitant, birdlike brush. "Han, please, what does it matter? Don't you see what we have done? It worked, Han, we have changed all of history, that's all that's important!"

I shook my head slowly, and I couldn't take my eyes off of Akan. Pharaoh. "No. It was supposed—to be me."

Nefar said, "Han, please. We have to get everything cleaned up. We don't have much time."

It began to occur to me that none of this had been a surprise to her. She had known what Akan planned to do before he did it. *In the end there will be only two.*

Urgency, fury, and disbelief mixed with the beginnings of horrified betrayal and I gripped her arm roughly. *"Why?"*

It was not regret that shadowed her eyes so much as impatience, and . . . pity. "Han, think about it. Akan is far more suited to be pharaoh. He has the intellect, the ideals, the *purpose* . . ."

My bewilderment began to fade into something far colder, far sharper. Something very close to understanding.

My voice was curiously flat as I said, "But not the courage to do murder."

My eyes moved slowly around the room, seeing it as though for the first time. The blood-spattered curtains, walls, floors. The servant girl sprawled in a corner where Nefar had dragged her, the palmetto leaf forgotten on the floor. A pool of blood as thick as oil on the floor by the gold-painted bed, and upon that bed the body of a man who once had lived and drawn breath and ruled the most powerful nation in all the world, lying with his chest torn open and only a puddle of congealing blood where once his heart had been. The room stank of death and illness and terror.

I raised my eyes to Nefar. Blood speckled her face like fly droppings, and on the front of her tunic it had left a bright scarlet serpentine blaze. I felt gorge rising in my throat, yet I could not be certain whether it was backed by rage or disgust. "You knew." I could barely spit the words out. "You planned this, the two of you—without me."

Nefar's eyes were desperate with entreaty. "Han please, be reasonable. You know this is for the best! What I do, I do for us—for the sake of the magic, for what we were meant to become, for our destiny!"

Ah, at last, a name for the pain that stabbed through my chest, twisted in my belly, and carved raw flesh from my throat. Betrayal. Cold and black, hot and red.

I heard the splash of water as Akan left the pool, but when I turned it was not Akan at all, but the Pharaoh walking toward me in his odd ugly body with his peculiar hitched step. And when he spoke it was not with Akan's voice, and when he lifted his hand it was not with Akan's gesture. I took an involuntary step back, repulsed.

He said my name, "Han—" And then he stopped, as though startled by the sound of his own voice. He looked down at his own outstretched hand and his eyes filled with wonder. He spun and looked urgently around the room until he found a mirror of polished copper; he held it up to his face. He gazed into that reflection for a long silent time, and then he let the copper slip from his fingers with a clatter.

He looked at Nefar, lips parted in amazement, eyes glowing. "What we have done," he whispered. Then to me, "Han, what we have done! How can you bicker over petty differences when you see what we have done! And this is but the beginning!"

He pressed both hands to his face, that face that did not belong to him, and then with an exclamation of joy he flung open his arms and Nefar rushed into them. They embraced fiercely, wondrously, and I watched.

I said, "You used me. You used my strong arm and my will to get you to this place, and then you stole from me the victory."

Nefar and Akan separated, the delight in their faces fading to confusion, and it seemed genuine.

"The victory is ours, Han, together," Akan said.

"Nothing has changed," Nefar insisted. "We still will rule together, the three of us. You will be our priest, our vizier—"

*And you will be his queen!* I wanted to roar at her. *His bride, his lover, his queen!* The fury was so bitter I choked on it.

"This is what we worked for, what we dreamed of—"

"What you dreamed of," I said. The words came slowly, as though they were churned up from the core of me through a thick syrup of fog, and I had not the strength to make them forceful. "What you needed me to achieve, but can never share."

I saw the truth of it in Akan's eyes, in the way he glanced at Nefar and the way she removed her gaze in shame. But when he looked back at me the sorrow in his face seemed genuine. "Han," he said, and reached for me.

I tried not to shrink back. Curiosity, perhaps, or even a last desperate surge of hope, persuaded me to stand still, to accept his touch. His fingers brushed my cheek, and I felt the smooth cool caress of an unfamiliar hand . . . and nothing else.

Like a snake of ice coiling around my spine, words returned to me again. *In the end there will be only two.*

I backed away from them. Nefar caught my sleeve but I pulled it away. I heard her voice but I did not stop. Had I turned back, I think I might have killed them both.

I do not know how I left the palace, whether I used magic or whether I used force. I know only that I left—the room, the palace, the city of Thebes, and eventually Egypt.

And I did not look back.

# Ten

At twenty-five years of age in a time so long ago no accurate memory of it survives, I was a great and terrible wizard. I could take the elements of earth and the elements of air and grind them into a powder that would give a man the face of a donkey or the scales of a snake. I could turn my will inside myself and take wings for flight; I could be seen or not seen as I willed it; I could raise my hand in anger and cause lightning bolts to strike; I could turn a vain woman into stone with but a single look.

These were but simple matters of alchemy, of formulae executed in a certain and precise manner to obtain predictable results, and I was a master of the science. It was the alchemy I did not understand—the alchemy of the human spirit—that almost destroyed me in the years that followed my flight from Egypt.

Akan took inside his body a horrible potion that transformed his appearance—indeed, the very essence of his physical being—into that which belonged to someone else. It was a dark and dreadful Practice. But how much more dreadful is the transmutation of the human soul from something that has known hope, and joy, and faith, into something that knows only hate, and wants only to destroy. There is in all of alchemy no formula to accomplish this black mutation. It can only be achieved through bitterness and grief and betrayal. There is no ritual to perform it, no talisman to protect against it. It can only be done to oneself.

And so without wanting it or intending it I became over those next years something I barely recognized. I awoke in the morning with a cold black emptiness in my belly, and I took the emptiness to bed with me at night. To fill the hours in between I strode across the face of the known earth, destroying or maiming anything that stood in my path. Where there was a battle to be fought or an army to be led you would find me at the front of it, bringer of death, mocker of death. I cannot say how many times I felt the slice of the arrow or the stab of the sword pierce my heart, nor can I say how many were slain for the sake of that emptiness in my belly.

Where once I had feared pain, now I sought it, for no mere pain of the body could stand in measure against the great vast anguish in my soul. Sometimes, for my own amusement, I would make deep cuts in my wrists or gullet and let my blood flow into a basin, speculating upon how much of it would be filled before the wounds healed themselves. On other occasions I might go at night into the roughest encampments of desperate dangerous men seeking nothing more than to be roused to anger so that I might kill them with my bare hands.

Once in a marketplace the shrill voice of a vendor woman annoyed me, and I stripped her voice from her with a look, leaving her croaking and clawing at her throat like a crazed wild bird. In a tavern in Persia I did not like the way a man at a near table gazed at me; I raised my two fingers and burned his eyes out of their sockets.

There was no poison I could not make, no man I could not defeat, no woman I could not have. There was no writing I could not decipher, no mathematical equation I could not comprehend, no feat of engineering I could not perform. I was held in fear and awe wherever I went. Even now, should you dig deeply enough into the dusty layers of the ancient past, you will find stories of my exploits, for they were known far and wide. Yet the emptiness remained.

I traveled to Mesopotamia and India and the jeweled isles of Crete and Minos; I tasted the marvels of the Far East where few of my heritage had ever been before, and I wallowed in the drunken self-indulgence that was Babylonia. I added to my repertoire of knowledge in the arcane arts, and to my collection of rare and valuable catalysts, elements, and ingredients, and I took grim and greedy pleasure in acclaiming myself the most accomplished, the most powerful magician in the world. Beyond Nefar. Beyond Akan.

And sometimes, when I could bear it, I thought how their eyes would light with envy should they see what I had become, what I had learned, what I could do. What I could offer them. What I could take away.

Sometimes I thought of how I should ride into the royal city on an elephant painted gold and dressed with jewels, how I should shout their names with a voice of thunder, and how they would run down the palace steps to greet me . . . and how I would raise my arms and call down sheets of fiery rain to consume all they had built. Sometimes I conjured in my mind every dark spell I knew to cause them suffering, and imagined how I should delight in invoking each and every torment. And sometimes I thought that tomorrow, yes, the very next day, I would set a course for Egypt, and I would push my way through the palace guards, and I would throw myself, weeping, at Akan's feet and bury my face in Nefar's soft sweet belly and beg them to love me again, implore them to fill the emptiness and make me whole again.

But I never did.

Perhaps you have heard of it, the magical city they called Amarna, and the poet-king who ruled over it. Did the legends survive of flying machines and gleaming glass towers, of globes that held the light of a hundred candles and illuminated the city at night so that it glowed like a great floating moon on the sands and was visible for leagues in all directions? Music that needed no musician to play it, and walls that belched forth steady streams of cool dry breezes on even the hottest days; rain that came from cloudless skies, words that were written upon the air. Do they speak still of the great leaps in medicine and agriculture, in art, literature, philosophy, and science? Do they remember the magic? Or has that, like so much from that time, been erased with the history that we, its creators, wrote?

Wherever I traveled I heard the tales of the gentle, scholarly pharaoh and his beautiful queen, how they adored one another, how he forsook all other wives but her, how they had brought prosperity, tolerance, and enlightenment to all the land. Each word was a dagger in my heart. Yet I thirsted for those words like a man parched in the desert who licks the dew from a poisonous flower, I craved them, I lived upon them. Their story was my story; their triumph my triumph, and I longed for it with the pure and simple yearning of a child for its mother's breast.

Yet in the end it was not the longing that sent me home. It was a ghost.

There was in Crete, that land of bright sea and green hills, a tavern where they sold cheese and meat roasted on olivewood sticks, and strong red wine by the cup. I liked to go there on occasion, and I had just returned from a war I do not recall on a ship powered by long-muscled slaves. I was hungry.

I came into the tavern on an early morning, and not many were about. I pushed aside the dusty curtain and let my eyes adjust to the dimness while my mouth watered with the aroma of fresh-roasted meat. A man sat alone in a corner where the shadows were deep, but I paid him little heed at first. I called out for the shopkeeper and scooped my fingers into a skin of cheese that lay on the table. It tasted sweet and cool. I found a clay cup and filled it with wine from a jug.

As subtle as a breeze and just as swift, something moved beside me. I spun around, and looked into the eyes of death.

His face was handsome and unmarred, a sunny golden brown; his hair, which I had last seen flaming and crackling and melting from his skull, bore the rich dark luster of good health. His lips were curled into an all-too-familiar mocking smile. He said, "Han. How good to see you looking so well."

The cup slipped from my fingers and bounced on the dirt floor, splattering wine on my feet. A single word was expelled from me, like a breath after a sudden fall, like a prayer when all else has failed, barely a whisper and barely a thought: *"Darius."*

And then, on the next inhalation, as my senses returned to me, I took a quick step backward and raised my palm. "Enchantment be gone from me."

I closed my eyes briefly, and when I opened them again he was still there, laughing softly. "Surely you can do better than that, for all my years of tutelage."

I swept up my arm in a rush of instinct and panic and snatched from the air a thunderous crackle of electrical flame, flinging it toward him. In an instant his eyes darkened and my flame met an invisible shield of negative force that caused it to explode harmlessly in midair, filling the room with smoke and the taste of ashes.

"And so," he said in mild admiration, "I'm pleased to see your years of travel have not been wasted."

I could see the nubby weave of his cloak and the rim of dust where the hood fell across the shoulders. I could see the slight shine of perspiration upon his cheeks and the slow steady pulse of a vein in his throat. I could smell his sweat and the days of travel that lingered in his clothes and on his hair. If it was an illusion, it was a masterful one. If it was something else . . . it was the something else that terrified me.

I had heard of all manner of corrupt and unclean creations of the magical arts: rotted corpses who breathed again; homunculus-soulless lumps of artificial life that resembled human beings but were created by alchemy rather than nature—even spirits brought back to assume human form. I had seen none of these with my own eyes, but had no reason to doubt they were possible. And nothing that came to me in the form of a man I had helped to murder could mean me well.

I said hoarsely, "Who are you? What has sent you to me?"

He shook his head sadly. "Ah, how short the memory of youth!"

With my heart pounding in my throat I turned toward the table, as casually as I could manage, and reached for the jug of wine. "Then share a cup with me, and refresh my memory."

I uncorked the jug as though to pour, and in the same movement I spun around and flung the contents at him. It was a clumsy effort but effective, and gave me just the moment I needed to summon my inner forces in an explosion of will and transport myself out of the room.

Such apparent dematerialization is not a difficult concept to master, being composed of more illusion than of actual transference of matter. It is simply a matter of throwing up an invisibility shield and moving at what some might call superhuman speed; I had used it before to get myself out of tight situations. I did not expect such a simple trick to enable me to elude the creature for long.

I rematerialized in the alley outside the building, and had to take a moment to regain my strength. I cast my mind about for some sign of him but found none, and that disturbed me. I spun out an invisibility shield around me and moved as hastily as possible away from that place.

I kept a house on Crete, a long rambling structure atop a cliff overlooking the broad Mediterranean below. Two hundred steps, carved precariously into the cliffside, led from the village below to its door, a fine deterrent to thieves and doers of evil who might think to creep upon me in the night. I raced through the village and toward my sanctuary, gasping with the effort of the exercise and maintaining my shield. Midway up the cliff I rounded a sharp turn and Darius was sitting there, cross-legged, smiling at me.

In a situation like this one's choices are limited, even for someone who considers himself—perhaps even rightly—the most powerful magician in the world. The potions, spells, and incantations that can destroy an enemy require time to prepare and perform; the transmutations that might allow escape cannot be accomplished in the instant that lingers between life and death; illusions would be ineffective on a spirit, as would the powders that could blind, paralyze, or kill that I kept close on my person.

I chose the only course left open to me, and flung out from my mind a powerful burst of energy that blasted across the cliff surface and should have sent the creature flying, in pieces, toward the vast bottomless sea below. Shards of rocks exploded in all directions and dust billowed up like a cloud; the percussion sent me to my knees, clinging to the cliffside for balance. I stumbled onward, leaping over the gaping cavity where Darius had sat, coughing in the dust-thickened air. And as I passed I saw Darius, levitating calmly several arms' lengths away from the cliff surface, with nothing between him and the sea but a sheer expanse of air.

I reached my house with muscles trembling and sweat dripping from my body, gasping like a wild man. I bolted the door closed behind me, and Darius was standing beside an open window, a goblet of wine in his hand, waiting for me.

He lifted the goblet with a welcoming, inviting gesture. "We were about to refresh each other's memories, I believe."

I felt droplets of ice form in my bloodstream, even as the flush of exercise and shame still burned my skin. Powerful magician, indeed. Master of sorcery invincible, wizard of terror—until confronted by the ghost of my own past, and then I fled like a child who hears a noise in the dark. I was humiliated, angry, embarrassed—and still afraid.

"What manner of creature are you?" I demanded slowly.

Darius sipped his wine, shook the dust from his robe in a theatrical gesture, and made himself comfortable on a low round hassock in the center of the room. I wondered where the servants were, the caretakers who tended the place in my absence. I wondered who had opened all the windows to the morning light and sea breeze, and what manner of spell he had used to find his way here before me. My mind was spinning with nonsensical wonderings.

"The same as you," Darius said, and sipped again from the cup. "A mighty magician, a powerful sorcerer, a talented Practitioner of the great art of alchemy." He lifted his gaze to me above the rim of the goblet. "A man who cannot die."

At some point I came farther into the room, I drank wine from a cup, I sat close enough to him to assure my senses, such as they were, that what I saw was made of flesh and bone, that the voice I heard was conducted through the air and not merely inside my head.

He said, "As you grow older and more accomplished you will find that you will be incapable of being deceived by illusion—even performed by one as adept as I. Our senses adapt with age, you see, become more acute and quicker in their perception. We can see and hear things ordinary humans can't. Even now, should I try a trick on you, it would appear clumsy and inept, and you would laugh. Like so."

He lifted his glass and tossed its contents at my face. But it was the oddest thing: the ruby droplets of wine seemed to crawl toward me, flat and dry; not wine at all but more like a drawing of wine that moved at ridiculously slow speed. If I had wished, I might have stood up and walked away before the wine reached me, but there was no need; it dissolved into nothingness before it touched my face.

I looked at Darius. "You would have me believe then that your appearance here is no illusion."

He sipped his wine, which of course had never left his cup. "Nor am I reanimated from the dead, nor fashioned only to look like the man you once knew, nor am I the result of any other arcane manipulation—not even one as clever as you and your friends devised for the Pharaoh."

I swallowed hard and my throat felt coated with sand. I stared into my glass but could not imagine bringing it to my lips, taking wine into my mouth, actually expecting it to stay on my stomach.

I said, "So that is why you have come. To punish me for my part in the crime."

And even as I spoke it I was aware of a certain relief at the thought, a relaxing of muscles that had been angry and afraid and poised for flight for years; a peace, almost, at the possibility that my suffering might soon be ended, the emptiness gone.

He said, "Our role is not punishment, Han, nor revenge nor manipulation nor acquisition. Our role is justice, and balance."

Abruptly, I was angry again. "*Our* role? I have nothing to do with you, nor with the depraved philosophies of your so-called temple! Do not come here, murderer of children, and tell me what my *role* is!"

Darius was unmoved by my outburst. "I have come for two reasons, neither of which is to judge you. Be assured that this will not be the last transgression you will make against your teachings, and know that even in your darkest ponderings you have not yet begun to imagine the kinds of crimes that I myself have committed in the course of my many lifetimes."

And there it was again. *My many lifetimes.* With my own eyes I had seen him die a horrible death in the flames; I had seen his skin melt from his face and his eyes burst in his head . . . just as he, no doubt, had seen me. Was there any other reasonable explanation for his appearance here than that he, like me, had been reborn in the flames? Could we really have been so foolish as to think we were the only ones in all of the world to possess this gift?

I stood slowly and took my knife from my waist. He did not waver or flinch as I approached him, blade drawn back. In fact, he sat back and opened his robe, baring his chest. His eyes did not leave mine, and for a moment my courage almost faltered. But it was a moment only.

I brought the blade down in a quick hard slash across the musculature of his chest, not a killing blow but severe enough to tell me what I wanted to know. He gave a grunt of pain and his eyes went hazy, but not a drop of wine was spilled. Flesh opened like a seam in a garment, layers of skin and pink muscle and dark ligament, and the seam began to well with blood. But before more than a few bright trickles had marred the surface of his chest the wound began to close, knitting into a thin pink scar that faded before my watching eyes.

"True," I whispered, and more than that I could not have spoken though I summoned all the will at my command.

The knife slipped from my fingers and clattered to the floor, leaving a smeared red stain on the marble. I backed a couple of steps away, staring.

Darius brushed the blood from his chest with his fingertips and closed his robe. I turned abruptly away and took up my cup, draining the contents in a series of long deep swallows. I refilled the cup, but it was a long time before I could face him again.

I think that was the first time I really understood what it meant to live forever. And the understanding brought me no comfort.

I said at last, on a long slow breath, "It was you who came to us in the desert."

"Yes."

"Why?"

He shrugged. "Without me, you would still be hiding in caves and eating lizards."

"But we tried to kill you."

"Yes," he said simply.

A moment passed while I collected my whirling thoughts.

"Are there others?"

He did not answer right away. When he spoke his voice was solemn. "There are always at least two of us on earth at any time. There always must be."

All I could think to say was, hoarsely, "What do you mean?"

"Balance," he replied. "Nature will seek its balance, whether we wish it or not. For example . . ." He sipped his wine with the casualness of a man conversing about the weather. "Only another immortal can kill one such as you or I. Balance."

I forgot, for several seconds, to draw a breath. "Do you mean—I might have killed you with my knife a moment ago?"

He shook his head, his expression indulgent. "No, it must be done with intent, as must everything else. And you did not intend to kill me with your knife."

My eyes narrowed. "You are a fool to tell me this."

"Perhaps." And though he smiled, his eyes seemed tired. "You will not believe it now, but the day will come when you no longer regard death with indifference, nor take pride in your immunity to it. You will, in fact, come to welcome it, to long for it like a lover who has eluded your embrace."

I thought of Nefar, and I said, "I have known that day already."

But even as I spoke I was aware of a certain wariness, for it had just occurred to me that, whatever power I might now have over him, I was looking at perhaps the only man on earth I had reason to fear.

He said, "Don't worry yourself, Han, I didn't come here to harm you. And you needn't look so startled, in a hundred years or so your skill at reading the thoughts of others will be as great as mine. It is one of the first things you will learn."

There was an edge to my voice. "Is that why you have come here? To teach me?"

"Actually, yes. It was regrettable that you . . . left the temple before your education was complete. It is in fact unacceptable. I am here to help you."

"You have nothing that I want."

"Ah, but I do." And he held my gaze steadily. "I have answers."

"I have no questions I wish to put to a liar and killer of children."

"No?" A slight lift of his eyebrow displayed his indifference. He finished his wine and got to his feet. "Then I'll away. Perhaps we'll meet again in a hundred years or so."

I wrestled with anger and stubbornness and the dull empty sound of endless years marching into the future until he reached the door. I said, in an explosion of words I seemed to have no power to contain, "What was the House of Ra?"

He turned and spread his hands palms up, an expression of peace and patience settling over his face. "The story is long, and we're both weary from our travels. Set a table, bring more wine, and let us talk."

**I**t was an ancient place when I came there, a hundred lifetimes ago."

The remnants of our feast were scattered on the stone table between us: dates and crusty bread soaked in olive oil, herb-roasted lamb and bowls of nuts. The torchlight burned low and the second jug of wine was empty. I uncorked a third.

"No one knows how it came to be in the beginning, nor who established it there, but its purpose then as now is much as you have always known: to preserve the arcane knowledge of the world, and to train the guardians of that knowledge as Practitioners in the powerful arts that govern Nature." He dropped his eyes briefly. "Of course, now there is nothing to preserve, no one to train."

I swallowed a sudden bitterness in my throat, fighting the guilt. "And for all the centuries those—Practitioners, the Masters—have renewed their power with the ashes of innocent flesh."

He remained unmoved. "Acolytes are gathered from around the world, chosen for certain signs, whether of heritage or precocity, that they will grow into adeptness. It is something one is born with, you see, just as one is born with a predisposition to be short or tall, but there is no way to tell until it manifests itself. Very often the children of those who have proven themselves adept will manifest the same abilities, but just as often they will not. And sometimes an adept will appear from the general population, and we will hear of him through rumors of unusual circumstances surrounding his birth or childhood—to be born with a caul, for example, is often an encouraging sign, or to converse with unseen beings or animals as a child or to manifest certain small examples of spontaneous magic. These things will attract our attention, and we will request the parents relinquish the child to our tutelage. And why should they hesitate? The life we offer their offspring is one most families only dream of—a station in the priesthood, luxury and security for themselves and all their relations."

"Except there is no priesthood," I said sharply, "at least not from the House of Ra. I have traveled the world and met not a single priest who has been trained there, or who has aspired to train there. You lie to the families, and you murder their children. No one ever leaves the House of Ra."

Darius smiled. "I have left the House of Ra. You have. Nefar and Akan have. Others have, through the ages."

Though I knew my curiosity would only entertain him, I could not prevent the question which had shadowed me, off and on, my entire life. "And my family? Who were my parents?"

Darius said without blinking, "Your father was a powerful Practitioner. Your mother was a street whore. They are gone now, and of no concern to you. You were born in a ditch on the side of the road and left to die by a mother who was barely aware she had dropped you. You would not have lived a week had we not found you."

Perhaps it was the wine, or the lateness of the hour, or the simple strangeness of the day, but I felt no reaction at all. I was no longer certain why I had asked.

"And so," I said dully, "I was plucked from an early death in a muddy ditch to become fodder for your fire in later life." I lifted my glass to him lazily. "Forgive me if I do not seem as grateful as I might."

Impatience flashed across his face. "Curse your ignorance, Han, how can it be that you still do not understand? No one was forced to take the Passage! They came to us begging to be proven, knowing full well what they faced!"

"Mirisu did not beg to be thrown into a pit of fire!" My voice rose as the images of that horrible night came flooding back to me. "He did not beg to become a human sacrifice to your glory!"

"Of course he did," replied Darius dismissively. "No applicant takes the Passage uninformed. And no applicant has ever doubted for a moment that he would survive it."

I stared at him. "You lie."

He gave an impatient shake of his head. "Use your reason, boy. By the time an acolyte is ready to take the Passage he has performed a thousand miracles, seen a hundred impossibilities become manifest. He has trod across an ocean without dampening his feet, he has flown without wings, he has crawled on the belly of a snake and soared through the treetops with the birds. Should he then doubt for one moment that he can walk through fire unscathed? Would you have?"

For a moment I was rendered wordless as the implications and the likelihood of his assertions tangled through my head. "But he did not survive!" I cried at last. "No one survives!"

And even as I said the words the cold fingers of truth were tingling down my spine. Darius looked at me steadily, and he said, "You did."

I whispered, "No," not because I denied what I knew he was about to say, but because I did not want to hear it. Could not bear to hear it.

"The ritual Passage of fire is the only way an acolyte's true nature can be proven," Darius said quietly. "And wouldn't you, too, agree to take it—if the recompense was eternal life?"

I wanted to challenge him to the lie, to fling back at him the mastery of prevarication about which he had so often bragged; I wanted to deny his words with storm and thunder and challenge him to prove them upon penalty of his own immortal life; I wanted to rise up from my chair with a roar of rage and fling myself upon him, tearing at his eyes and squeezing closed his throat. I did none of those things. And I did not need to call upon superhuman powers of mental perception to know that he spoke the truth.

"We were wrong." I heard the words echo around the room, in a strange quiet voice that could not have been my own, but somehow was. Even as they faded away I could not recall having spoken them.

We were wrong. The ritual we had seen had not been sacrifice but willing fulfillment. We had destroyed the temple, Masters, the sleeping students, the collected knowledge of a hundred thousand generations, and we had justified it in the name of right, in the name of self-preservation, in the name of defending ourselves and the world against a much greater evil. But there had been no evil. We had never been in danger. All was as it should have been . . . until we interfered.

I lifted my goblet and saw, with a distant dispassion, that my hand was shaking. I set the goblet down again. There was no room in my throat for wine to pass, and every breath seared like acid.

Darius went on, "The fire, you see, is both a test and a trigger. Many are called to the Great Work, but few are chosen to become genuine Practitioners, for all immortality. Only through the Passage of fire can the healing essences of the body be activated, and only by facing his own death can a Practitioner achieve the potential of his spirit. This you would have learned had you come into your Passage in the fullness of time . . . this, and many other things."

"We destroyed everything." My voice was hoarse, and the words themselves felt like ragged shards of glass, scraping their way through my throat. "All those deaths . . . because we were young, and stupid, and intemperate." I took a breath and let the words settle in the room, heavy and still. Then I raised my eyes to his. "And now you have come to mete out my punishment. To torture me, perhaps, and then to kill me, as only you can do—as no doubt you have already done to Akan and Nefar."

He shook his head kindly. "I have told you before, revenge is not my purpose, and you have written your own punishment. When you have lived as many years, you too will discover a certain comfort in the rhythm of balance, and such petty motivations as revenge, and lust and greed are simply . . . irrelevant."

He refilled his goblet and stood, walking a few paces away, where he stood for a moment, gazing toward the darkened window and the moon-softened sea below. "What you fail to understand, Han, is that we the Masters bear as much responsibility for what happened as you do. We knew the danger of bringing the three of you together when only two should have been chosen. Yet it is the nature of alchemical magic that those who are drawn to its practice are afflicted with an insatiable need to experiment, to discover, to challenge what is accepted and to seek newer and greater challenges. Within the three of you we knew we had the potential for something never before seen among our kind. We thought we could guide it, control it, and give to the world a power more glorious than even we could imagine." He paused, and glanced at the wine remaining in his cup, and I thought how like Akan he sounded with his grand dreams and altruistic longings. "But we were wrong. It was against nature, and we were wrong."

He turned now and looked at me again. "This is your heritage, Han. This is how you and all those who have been forged through fire before you are charged. Your calling is to gather wisdom and disperse it judiciously when you can. Throughout history you will sit at the right hand of kings and warriors, you will give counsel, you will influence events that shape the course of mankind—and always you will maintain the balance. Today you will give the call to war, tomorrow you will herald peace. Today you betray a king, tomorrow you give rise to a dictator. You will cure a leper and withhold the potion from a dying child. You will never know, most likely, whether what you do is for good or evil, and it won't matter in the end, because that is simply the nature of life.

"You will never rule," he said, and his voice grew hard, and as cold as stone in the darkest hour before the rise of day. "You will never control by force or by direct interference. The most important rule of balance has always concerned the freedom of choice, and to take away that freedom of choice by a misuse of your power is the darkest crime against nature. Be sure you will be brought down for it, for remember, there are always two of us."

I drew a long slow breath, and found I could barely summon dread of the consequences I knew were coming. "Already we have broken that rule."

"You have tried," he said in the manner of one making a correction for a small grammatical error.

Curiosity tugged at the strange lethargy that had seized my limbs, and I raised my eyes to him.

"I told you there were two reasons I had come," he said. "The first was to complete your education, to the best that I am able, and the essentials I have already imparted to you. The second was to bring you a message from Nefar."

Of all that he had said this night, of all that had happened this day, these words alone had the power to propel me from my chair, heart leaping. "Nefar? You have seen her?"

"She begs you to come to them. You've been away a long time, Han. You haven't heard the news from Egypt."

My heart, stilled with anticipation for so many beats, now began to thunder in my chest. "I've heard news," I insisted. "I've heard news of prosperity, of bounty and riches beyond compare. I've heard how art and music flourish and how the foolish gods have been abandoned, and how desperately in love are the new king and his wife. I've heard—"

"You haven't heard how armies march across Egypt and ravage its lands and how the Pharaoh, in his glittering walled city on the river, is incapable of preventing them. You haven't heard how the priests of the old gods are even now gathering armies to rise against him, but most importantly of all, Han, you haven't heard what is happening to Amarna itself . . . to the Pharaoh. They have done their best to keep it secret, but they cannot protect themselves from the truth much longer.

"Your magic was imperfect, Han," he said. "The power needed for such a grand enchantment cannot be manufactured from half-remembered texts and experimental formulae. Only age and experience could have completed the spell. Like the falcon, like the bridge, your magic was flawed, and the center could not hold. Already it has begun to unravel, everything you set into motion is crumbling to dust. In mere weeks Nefar and Akan will be revealed for the imposters they are, and the priests will tear them apart."

I found I was breathing hard. "They can't be harmed by the priests, or by any army living, any more than I can."

Darius said, "You forget. The body Akan occupies is not his own, and I assure you they can be harmed. This is only one of the reasons the dark magic you attempted is forbidden."

I remembered then the Darius I had known at the House of Ra, who taught by trickery, whose mastery was mostly of duplicity. I knew that, for however true his earlier sayings had been, what he spoke now could be a lie designed to entrap me—and Akan and Nefar—and bring us all to account for what we had done. Yet there was a certain logic to what he said, a grain of possibility I could not ignore.

"Why should you care about this?" I demanded. "Why bring me such a message? You have said already that our magic has broken a cardinal law of balance, and that such a thing never goes unrighted. Yet you would have me return to make the spell whole again and restore the illusion you've just declared a crime?"

"I would have you do no such thing. I am telling you only that Nefar has sent for you, because she knows what Akan will not admit—it will take the three of you, united again, to undo what has been done, and to restore Akan to what he was."

I swallowed hard, and tried to mask the warring emotions that surged inside me. To return to them, after their rejection of me. To save Akan, after his betrayal. To be needed by them. To return to

Nefar. To be linked with her once again, to be joined once more in power and glory in the performance of our art, to feel the miracles exploding from our wills and into reality. To return to her.

If there was even a chance that Akan was in danger, even the ghost of a possibility that Nefar had sent for me, I had to go. I think Darius must have known from the beginning that I could not refuse.

Darius said gently, "I have told you before, Han, I can no longer deceive you. Touch my thoughts, find the lie if you can. Go ahead. Try."

It was as though, having been invited, I simply remembered how to do this thing, much in the way a muscle, once trained, will resume its former shape even after neglect, with a little coaxing. I felt my mind, like a question, slide toward his, and I felt the jumble of answers in images and snatches of sound, as though they were my own memories. Crops dying in the field, bloated animals lying dead in the roadway, angry, hungry people gathering into a mob. A glimpse of Nefar's face, her eyes desperate, and her voice: *His name is Han, they call him the Dark Warrior. You must find him and bring him to me—*

I looked at Darius. "You could have put the images in your mind to deceive me." But I did not think he had. And I knew something else, instantly. "It was not you to whom she spoke. Nefar didn't send you to me. You haven't seen her."

Darius said, "The palace and the grounds are protected by your magic, remember? You ensured that no one who practiced the Art could approach. A clever foresight, by the way, and one I'm not certain even I would have thought of. That part of the spell still holds—for now. I couldn't get close. But I heard her thoughts, and I met her messenger." Darius smiled. "He had no intention of carrying out his queen's orders. Your reputation is a terrible one, and he was more afraid of you than of her."

I was silent for a while, trying to sort out the thoughts that raced around in my head. But in the end there was no decision to make.

I stiffened my shoulders. "It will be an easy enough matter to discover whether you speak the truth. I will return to Egypt. If all is as you say, I will know it long before I reach Amarna."

He nodded. "I will accompany you if I may. There is still much I have to teach you, and the journey will go more quickly if we are occupied."

I hesitated, but saw no way to stop him. "We'll depart on the morrow."

I went to the door, my head filled with preparations for the journey and my body longing for my bed. Then I looked back. "It is Nefar, isn't it?" I inquired quietly. "Akan and I—we are powerful, but Nefar has always been the catalyst that multiplies our power, the way a glass magnifies the sun and makes a fire. It wasn't just the three of us who were your mistake. It was Nefar."

He did not answer. But he didn't have to.

# Eleven

As soon as I set foot upon Egyptian soil I saw that Darius had not lied. Fields of grain stretched toward the horizon, each stalk three times the height of a man—each stalk as black as soot, putrefying in the sun and crumbling to dust at the brush of a hand. Ripe fruit weighed down the branches of trees—and burst open at a touch, roiling with worms. Livestock lay dead of thirst on the very banks of the Nile, and the waters gave off the foul odor of dead fish and rotting flesh. The cities were filled with disgruntled tradesmen, crying children and their thin, angry mothers, soldiers on the move. Remnants of a disenfranchised priesthood had lost no opportunity to whip the populace into a frenzy of anger against the Pharaoh, and already there had been riots in Thebes.

It was the same wherever we went, and as we traveled the two hundred miles up the river toward Amarna my sense of shock deepened into despair. "We were so careful," I said at one point, but even my voice sounded small against the vastness of our failure. "We worked so hard to think of everything. . . ."

Darius said nothing, for the answer was obvious. We hadn't thought of everything. No one could have.

Ah, but it was the beautiful city of Amarna, where the possibilities were most striking, the failure most painful, that *almost* stabbed like a blade through the pit of my heart. There was a moment, as I stepped through the gates, when I could see with my mind's eye how it once had been—how we had planned it to be. The gleaming stone walls, painted in murals of azure and gold; a central lake reflecting the soaring columns of the temple, and upon the lake exotic waterfowl in all the colors of the rainbow. Streets cobbled in pink marble and mortared with bronze, a central fountain whose waters tumbled from ten stories high to splash over the statue of two males and a female, their joined hands raised high to balance the triglobed symbol of infinite power—*The Alchemists*. From that fountain little rivers rushed and rambled to perform their separate duties—to turn the wheels that propelled the force that generated electrical energy, to water the hanging gardens and the fields of grain and fruit, to clean the streets and sweep waste from the homes, to assauge the thirst of families and livestock, to fill the pools and the baths, to clean itself and begin the cycle anew, a masterful feat of imagination and engineering.

In the eyes of my heart I saw what I could not with the eyes of my body: tall feathery plants in colors of rich blue and bright pink and royal purple which sang when touched by the breeze like a celestial chorus and whose only purpose was to be beautiful; healthy brown children of age two and three playing games designed around complex mathematical concepts and making happy discoveries with alchemical formulae. Centers of art on every corner, poetry quoted by street vendors, music floating through the air. Families laughing together. Lovers delighting in one another. Life at its fullest, rich and sweet in the land of the never-ending sun.

What I saw were streets that were almost deserted in the middle of the day, a stone wall that crumbled to dust with the brush of my hand, brilliantly painted columns fading to gray. A vendor's cart had been overturned and abandoned, and a great quantity of black and shriveled fruit spilled from it. There were flowers wilted in giant urns, palms without leaves, and the sound of the wind rustling through dead brown foliage was the clatter of bones when a skeleton walks. A hunchbacked mother quickly drew a child with a deforming growth on her face out of our path; an armless beggar looked up at us with tired eyes. Swaying in the heat and foaming at the mouth was an exotic-looking beast whose striped hide hung in dry, scaly strips from its frame. Giant flies buzzed around the raw flesh exposed by the deteriorating skin.

The mammoth fountain spewed forth a thick gurgling stream of mud that dripped down over the broken remnants of the statue and filled the canals with a slimy, foul-smelling ooze. Clouds of gnats and mosquitos swarmed over the sludge-filled tributaries and as I approached the statue I had to draw the hood of my cloak over my face to avoid inhaling them.

The two males in the statue had lost their arms, so that their hands were no longer linked. A chunk had been eaten away from one of the boys' faces, and the trail of mud that slid down the girl's face looked like tears. I reached out my hand to touch the girl, and my arm was quickly black with biting insects. When I touched the carved stone fold of her skirt, a portion of her leg crumbled away and splashed into the mire.

I turned away, my throat so thick with pain and disappointment I could not speak. Guilt stabbed at my stomach like a swarm of hungry vultures plucking at my flesh. Had I stayed, might I have prevented this? Had my selfishness and anger led to this, the destruction of the grandest dream that had ever been devised?

And yet I would be lying if I did not confess a shameful sense of vindication, a small ugly weed of satisfaction that raised its stubborn head above the decimated landscape of my hopes. And it was the shame as much as the shock that kept me silent as Darius and I walked the dusty, crumbling streets to the palace.

The palace gates were unguarded, and hung open on broken hinges. A mosaic mural of the beautiful queen had been fashioned upon one gate out of semiprecious stones, but the stones had begun to revert to sand, and were falling away, leaving gaping holes in her profile. Weeds grew through the cracks in the paving stones that once had been elaborately painted and gilded to form a landscape depiction of all of Egypt; nothing was left now but muddy chips of cracked paint and broken stones.

I stood at the gate and found I did not have the courage to go forward.

I, who had slain a hundred men in battle and dozens more in temper. I, who could stand upon a street corner and command a spell that would send an entire city to its knees in fear of me. I, who looked death in the face and laughed every day of my life, could not find the fortitude within me to walk inside those gates and face the final evidence of the grandest defeat of all time.

I said, "I don't know how to fix this." My voice sounded hollow.

Darius touched my arm. His face was calm, his voice quiet. "I do."

I said the words that would remove the protection spell and allow Darius to walk through the gates.

The grand courtyard, which should have been filled with admiring courtesans and visiting dignitaries who were being entertained in the grandest style of the best of Egypt, was all but deserted. The pool was filled with stagnant green water and rotting plant material, the date trees were shriveled and dead, and large, stinging blowflies buzzed everywhere. As we went deeper into the courtyard we heard the sound of sobbing and saw a woman bent over the body of a dead child.

Within the walls of the once-grand palace itself there was more of the same. Fine hangings and silk curtains were draped in tatters over rotting wood walls, a fine haze of dust from crumbling stone hung in the air, and our footsteps echoed in the emptiness of the corridors. The great decorative trees that once had cooled and cleaned the interior air were nothing more than blackened stumps, the brilliantly painted walls and floors faded and dull. We met few people along the way, and those were fleeing with what meager possessions they could salvage. Everything felt cold, and still, and dead.

We found them in the royal bedchamber. This room, their last refuge, was still mostly intact—polished marble floors, rich fabrics, gold and azure and crimson paintings on the walls. The enormous bed was designed to look like a barge floating upon the Nile, painted in gold and hung with layers of silk curtains from prow to stern. There was a figure in the bed, looking very small and almost swallowed by the vast sea of linens, but I could not make out the features through the bed hangings. It was Nefar I saw first, and the sight of her stopped my heart in my chest.

To this day there are those who use her name as a standard of beauty, relying upon the state portraits of her in elaborate costume and jewelry—high heavy wigs, deeply kohled eyes, and rouged lips, her delicate neck weighed down by heavy necklaces of gold, her ears decorated with elaborately worked earrings. This is the portrait the world holds of beauty at its height, of perfect features and fine bone structure, of wealth and privilege and splendid excess.

But the picture of beauty I hold in my mind is as she was at that moment, a young girl with dark hair unbound about her shoulders, loose robes falling to the floor, devoid of paint or jewelry, turning from the window as I entered the room. Her hand was at her throat, and her eyes were bright with tears. "Han," she whispered.

And then she ran to me and flung herself into my arms and I embraced her as though I were holding on to the edge of a cliff in a high wind, and her arms crushed my chest and my neck and her kisses were wet upon my throat. "I watched you come—I could hardly believe it—I've searched so long, hoped so hard . . . why did you desert us? How could you leave us? We have begged for you to return! Oh Han, thank you, thank you for being here! We can save it, we can save it all now that you are here!"

Oh, the words I'd longed to hear, and dreaded to hear. The sound of her, the touch of her, the smell of her—they filled my senses until I was drowning in her, melting in her, wrapped and smothered and imbued with her. I took her in like a starving man at a feast, greedily and in great gulps; I held on to her until I feared I might shatter her bones with the strength of my embrace. And then she said those words, *We can save it all now that you are here,* and the great fever of joy seeped from my bones and was replaced with something dry, and chill.

I took her face in my hands, I looked into her bright, pained, hope-filled eyes, and I said, "No, Nefar. We can't."

She took a step away from me, but I saw in her face that my words were no surprise to her. She begged me, not to unsay them, but to make them untrue. "You don't understand," she whispered brokenly. "Akan . . ."

From the bed the figure stirred, slowly parting the cloud of drapery. "Han." His voice sounded hoarse, and unsteady. "Look at me."

He swung his legs over the side of the bed as I approached. "I rarely leave this bed anymore," he said. "It isn't painful, really. But . . . it wouldn't do to let people see me. I can't bear to let people see me."

He wore a long-sleeved white robe with a deep-cowled hood, and he seemed to be speaking from the depths of the fabric. I couldn't help noticing that the white robe was streaked with pink stains in places, as though from sloppy eating habits. And then he lifted his hand and pushed back the hood.

His face.

His face was beginning to dissolve.

As though his skin were a clay mask melting in the heat, it was beginning to lose its cohesion and slip away from the structure of his bones in gelatinous globs. Where his nose once had been was only soft oozing tissue. The flesh of one eye ridge had dripped into the socket, and the eye had melted away. I could see the weeping musculature of one cheek and the blue-white membrane over a temple. I realized that the pinkish streaks I saw on the robe were not food stains, but the remnants of his flesh, dropping away in strips.

I recalled the poor striped beast I had seen in the city, the creature never invented by nature, with its hide peeling away and its flesh being eaten by flies. I barely restrained a shudder.

Before I could move away, Akan grasped my hand. His hand was wet and slippery and I dared not look at its condition, but his grip was firm. "Everything is going to be all right now that you're here, Han. This is just a small thing, a minor adjustment. It worked, for all these years, it has worked, and it was magnificent. You should have seen it, Han, and you will see it when we make it right again. Just a few corrections, that's all that's required. . . ."

"No." I pulled my hand away, resisting the urge to scrub away the remnants of his moist gummy flesh from my fingers. I made myself look at him, at the hideous creature that was not Akan and not Pharaoh, nor even a replica of either, and I repeated, more firmly, "No.

Akan, we were wrong, we made a mistake. This magic—it can't be repaired, it's like the bridge that failed in midair. We don't have the skill, we don't have the experience—we don't know *how*, Akan, we only thought we did. There is a world of things we don't know, that we may never know, and this is one of them. We were wrong about the House of Ra, about the Passage, about the Masters. It wasn't a sacrifice, but a proving, and we weren't the only ones to come out of the fire changed—there are others like us who can't die. I've brought one of them with me. I've brought the Master Darius to help you."

I spoke all this in a rush, almost in a single breath, and as I finished Darius stepped forward, seeming to materialize from a corner where the shadows were the same color as his robes. Akan said, "No," and it was a harsh, strangulated sound that was almost lost in Nefar's gasping cry as she whirled to face Darius.

Darius said, "Han has spoken the truth. What you've done here is ambitious, magnificent, brilliant—and incurably imperfect." He moved closer, his voice gentling. "Did you never stop to think, Akan, why it might be that the Dark Arcana were a forbidden rite? Don't you imagine that, of all the eons of knowledge that have gone before you, of all the Master Practitioners who have studied the art, if such a thing as you have tried could be accomplished, it would have already been done? The Dark Arcana are forbidden simply because they *do not work*. Nothing that strives against nature, instead of with it, can succeed in creating anything but chaos."

Akan said hoarsely, "You're wrong. Our purpose is to manipulate nature, to make possible what once was not."

"Our purpose," said Darius, "is to maintain the balance."

Something began to stir inside me, a small worm of discontent that I couldn't define or recognize, something important yet uncertain, something I should have understood the moment Darius began to speak, yet I did not. *Our purpose is to maintain the balance. . . .*

Nefar said, "You're alive. How can that be?"

He came to her. "It is a dull story. I will tell you a more interesting one. It's about a great Practitioner who lived a hundred lifetimes or more, who lived so long he grew tired of living. He had women, one after another, and he had many children, most of whom died. But it happened that in a single lifetime three of his offspring were born alive to separate mothers, and this Practitioner, this great wizard who could do anything but die, saw in each of his children a promise of something remarkable. And suddenly his life did not seem so long, his days so dull. The laws of balance required that he save only two to be tutored and tested in the ways of magic. But he could not choose which of his children to leave behind. So he brought all three to the House of Ra."

*It was against nature.* The words echoed in my head, and my uneasiness grew. My heartbeat grew fast, and heavy, and I could not say why.

Darius cupped Nefar's face in his hand, and looked at her tenderly. Her gaze was tilted up to him, wide and puzzled, her lips slightly parted. They looked, in that moment stolen from time, like lovers. He said softly, "You were my favorite child, Nefar."

*It was Nefar, wasn't it? She was the catalyst. . . .*

I cried, *"No!"*

I lunged for him, but too late. One moment she was standing and gazing at him, a question on her lips, heart beating, breasts rising with breath. A small movement of his hand and every vertebra in her neck was crushed and severed from her spine. Gently, he laid her head upon her shoulder as she sank like a doll on broken strings, to the floor.

Nefar had never walked through the fire, and only Darius would have known that. Her death was a simple thing.

I heard Akan's shout of horror but it was dim and distant, as small and insignificant as the mewling of a cat against the great thunderous roar of rage that built inside my chest, that fought its way up through my throat and exploded from my lips. It raced throughout the room like a living creature gone mad, it slammed into the rafters and shattered against the walls, my pain, my fury, my guilt.

For I had brought him here. I should have known his intent, he had given me every opportunity to know his intent, and I had brought him here. I had brought Death.

I remember he looked at me, and he said, quietly but distinctly, "It was the only way, Han."

And he never lifted a hand in defense as I threw myself upon him in the blindness of my fury, as with my hands and my anguish I tore open his throat, I crushed his ribs, I ripped apart his flesh and I ripped out his heart. Only another Practitioner can kill an immortal. He had told me so himself.

Too late I understood. By creating this magic, by manifesting the Dark Arcana, we had committed a crime against nature and the laws of our kind. Darius had never intended to help us restore the magic; his only mission was to make certain we could not perform it again. He might have killed me, or Akan, but Nefar was the focus of our power. Without her, we were . . . ordinary.

And our magic had no power.

Akan flung himself to the floor beside Nefar's limp and broken form. His face was beginning to heal itself, and as it did the features we had stolen from the dead Pharaoh were fading away, and his own features were being restored. He did not notice. His face was twisted with anguish and disbelief as he gathered Nefar in his arms.

I staggered a few steps back, drenched in the blood of my parent, staring at the mutilated corpse of the man who had taught me the only truths I would ever know. He had known he would never leave the palace. In order to restore the balance, he had sacrificed himself. And I had been his instrument.

Akan roared his grief to the sky as he gathered into his arms the limp and broken body of Nefar. But I had killed my beloved, and my father, and I could not weep. I sank to my knees in a puddle of blood and I stayed there, wordless and staring, while the day died around us and the night wrapped its cloak around my soul.

*Part Two*

# THE AGE OF DISCOVERY

✣

## VENICE

## 1586

# *Twelve*

And so the triad was broken, and the magic undone. The great miracle that might have been human civilization never again approached the grandeur that was Amarna. Art and science sank into the ordinary, the great transformations in society and religion were forgotten, and the secrets that could have changed the world were buried forever beneath the ruins of fallen gods.

Watch now as the years roll forward. Civilizations rise and fall like waves surging in the sea, now mighty, now cresting, now swallowed in the vast still waters of time. Prophets come and go, and even the pyramids sink beneath the sands of storms long ago forgotten. Soldiers ride forth in metal armor to conquer and to claim, and return with treasures from exotic lands. Populations stagger and fall. Cathedrals rise. Libraries burn. Wars are waged and won, disease flares and fades, technology falters and advances and hope, like a fragile spark sheltered from the wind, begins to catch and hold and flame again.

And yes, look closely, and you will see my shadow flicker across the landscape of time now and again. I made mistakes. I did evil. I did great good. But I will tell you this, whatever I did, and by whatever means, it was always in a diligent effort to keep the vow I once so recklessly tossed aside, to live by the laws that guide those with power. I did whatever must be done to keep the balance, often at the cost of personal pain, for never again would I make the mistake of letting my emotions rule my will.

I took wives and lovers, and watched them die, and in my own way—in the thin shallow way of mortals—I loved them all. My seed never quickened in the womb of mortal woman, and I came to understand that it never would, and eventually to be grateful for my own fruitlessness. To know a child of my flesh, to love that child and hope for it and then to watch it die—not once, but over and over again—surely that was a punishment even I did not deserve.

There were times when I thought I would go mad from the loneliness. To live a hundred years . . . ah, that is something. But to live two hundred, and three, and then a millennium and to find no one in all that time to whom you can say, "Yes, I remember when we were children . . ." or "I recall as a young man . . ." It is loneliness like no other.

I accumulated a great deal of wealth over the centuries, and I learned how to pretend to age and die, and then to return as my own heir to claim what was mine. I had houses in all the known world and filled them with treasures that appealed to me, and I took pleasure in them for a time, then grew bored. With no one to share them with, no one to appreciate the wonder of all I had seen and done and the memories each trinket evoked, no work of art gave inspiration, no gemstone shone.

There was a time, in Rome, when I thought I caught a glimpse of one who could have been Akan, inciting heresy among a religious sect there. For years after that I was obsessed with finding him, but either my skills were lacking or he did not wish to be found. Again, in Constantinople, I heard word of one who might be he, and I traveled across continents to seek him out, but in the end I was mistaken. For centuries I abandoned the search, and for some great long periods of time I even imagined I did not miss him, that I had no need for others of my own kind, that I was content on my solitary path, living the lives I had designed for myself. But I did not forget.

I next heard of Akan in the fourteenth century where he lived as a Frenchman and practiced openly as an alchemist; he gained a reputation as a beloved philanthropist and his name is revered still. And why, you may wonder, didn't I go to him then? From the great loneliness that assailed me, why didn't I seek him out? Well the truth is simple and mundane: For all my magical powers I am still but a man, and I did not know it was he.

Only years later, when I began to hear rumors of the great alchemist who would not die, who had been seen around the world dozens, even hundreds of years after he ended his life in France, did I begin to suspect the truth. But by that time it was too late; he had disappeared again.

In sixteenth-century Italy the arts of the alchemist were both celebrated and feared. The Old Magic had been driven underground during what is commonly known as the Dark Ages, its practitioners persecuted and destroyed until only a handful remained who knew its secrets, and even fewer who remembered its truths. But in Italy a great renaissance of learning was born, a remembering of ways lost, a reverence for the beautiful and the mystical. It was there, in the dark rich broth of creation and decay that is Venice, that I met Akan again.

And so how, you may wonder, did I find him at last in Venice? The fool wrote a book.

Time had not changed him much, my Akan. Still he sought to enlighten. Still he believed in the power of Truth. Still he sought to reconstruct what had been lost . . . and still he did so without regard for the laws of common sense.

To be honest, I didn't read his book. I was at this time indulging my newly discovered passion for building, for the designing of magnificent palaces and soaring cathedrals. There is in such an endeavor the constant strife to create perfection from imperfect matter, the yearning to touch, even for a moment, the divine with corporeal hands. The transmutation of a thing of beauty from the ethereal concept into the physical world of stone and mortar and glass seemed to me then, as now, the ultimate alchemy.

My buildings were my obsessions, and I practiced little magic. But I heard about the magical writings in occult circles, this great gift to the world, this "Wordless Book" as he called it, whose cryptic illuminations contained what was supposedly the formula for creating the philosopher's stone. Ah, that philosopher's stone again. Only amateurs took it for a literal thing. And only Akan would think to use it as a symbol for some far more probable magic.

I warred within myself for almost a year. I plunged myself into my work, I tried to forget I had ever heard of the eccentric magician who some claimed was the last of the great Practitioners, an alchemist who had discovered the secrets of eternal life and who had secluded himself in Italy to write those secrets down.

I was afraid he wouldn't see me. I was afraid he still hated me. I was afraid that, after all these cold and empty years of searching, I might find my brother at last only to discover his back was still turned against me.

But there is within the human heart a power more compelling than reason, stronger far than fear. It makes cowards of kings and soldiers of priests and makes heroes of the faintest of men. It has been called love. But its root is simple loneliness.

And that is how the spring of 1586 found me upon the steps of a villa near *Ponte di Sospiri*, with the waters of the canal lapping gently below me and the sound of the oarsman retreating behind me, on a night that was swathed in mist and tasted of seaweed and old magic. That this was the house of an alchemist would have been obvious, perhaps, to no one but another alchemist. The billows of chimney smoke that polluted the skies in cities like Paris and Prague where alchemists—often called puffers for obvious reasons—were so thick that entire streets had been devoted to them were missing here. I could smell the faint acid fumes from a fire that burned so hot its smoke was all but invisible, and I could hear the low bass thrum of an alchemical laboratory deep within the bowels of the house—but only because my nose sought the scent, only because my ears were attuned to the sound. On the front door, aged with the moisture of decay that has been slowly nibbling away at Venice since its inception, was a painted aniron snake swallowing its own tail. Many might recognize the symbol, but only two men living could trace its origins back to the House of Ra. I was one. Akan was the other.

There is a substance which, when mixed slowly with nitric acid and applied with the intent of a magician to a solid object composed of earth elements—such as stone or wood—will cause the molecules of that object to separate, briefly, so that another object might pass through. I used that formula to slip my hand through the solid stone of Akan's door and lift the latch that protected against unannounced visitors.

I slipped silently inside the darkened house, wrapped in a shield of invisibility to protect myself from any servants who might be about, and swathed in an enchantment of defense to protect myself against what I could not imagine, I began my explorations.

I had with me a small glowing globe that, at my will, could cast a light bright enough to illuminate a banquet hall, or dim enough to be all but unseen by anyone but myself. I used it to light my way through the unfamiliar surroundings, diffusing it with my invisibility shield so that it would not unintentionally awaken the sleeping occupants of the house.

I moved the light over fluted columns, casting amber shadows on plastered walls and magnificent trompe l'oeil friezes depicting scenes of long ago. The floors were polished pink marble inset with lapis, and the domed ceilings were painted with cherubs. I admired the tall windows and the curved archways and the floating staircase of elegantly carved marble that bisected the great hall. I recognized in its design some of my own influence, and it amused me to think an apprentice of mine might have built the house in which Akan now dwelt. Amused and disturbed me in a way I could not, at that moment, precisely define.

The great sleeping silence of the deepest hours of morning lay over the house and I myself might have been a ghost within it, floating through the halls and the still-empty rooms, leaving nothing but a trail of foggy light so faint it might have been nothing but a figment of a dreamer's imagination. Yet I knew Akan was within. He was my brother, and I could feel him as surely as I could feel my own heartbeat, low and heavy in my chest.

I followed the staircase to a grand reception room draped in gold and red and flanked by six sets of arched doors that could be opened to form one enormous ballroom. There was a dining area overhung with chandeliers so finely cut they looked like the delicate weavings of spiders in the dark. There was a music room and drawing rooms that smelled of fresh flowers. The house was in every way what one would expect from a wealthy young man of taste and importance who knew how to maintain his place in a society that was anything but ordinary.

Another staircase, this one of cypress carved to resemble a flowering trellis that flowed upward, led to a set of rooms done in red velvet that smelled of wine and sex. I cast my light briefly over the two sleeping boys entangled among the bed linens, but there was nothing there of interest to me. Next to it was an artist's studio with a half-finished canvas featuring one of the boys. Other rooms were empty. In another room a woman slept with red curls scattered across the pillow and arms open wide, but the man who snored on the creamy mound of her breasts was not Akan.

I came at last to the room I sought. I stood still, shielding my light and my breath and my essence of life, and I studied it.

In the life of man, whether that life be a hundred years long or a thousand or ten thousand, memory is a peculiar thing. Certain events seem frozen in time, as clear to the memory as they were in the reality, others are as ephemeral as though they never happened at all, and the clarity of the memory seems to have no relationship at all to the importance of the event. I should be able to tell you whether or not I knew Julius Caesar; I cannot. But I can describe to perfection the way the Tiber River smelled on a winter day a hundred years before he was born. It seems logical that an increased life-span might be accompanied by an increased capacity to remember what one has learned and experienced, but that is not the case. One learns to rely on other methods for preserving that which is precious.

The walls of Akan's private sleeping chamber were covered with paintings, and I knew immediately what they were: his memories. There were a few landscapes and seascapes, but by far the overwhelming majority were portraits. And most of those portraits were of women. They were his wives.

They were captured in various stages of life from young bride to plump matron, and their fashions spanned the centuries. All were beautiful, richly attired, artfully portrayed. And yet there was something about them, about the collection as a whole, that caused an uneasiness in me. Try as I might, I could not determine what it was.

Akan slept alone in a large bed draped from the ceiling against the insects of Venetian summers and the drafts of its winters. The heavy tapestry curtains were drawn back against the wall now, and through the haze of gauze netting I could see him as clearly as my mind remembered him: sharp, unlined features, peaceful now in repose, dark hair, worn shorter now than it once had been, his form long and lean beneath the fine woven bed linens. His breath was deep and even.

After so many centuries of waiting and wondering, the moment itself seemed rather anticlimactic. I felt neither a great stirring of joy nor a vast disappointment; not relief nor amazement. He was little changed. I was not surprised.

I moved from the room as silently as I had entered. I wanted to see his laboratory.

I descended the stairs again to the ground floor and turned to the left, toward the low heartbeat of a hot-burning furnace, and the smell of chemicals both familiar and arcane, tantalizing my curiosity and, in some odd way, my dread. I followed the sound and the scent to a large sitting room that was comfortably outfitted with brocade sofas and polished tables and lamps formed of artfully blown red glass. A bound leather book was open on the desk as though he had just finished writing in it, but when I glanced at it I saw it contained nothing more interesting than household accounts. Beyond this room, through some manner of entry that would be hidden to the casual observer, lay his laboratory. I saw no door.

My attention was drawn, instead, to the walls, which were decorated all around with a complex and multidimensional mural depicting the various stages of the life of an alchemist. I could imagine it would amuse Akan's sophisticated friends, whether they were of the magical or worldly bent: Here a poor puffer chokes on his own smoke, there he flees from a laboratory explosion; here he begs a stingy patron for a few coins, and there he chortles over the mountain of gold he has created while the patron bangs upon his door from the outside. Few would bother to study the elaborate and multifaceted painting in detail. But there was something about it, like the portraits in the bedchamber, that disturbed me.

I widened the beam of my light, and I moved closer.

The mural was crowded with figures, with action, more than the eye could take in upon cursory glance, more than, perhaps, could be completely understood after even hours of study. The foreground was filled with the amusing scenes I have described, but the background kept up a running narrative of a much more serious nature.

In the dungeon of the wealthy patron's castle, portrayed in a dimly lit corner of the canvas, the alchemist labored over a distillation in which a tiny scalp, complete with flowing strands of hair, could plainly be seen floating. He held his hand over the vial and dropped blood from a fresh wound into its contents. From an upper window a street scene depicted an apprentice chasing down a small, malformed humanlike creature with a knife while horrified onlookers drew back to clear a path.

I scanned other scenes, in no particular order, and realized that similar occurences were depicted at various times throughout history—the alchemist is consumed by some secret work, blood and body parts encased in animal bladders or glass bottles form part of a dark formula that somehow goes wrong and must be destroyed. In one scene a woman cowered, weeping, in a corner, with her hand raised as though to ward off an attacker. In another, a peasant girl, her belly visibly swollen with pregnancy, slept on a cot while the alchemist labored over a table cluttered with books and bottles. In the painting, the low-burning light from the candle cast its light over the table and the beleaguered alchemist so that one did not notice without close examination that the hands of the woman in the background were tied to the iron frame of the cot with a rope.

But perhaps the most intriguing detail of all was contained in a ballroom scene in which the alchemist was being honored by his patron for his apparent success. The ballroom was filled with stylishly dressed men and women who laughed and danced and lifted gold goblets toward gold-painted ceilings while velvet bags spilling gold coins were tossed casually about. On a gold-trimmed table in the far left corner was a decorative object covered with a glass bell. Upon closer examination one saw that the bell encased an open mussel shell. Rising from the soft, vulvalike flesh of the shell was a fully formed, beautifully naked, dark-haired woman. The woman was Nefar.

I knew then what had pricked at my recognition about the portraits in Akan's chamber. All the women in the paintings, all of his wives, had had dark hair and dark eyes and fine-chiseled features, and though they did not resemble each other in any other way, they all resembled Nefar as much as was possible for one human being to resemble another.

I swept my beam along the mural until I saw it: a scene from that time in Egypt. The foreground I barely noticed, but in the background a Pharaoh and his bride ascended a staircase that seemed to disappear into the sky. The Pharaoh was Akan. The bride was Nefar.

My light caught the hint of a straight line near the painted staircase, as though the plaster were beginning to crack. The door to the laboratory was concealed by the complexity of the painting. I moved toward it.

I saw nothing, not the flicker of shadow nor the rush of movement, but I felt the brush of breath on my neck before I felt the steel blade. "And so, old friend," Akan said softly, "have you decided at last to die?"

# Thirteen

I turned my head slightly, but saw no fingers holding the knife blade to my throat. I did, however, feel the thin cleft opened in my skin by the movement, and the slick moist blood seeping into the impeccably white ruffle of my collar.

I said, "Quite good. You've turned my own invisibility shield against me."

"You surely didn't think it would deceive me."

"I didn't intend it to."

"Answer my question."

In my pocket was a small stiletto blade painted with a poisonous oil and swathed in a leather sheath. My fingers slipped the blade from its sheath. "No," I said slowly. "I don't think I will die tonight."

Abruptly, he released the pressure of the knife on my throat. "Why not?" he demanded.

"Because," I said, "I haven't done what I came to do."

He was still so close that I could feel his muscles tense. "What is that?"

I released the invisibility shield. Cautiously, I turned to face him. "I came to see you."

He bore little, if any, resemblance to the figure I had seen sleeping in the bed, which I now realized had been an artful illusion. His hair was long and thick and streaked with gray, his figure strapped with hard bands of muscle that had not been present as a boy.

Though our physical appearances had been more or less arrested at seventeen, I had discovered over the years that I tended to project an image that reflected the way I thought of myself. I could only assume Akan did the same, for there were lines in his face that could not possibly have been the result of natural process, and the lessons of a hundred decades weighed in his eyes.

He said, "I'm glad."

The knife clattered to the floor and he opened his arms wide, stepping forward to embrace me. We held each other long and hard, and for a moment—for a single, pure moment out of centuries of loss—we were as we once had been: innocent, joyful, together.

We moved apart at last, and Akan stood back to survey me. He didn't speak for a long time, but I did not need to use my magic to read his thoughts, for they were my own—sorrow over the passage of time, and wonder that it seemed so little time after all, and disappointment, in some peculiar way, that our reunion should not have been accompanied by more fanfare.

His eyes traveled to my throat, and he said, "I've ruined your whites."

I touched the bloodstained ruffle negligently. The wound had already healed. "Not the first time, as I recall."

A flash of shadow troubled his eyes as we both were transported back to a rooftop in Cairo, and then it was gone. He scowled. "Why do you steal into my house like a thief in the night?"

"Why do you lay traps for me in rooms filled with illusion?" I returned.

He smiled. "I only allowed you to see what you expected to see. I thought the drunken boys were a particularly piquant touch."

I looked at him for a moment in silence, then shrugged. "Clever," I admitted. "I wouldn't have thought of it."

He looked pleased. "Come, Han, sit." He extended his arm to me, inviting me to one of the low couches near the center of the room. "Drink with me, talk with me, or simply be with me and let me realize you are here. I've hoped so long for this day."

I hesitated, then inclined my head. He moved toward a table where a tray held decanters of wine and crystal glasses, and I slipped the little poisoned stiletto back into its sheath.

I said, "I might have easily been found, you know. I've traveled all of Europe in the past generation, and everywhere I go my name is known. Ask anyone of note in Florence where I might be, or in Paris or Rome, and here in Venice even the Doges owe a debt to me. Had you wished to see me, you need only have sent word."

"As you might have sent word to me when I lived in Paris as Flamel two hundred years ago?" He shook his head, his back to me as he poured the wine from a decanter that was shaped like a swan. "Ah, Han, the existence we lead is a complicated one."

"I did find you once." He added as he turned, "In Rome."

I looked at him sharply. "Why didn't you—"

He handed me my glass. "Don't you remember? You were a centurion in Caesar's army, and I was the heretic you were charged with eliminating."

I made an impatient gesture with my wrist. "As though such a thing would have consequence between us."

Akan gazed at me steadily. "Can you read my thoughts, Han?"

"I wouldn't presume." It was a lie, and he recognized it with a smile. He had blocked his thoughts from me, as I had from him.

He gestured to a tall painted chair with plush cushions, and when I was seated, he took the chair adjacent to me. "I know about your knife, by the way," he said, sipping his wine. "You were wise to bring it, although I think the poison might be a bit much."

"I decided to err on the side of caution."

He smiled, but it was a bleak thing, as was his voice. "So many years."

Silence. The thrumming of furnaces. I tasted my wine. He stared at his.

"I betrayed you," he said abruptly.

"Yes," I agreed. My manner was calm and steady, and I did not take my eyes from him.

The expression on his face was the reflection of centuries of torment, worn down now like a once-mighty rock battered by the sea. "It was for her, you know. For the love of her. When we were together, the three of us, it was magnificent, and the ecstasy was beyond anything I could have imagined, but there was a part of me, always a part of me, that yearned for her, to possess her, alone, in the union between a man and a woman. To be the most important thing in her life, to be her only partner—to be loved by her." He looked down at his glass as though suddenly remembering it was in his hand, and he took a sip. "She would be the consort of the Pharaoh. So I must be the Pharaoh."

It was a moment before I could think of anything to say. He spoke of a time before the city in which we sat had even been built, and he spoke of yesterday. He spoke of passions I had long since ceased to feel, and, by speaking of them, he brought them all back in a swift, hot rush as sharp as the blade of a knife.

I said, "You wanted, therefore you took."

"Yes." He did not look at me.

"And was it worth it, Akan?"

Again the long, sad smile. "Shall I tell you the irony, Han? Then perhaps you will not hate me so. I wanted to be the husband of Nefar, to share her bed and father her children and yes, to create the power of sexual magic between us. But in order to do that I had to sacrifice my perfect, healthy young body. And the Pharaoh whose form I assumed . . ." He tilted his glass toward me as though in salute, while his lips turned down wryly. "Was impotent."

I sipped my wine and I sat in silence and I tried, in those next moments, to think nothing at all. Could I condemn him for feelings with which I myself had burned all those years ago? Could I celebrate his loss when it had been mine as well, or congratulate myself for having been spared the torment he had known while living in the twisted ineffectual body of the Pharaoh who could never possess his beautiful bride?

Tentatively I probed for some sign of the triumph I should have felt. I had been betrayed and my betrayer had been denied his prize; I longed for the satisfaction that was mine to enjoy. I searched for the anger his confession should have resurrected: the waste of a life destroyed, the loss of magic, the death of the father who could have unlocked all the mysteries of our strange existence for us. Nefar, dead upon the ground. My beautiful Nefar.

I wanted to be angry, I wanted to be outraged, I wanted the sharp sweet taste of revenge to be strong in my mouth. But passion, I had learned already, is an ephemeral thing and does not stand the test of time. I could not be angry with Akan; I could not be smug in his misfortune. All I felt was a soft swelling cloud of sorrow for all we had lost, and the aching empty pit in my heart where Nefar had been.

I said at last, softly, "If I but had that time to relive, I would spend more time dancing on rooftops, and less with mad grand schemes that were doomed from the start."

Akan's eyes became opaque, and his thoughts shielded from me. If we had shared anything in common through the long and twisted years that separated us, it was only the pain of a memory frozen in time. That understanding was as bleak as any I had ever known.

Akan arose, and crossed the room, and stood before the muraled wall as though seeking inspiration from the scenes portrayed within . . . inspiration, or something else. When he spoke I had the very certain feeling that what he said was not what he had originally intended.

"Have you crossed the sea to the wilderness, then?"

I said that I had, and had lived almost a century with the natives there. We talked for a time about mighty rivers and soaring forests, about odd creatures on secluded islands and the truths and superstitions that were shared by the tribes of natives we had met. An excitement grew in me as we talked about healing biles and conducting stones and the discoveries we had made in our travels, the magic we had made from our own knowledge, the games we had played, the gods we had been. All that I thought was known to me alone, he also knew. All that I thought I alone had seen, he also had seen. The secrets I held because there was no one in all the world to understand were not secrets to him. Where I had been, he had followed, even as I had unknowingly trod in his footsteps throughout the centuries. Ah, what inexpressible comfort there was in that. What quiet joy.

When our voices were hoarse with talking and the pleasant fatigue of two thousand years relived settled over us, we sat in silence for a time, content in the other's company.

After a moment he said, "Have you ever met any others . . . like us?"

I hesitated, and shook my head slowly. "There have been rumors, I have hoped . . . but no. I've never met another."

He gazed at the low burning flame in the oil lamp. His voice was like a sigh. "Nor I."

He asked abruptly, "Have you any children?"

I said that I had not.

He smiled. "Perhaps barrenness is the price we pay for immortality."

"Or perhaps," I suggested, "prolificity was limited to our father. Three of us in one generation, sired by a single man, cannot be a common thing. Perhaps whatever magic he used to conceive us has taken its toll on our own ability to reproduce."

"Balance," said Akan softly.

And then he said, "Can you recall how it was the first day we flew together? The magnificence of having transformed, of soaring high above the ground, of *being* a bird? How the whole world opened up before us, how you suddenly realized nothing was impossible, that there were no limits in all the world to what you could do?"

I smiled sadly, remembering.

His voice lowered a fraction. "And do you recall how it was when you realized you could not die? How your mind was so filled with possibilities it seemed not even a thousand lifetimes would be enough time to do and see and experiment and accomplish? Didn't you imagine such splendor, such achievement that even now, Han, even now, doesn't it make your soul ache to think of it?"

"Yes," I whispered. And I didn't want to remind him that in the days that I dared imagine such things I thought in terms of *us*; the three of us and what we created between us. The power that was ours, together, and that made us, together, undauntable.

"We never thought of failure," he said, reading my thoughts. "We never thought of limits. Such things were unimaginable to immortals." And he gave a soft short laugh. "I never thought that after two thousand years I would still be cooking chemicals and muttering incantations like a common pledgling of the temple. And I venture to say that, when you looked two thousand years into the future from the sands of Egypt, you did not see yourself building palaces of mortar and stone."

"I saw myself waving into being bands of winged seraphim to do my bidding," I replied lightly. "Had I known omnipotence did not come with immortality, I might have thought twice before accepting the bargain."

He smiled at my attempt at levity, but the smile faded too soon. "So much was lost," he said. "If we had had even a fraction of the knowledge that was destroyed with the temple, imagine what we might have accomplished by now. Instead, we have had to learn it all over again."

He left unspoken the other *if*. If Nefar had not died . . .

I said, "There is your 'Wordless Book.' You must have preserved a good deal of all that you ever read in the temple within it."

He chuckled, but there was no amusement in his eyes. "Ah, my friend, that's the tragedy of it. My memory is not what it once was, and what I write now is but the merest shadow of what I once knew."

I frowned. "You have been keeping records of what you read in the temple since we were in Egypt."

He waved a dismissing hand. "Lost, long ago. The trouble with immortality is that one can never picture with any accuracy exactly *how* long it is. I did not imagine in my youth how difficult it would be to preserve anything for a thousand years, and I thought I could afford to be careless when I believed I could reproduce what I had lost. I never thought I would . . . forget."

A puzzled look crossed his face, as though even now he had trouble believing that he, who once could glance at a writing for a moment and copy it in exact detail days, weeks, or even months later, might experience this very mortal failure of the memory. But then the expression was gone with a shrug of dismissal. He sipped from his glass, and added casually, "Fortunately, the matter of the lost library of the House of Ra is not as urgent as it once was. I have found the copies."

I stared at him, at first uncertain I had heard him correctly. "You have found . . . but where? How can you be certain? There's never been any evidence at all that these copies ever existed. Are you sure—"

"I have seen them," he said.

He seemed completely and calmly convinced. It was a moment before I could demand, "Where?"

He laughed softly. "Come, old friend. Can't you guess?"

Again I scowled impatiently. "If you had the writings, the lost knowledge of the House of Ra, you would have copied them into your 'Wordless Book' and made them known to all the world. You would have set up your own temple and caused acolytes to come to you. You would have performed magic like none the world has ever seen. I know you, Akan."

His eyes seemed suddenly to glint with the shadow of a low hot flame, and he said softly, "I have."

"You have what?" I demanded.

But the odd light in his eyes was gone and his face was once again a smooth and pleasant mask. "I did not say I possessed the books, only that I had seen them. And they are genuine. But they are of little use to me . . . alone."

In the fading lamplight the figures on the muraled wall seemed to move, coming to sudden brief life in a secret little dance that, as soon as I turned my attention to it, was still again.

I passed my fingers through my hair. I wore it long then, thick and peppered with gray, and loosely gathered with a ribbon behind my neck. The movement loosened a few strands, which annoyed me. "The hour is late, and we've talked too long. I have no patience for this, Akan, and I am sorry. Perhaps tomorrow."

I saw something flash in his eyes, and a thought rippled across the waters of my mind like shadow lightning on the sea, too quickly gone.

"I have a bed prepared for you," he said graciously, rising to his feet. "You will of course make my home yours for as long as you are in Venice. But before you retire, I did set aside one item I thought might interest you. Perhaps it will amuse you in your dreams."

He crossed the room toward the muraled wall where I had noticed the door, and I thought he was going to take me to his laboratory. But instead of pressing whatever button might have opened the door, he veered slightly toward the left, to the heavy velvet drapery that concealed the window.

But when he swept back the drapery there was no window. Instead there was a trompe l'oeil door, skillfully painted to resemble an elaborately carved stone slab flanked on either side by brasswork sconces. In the center of the door was an Egyptian stela, beautifully preserved. The whole of it looked disturbingly familiar to me.

I got to my feet slowly and approached.

"Do you remember?" Akan's voice was soft but excitement tightened every muscle. I was acutely aware of his scrutiny as he watched for my reaction.

"The fountain at Amarna," I replied, remembering. I felt sick with remembering. "Two boys and a girl. . . ."

"But before that," he urged. "I took the design from another place."

Now I recognized it. "The doorway to the secret archives. There's something wrong," I added as I drew nearer. "It's incomplete."

Akan said, "It took me years to find the temple site again. The desert sands erase so quickly. I spent even more years with teams of slaves digging, hoping to find . . . I don't know. Some proof, perhaps that it had actually existed."

A moment of silence followed that was heavy with his own thoughts. I did not try to read them. I was far too absorbed with studying the door, and its single historical artifact.

"I found scraps and shards," he went on at last, "worthless charred splinters, proof of nothing. And then, at last, this. Of all that might have survived, of all I might have found, this alone came to me. Look at it, Han. You've seen it a hundred times as I have, but look at it now from the perspective of a truth we could not even have imagined when we lived in the House of Ra. There is a reason my instincts chose it, of all the other works of art I had seen, for the fountain at Amarna. Look at it."

The stela was slightly more than the circumference of a man's arms, where they joined to make a circle, formed of the sandstone that had been the most abundant building material in the time we lived in Egypt. Its ragged edges and incomplete painting suggested it had once been part of a greater work, but it did not matter; I recalled the whole very well.

The door that guarded the chamber of the secret archives—wherein lay the Dark Arcana—had been decorated with comparative simplicity with commemorative scenes from the lives of great Masters. Some, like Rhek the Flying Man and Seth, who had been credited with carving the course of the Nile, were easily recognizable to anyone who crossed the threshold of the House of Ra; others would remain forever a mystery. The portion of the painting I gazed at now depicted a man standing alone with his hands outstretched toward three children—two boys and a girl. The man wore a gold crown that was formed by the symbol of eternal magic—the snake that consumed its own tail. Bright drops of blood spurted from his heart, and showered his offspring.

"It was a prophecy," Akan said. His voice was taut, electric with subdued excitement. His gaze felt hot on my skin. "A great Master with three children, doomed to shed his blood for them. But look. Look what the children become."

The three children stood atop a bright blue globe which I recognized as a depiction of the earth. Their arms were upraised, fingers touching, and between them they balanced three linked circles: the symbol for the source of all magic, pure and seminal power which not even the greatest Master had possessed.

"We will dominate the world," Akan said. "We between us have the secret that all men, magicians and commoners, priests and philosophers, kings and slaves have sought since the beginning of time, and we have the power to bring it to all of mankind. We were destined to do so, don't you see? It was prophesied!"

I took a long slow breath. "Then you say I was destined to kill my father."

"He gave his life to empower us!" Akan said urgently, gripping my arm. "Look how the blood showers us, and becomes the symbol of our power."

I jerked my arm away angrily. "Darius gave his life to destroy us, to disrupt what we had become. He killed Nefar, remember? He killed her knowing that one of us—that I—would in turn kill him, and he did it so that we might never again unite and attempt to repeat what we had done at Amarna."

Akan turned from me and began to pace the floor. The passion that rose within him gave off a heat I could feel as he passed, a glow I could almost see. "We made a mistake at Amarna, perhaps many mistakes. We were young, our magic was not as strong as we believed. But it was strong!" He spun to face me, his face flushed and his eyes filled with radiance. "It was strong enough to change the history of the world had it lasted only a little while longer. It was only the execution that was wrong, don't you see? Not the concept."

He drew in a breath and I knew his words before he spoke them. I knew them, and I did not flinch from them. "My friend," he said. He came to me, and laid both his hands upon my forearms, gripping them lightly. "My only, dearest, and much-loved friend. We can do it again. You and I, united as we were meant to be, bringing the greatness of our magic to the world. It is our destiny."

Once again, the figures on the muraled wall danced into life from the edges of my vision: a child ran, a woman screamed, a flame flickered. I jerked my head around to look at the wall, but all was as before. Nothing moved.

I looked back at Akan. A disappointment filled me that was deep and hollow, and it wearied me to my soul. "We did nothing before, Akan, except create an illusion that was rotten from its center out. Two great Practitioners died and a civilization was destroyed because of it. We have no destiny. We are a tragic accident that was never meant to happen. I'm tired. I'm going home."

I was halfway across the room before he said, "Tell me, then, that you have not played god before superstitious tribes of dark-skinned natives, that you have not awed them with your magic to amuse yourself or to bring them a greater good. Tell me that somewhere in this world today some group of men do not worship you still, and that the knowledge does not thrill you in ways that you would admit to no one but me."

I kept walking, but without as much determination as before.

He said, "I have read the secret writings, Han. I know what went wrong. I know how to correct it now."

Ah, Temptation. Sweet as the voice of seduction, deadly as a viper's kiss.

I turned slowly and looked at him, silently, for a long moment. Studying him, probing gently at the firm shield of his mind, wondering. I said, without any expression in my voice at all, "You would re-create Amarna. In this age."

A slow secret light filled his eyes. "I would do better."

He moved toward me, the excitement that burned within him giving off an almost palpable aroma, hot and quick. "We stand on the edge of the age of miracles, Han. Never has the world been so ripe for the magic we bring. Oh, how my heart has broken over the years, watching empires rise and fall, watching civilization itself stretch toward greatness and then stumble into the abyss . . . watching mankind, like an infant learning to crawl, begin the journey again. And again, and again. For centuries I searched for a way to break the cycle, to resurrect the forgotten magic of the House of Ra and to bring it once again to a gasping, dying world. Over and over again I failed. But now. Now, Han . . ."

He was close to me now and I could feel his heat, taste the fan of his wine-scented breath. The aura of his power was a pulsing hot blue glow, sparks of magic straining to be released.

"For the first time in history all of civilization is united beneath the rule of a single god, and all mankind stands in awe of the notion of magic. They look to the stars and to the infinite workings of nature, they try to resurrect the lost arts of alchemy and they turn their minds toward ancient writings, seeking an answer, seeking secrets, seeking miracles. We can bring them those answers, Han. We can show them those miracles. We can give them the truth they seek. We are the guardians of the future, my friend, the keepers of civilization. We cannot ignore our destiny."

Ah, there it was again, and I could not deny it. A purpose, a reason, a *meaning* behind the centuries of aimless wandering . . . a destiny. I yearned for it, I ached for it, I wanted desperately to believe in the possibility.

I said, "Miracle workers have come before, and have departed. Truth has been given before, and has been forgotten. The estate of mankind has not been fundamentally changed because of any of them."

"They have come," he repeated urgently, "and they have *departed*. We will not depart! We will rule forever! We will be the fulfillment of every dream that was ever dreamed, of every prophet who has gone before us. We can restore Amarna, yes, in all its glory and grandeur, but not just in one small corner of a nation—in every corner of the world. And we can do more."

I could feel my own breath quicken in tempo with his, and I will not say I was an unwilling victim of his passionate persuasion. The temptation to be a god was as darkly compelling as it ever was. All these centuries I had spent trying to redeem the past by walking the narrow path set out for us in the laws of the Masters, but all I had ever really needed was the forgiveness of my friend . . . and to be free of the ghost of the woman we both loved. The power of Akan's argument was not what it offered for the future, but that it promised, for me, to restore the past.

I tried to smile, clinging to an ironic dismissal I no longer felt. "We would do more, would we? Uniting the globe under our rule for all eternity would not be enough? What more would you have us do?"

Akan was undisturbed by my sarcasm, if indeed he even noticed it. His eyes seemed to glow with a darker fire, and he stretched out his hand toward the stela. "That," he said softly. "*We* are the source of all power. We can unlock secrets of magic not even dreamed of before this day. We . . ." He drew a breath, pausing for the smallest fraction of a second as though, now that the time had come, he was suddenly unsure whether he wanted to utter the next words. "Can give life."

It was not that I did not understand. It was simply that, for that moment, I could not believe what I had heard. My eyes had come to rest upon a portion of the mural in which the alchemist labored over a sealed beaker. Inside that beaker was a perfectly formed human fetus.

I stared at it, unspeaking, for a long time.

Akan said softly, "It is possible, Han. I assure you it is possible. Darius could not do it. None of the Masters who have gone before could do it. Only we, Destiny's children, have the power to create human life from dust and ashes—and not just life, but *perfect* life, unmarred by disease or defect or human frailty. *This* is what we were created for."

With a very great effort I moved my gaze from the mural to the ancient painting on the door. Three children astride the world, balancing the source of infinite power between them. At last I looked at Akan.

"You forget," I said quietly. "Destiny gave birth to three. Now we are two."

Akan smiled. All the urgency, the passion, the great heat of excitement seemed to evaporate into the air. His shoulders relaxed, his face settled into genial lines. The secret within him was as thick as a lie, and it hung between us like a thorned veil.

"You came to see my laboratory, didn't you?" he invited pleasantly. "And I have been a thoughtless host not to offer to show you it myself. Come, please."

I might have walked away then. There was a part of me that wanted nothing more than to do just that, to turn my back on whatever might lie behind that door and to keep my memories of Akan as they once had been.

But there was a stronger part of me that had known even from the moment I first learned where Akan might be found, that all things past and present hinged on the turning of that door. That was, after all, why I had come.

Akan passed his hand over the Egyptian stela and a portion of the muraled wall to my left slid open on well-oiled wheels. Beyond was what, to the ordinary eye, might appear to be a cozy sitting room, with damask-upholstered chairs and marble tables and ruby-glassed lamps. The scene appeared to me to waver at the edges, however, and I knew it was a rudimentary illusion designed to foil the uninvited visitor should he manage to get this far.

As Akan and I walked through the door the sitting room disappeared altogether, giving way to the reality it concealed: the alchemist's laboratory. For a moment I stood still, looking at it.

Akan had reproduced the Chamber of the Passage from the House of Ra. We stood at present upon the ledge overlooking the great circular room. He had re-created details I had almost forgotten: the ceiling painted in cerulean blue, the tall marble columns carved with the faces of the great Masters, the lapis characters inset in the floor that formed an invocation of protection for all who took the Passage. Below us, in the center of the circle formed by the lapis characters, the fire pit surged and bellowed, giving forth the roar of heated winds and a thunderous throbbing heartbeat.

This was no illusion. The fire pit was his furnace, the generating source of the enormous energy that was required for the alchemy he performed. One of the columns was a cleverly disguised transformer, another concealed a conduit chamber for the conducting wires and tubes of coolant that ran from it. The laboratory itself was housed on the balcony where we stood: The walls were lined with books and shelves of supplies, the floor space taken up with long tables and writing desks. The entire space was brilliantly illuminated from above by glowing glass globes that lined the ceiling in a pattern that imitated the stars in an Egyptian summer sky two thousand years ago.

I was acutely aware of Akan's eyes upon me, hungrily waiting, watching for my reaction. Now he turned to the back wall and pulled down upon a lever that caused heavy doors to slide across the fire pit, sealing off its heat and roar. His faced was flushed and his eyes were bright as he came back to me. Perhaps it was the heat. More likely, it was the excitement of triumph.

"It took almost a century to build," he said. "I had to tear the whole thing down, house and all, three times because some new detail returned to me that I'd forgotten. And, of course, I had to dispose of the workmen each time." A shadow crossed his face. "It was regrettable, but necessary. There were too many secrets, you understand. I couldn't have them escape." And then he smiled, putting the unpleasantness behind him, and opened his arms wide. "But isn't it magnificent?"

Akan, genius. And madman. No detail escaped him, no memory died. How must it have been all these centuries to live with the obsession of a dream gone bad, a love lost, a torture by fire that wouldn't die? To live forever, and to know no escape from the pain . . . the pain of memory, the pain of disappointment, the pain of ambition.

I looked at him, and felt only pity . . . and a great, swelling sorrow. "Yes," I agreed softly, "magnificent."

His smile was filled with relief, and with kinship. "I knew you would admire it. All those years, striving and starting over, I kept discouragement at bay by imagining the look on your face when you saw it. You have not disappointed. Thank you for that."

He clasped my hands warmly for a moment, and I tightened my fingers on his in a sturdy, reassuring embrace . . . because I loved him, and because I think I knew, even then, that I had lost him. The thought of the loneliness that lay ahead was almost more than I could bear, and I would have done anything to spare myself that.

Almost anything.

Akan said, "And now I will show you what you have come here to see. My Great Work."

I said, "A work greater than your 'Wordless Book'? For that I have seen already."

He laughed, delighted. "How many of the great philosophers and magicians and scientists have sat in that very room and admired my painting and have never realized that contained within it was the formula for the greatest alchemy ever devised? Only you, Han. Only you have seen my 'Wordless Book' painted on the wall, with its secret formula for working the greatest magic ever known to man."

I was careful to reveal no emotion. "Magicians have sought to create human life since the beginning of time. All have failed."

He smiled. "And yet that was only one of the secrets that was hidden—and lost—in the House of Ra. Oh, I tried all the common formulae, made all the common mistakes—the blood of salamander stirred into the seed of a bull, the hair of horse boiled over a cold fire." His speech grew more rapid, his tone more intense, as his excitement grew. "I came very close once, and nourished a living fetus in the womb of a goat for almost six months . . . of course it did not survive. So many hopes, so many failures. In the end the answer was so simple, Han, so obvious, so perfectly reasonable—as of course all true magic is. Life can only be created from life, and nourished in the living womb of a human female. *That* is the secret that Nature has suckled since the beginning of time, but that only I have mastered."

"You have succeeded then?" My voice had a curiously flat quality to my own ears. It seemed almost to echo against the background thrumming of the furnace. "You have created life?"

His eyes glowed with passion, twin coals in a pit. "Don't you understand, Han? Life cannot be created. It can only be re-created! It is as we learned all those years ago, among the first rules of alchemy—that which is set in motion remains in motion, and nothing is truly lost." He drew in a quick sharp breath and his fingers closed hot around my wrist. "But come. Let me show you. I've waited so long."

I let him lead me then to the library alcove, past the tables and bubbling flasks, past the desk with its neatly arranged quills and papers, to a curtained niche that was framed by a marble arch. He lifted his hand and the curtains evaporated. Behind them was a stone wall. He waved his hand across the arch and the stone parted silently, sliding upward into the ceiling, downward into the floor. The interior of the niche was painted the same cerulean blue as the ceiling, the blue of gods, and it was lit softly from behind and above. On a pedestal in the center of the niche was a cask about the size of a small traveling trunk, elaborately carved in gold and inset with sacred stones of protection—amethyst and ruby, topaz and emerald.

"I have lost many things over the years," Akan said softly. "A hundred wives, as many lovers, too many friends. Joy, virtue, patience. Sometimes even hope. But this I have kept with me always."

He laid his hand upon the cask lightly, caressing it. "There is only one life I ever wished to re-create, Han. And that life will change everything." He opened the lid.

I thought I was prepared for the worst. I had not even begun to imagine it.

Inside that small cask, posed knee to chest in the way of the ancients, was the shriveled, naked, mummified form of a woman. The skin was like paper, so thin that the striation of the muscles could clearly be seen, and in some places, the bone. The roundness of flesh had long since dried away, the breasts were shrunken, the hips flat. Long ropes of hair, once dark, had faded to ash, as fragile as powder that a breath might blow away. But the face . . . ah, the face, was perfectly preserved. High cheekbones, eyes serenely closed, lips defying the rictus of death in their perfect composure. The skin had flaked off, the lashes and eyebrows were gone, even the ears had fallen away. But all his artistry had been employed to preserve the shape of the face. There was no mistake.

It was Nefar.

I felt the pressure of Akan's fingers on my shoulder, but it seemed a distant thing, without life or sensation, as though my flesh were wood and his fingers were stone. His voice, however, was preternaturally clear, his breath like a desert breeze across my cheek, stirring the fine hairs of my beard. His passion was a living thing, throbbing with its own heartbeat, glowing with its own heat, pressing itself inside my skin.

"Do you see now?" he said. "Do you understand what is possible? There will be three of us again, the triumvirate restored. Destiny has been returned to its rightful course and all things are possible—*all things*—through us! We will be together again, the three of us, as we were meant to be!"

I could not remove my eyes from her fragile, graceful features. In my mind a breath filled her lungs, a glow spread over her skin; shriveled muscles stretched and lengthened, graceful limbs unfolded. Eyes danced again, lips laughed again, fingers reached out for mine and centuries of wasteful wandering were gone, years of empty longing were forgotten. Loneliness had no meaning for me anymore, life was an eternity filled with promise.

I said softly, "The reason the Dark Arcana are forbidden is because they do not work. There is always a flaw. Didn't you learn that in Amarna, Akan?"

"Amarna failed because we were young and ill educated," he insisted. "*This* is our time, Han. Now we cannot fail."

"You brought me here," I said, "for this."

A great well of sorrow opened inside me, and was filled too quickly by the bitterness of betrayal and the disappointment of all I had lost.

I hated Akan for his sick, foolish notions, for destroying any hope we ever had of reclaiming the friendship we had once known. But he was no more the fool than I, for believing that the innocent joy we had known in Egypt could ever be restored, and perhaps the hatred I felt was really directed at myself. I had lost them both—Akan my friend, and the unsullied memory of my beautiful Nefar. I had lost the past, and I had lost the future.

He said, "I brought you here to share the moment. Because it's time, Han. It's time we were all reunited at last."

I reached out my hand, and lightly I touched the wiry strands of Nefar's hair. It was as dead as shredded bark.

I said, "No."

In a swift movement born of rage and loss, I snatched up the loathsome shell that once had been Nefar, that paper-light husk that began to crumble with my touch, and I swung toward the door. Akan shouted, "*No!*" and lunged at me, but I flung out a hand that cast the force of ten men from my fingertips; he was propelled back into the alcove.

He was caught off guard for only a moment, and he rushed after me. "Han, you don't understand! Listen to me!"

I reached the lever and twisted it hard. The doors of the fire pit ground open, releasing the hot winds of hell.

I heard Akan scream, "Han!" But I did not hesitate. I flung the mummified remains of my beautiful Nefar into the pit, and they were consumed before they touched the flames.

I thought I felt Akan pluck at my sleeve, but I tore away from him blindly. I pushed out of the room, out of the house, and into the mists of Venice. I did not look back.

# *Fourteen*

✣

Akan stood at the window of his bedchamber for a long time, looking out, seeing nothing. A woman's voice spoke gently to his back.

"You let him go."

"Yes." His voice was cold.

"Bring him back."

"No."

"We need him."

"We don't need him. He doesn't respect the work." He turned, his expression set and his eyes angry. "He was never one of us, he never understood the importance of our destiny. Never."

Nefar came toward him, her lace dressing gown flowing behind her as she walked, her dark veil of hair glinting in the lamplight. "You promised," she said.

"We don't need him," he repeated. "Our time will come."

Her eyes were full of luminous light, and as unfathomable as a midnight sky. She lifted her hands to his face, and cascades of lace fell away from her slender arms. She kissed his lips tenderly. "The time," she said, and it seemed to Akan that there was a note of regret in her voice, just before he understood what she meant. ". . . is now."

She dropped her hands to his throat, caressing. "Father," she whispered. "Beloved. I am sorry."

And she kissed him again.

* * *

I did return to the house near *Ponte de Sospiri* a day later. I don't know why. I tell myself it was regret that motivated me, the need for apology, or simple curiosity. But I suspect I was persuaded by a much darker need. I suspect that had Akan opened the door and invited me once again into his laboratory that I would have sat with him and talked long into the night, and secrets would have been told and agreements struck, and the magic that we made would have changed the world.

I know it would have changed me.

But when I arrived, the house near *Ponte de Sospiri* had burned to the ground, along with most of its neighbors. I never saw Akan again.

*Part Three*

# THE AGE OF REASON

NEW YORK CITY

1967

# *Fifteen*

She was Nefertiti, the Most Beautiful Woman in the World. Her face appeared on billboards, magazine covers, and in television commercials in every language of the civilized world. She was photographed on the arms of kings and princes, celebrities and politicians; at the most exotic beaches and exclusive night spots, at premieres and openings and the christenings of ships.

She ran one of the most lucrative cosmetics and fashion empires in the world and, like the queen with whom she had so much in common, her name was synonymous with all that was glorious. She was—in many ways—a symbol of the age in which she lived: outrageous, unfettered, larger than life—and completely inexplicable.

Anyone looking closely would observe that her beauty was not classical. Her high cheekbones were almost too sharp, her lips owed much of their luxuriant fullness to makeup, as did the drama of her dark eyes. Her figure was fashioned for designer runways, but lacked the delicate frailty that distinguished others of that ilk. There was an edge to her, in both appearance and manner, that was the antithesis of what the average male called beautiful. She was silk draped over a frame of steel, deceptive to look at, cold to touch.

And yet, in her presence, whether through the lens of a camera or in person, one did not see the sharp cheekbones or the hard angles. In her presence the features that, on another person, might have been simply pretty became breathtaking. In her presence the eye that saw the truth became blind and all that was left was the illusion . . .

which was, after all, the secret shared by beautiful women from time immemorial.

"Amazing," the man murmured as the film segment flickered to an end. The projector screen that had been filled with images of her, images of grandeur, flashed into rapid-fire black-and-white squares and then into steady white. Only then did he pull his attention away from the blank screen and onto the woman who sat across from him in the darkened room.

The transition from fantasy to reality was effortless and filled with wonder, for she had commanded the screen as subtly and as powerfully as she commanded the room. He arose and switched on a lamp, turned off the humming projector. "Absolutely amazing," he repeated, as gradually his eyes lost the stupor of hypnotic pleasure, gradually his dilated pupils returned to their normal size. "How do you do it?"

Her smile was slow and soft, an indecipherable mix of the whimsical and the sensual, utterly enchanting. "Magic," she said.

She lounged upon a white-silk sofa in a white-silk toga that was fastened on one shoulder with a diamond cluster. The material draped across her body in pleats and swirls as delicate as a caress, glowing softly against her golden skin. Her mass of dark hair was piled atop her head in a deceptively casual style, artfully selected tendrils waving against her cheeks. Diamond teardrops hung from her ears almost to her shoulders, and a silver pendant nestled in the shadow of her breasts.

Her arm was stretched over the back of the sofa, her long legs tucked under her. Now she rose with movements as fluid and graceful as a cat's, and crossed the carpet to the bar. A soft powdery fragrance emanated from her when she moved, like the gentle musk of some exotic, moonlit creature.

Her feet, noticed the man, were bare, narrow, delicately boned, soft-skinned, and perfectly manicured. Most models had hideous feet. Hers were beautiful.

She said, "The edges of the last six frames seemed a bit sharp to me, but you should be able to correct that in editing. Other than that, I don't think it's too early to drink a toast to the successful launch of a new campaign, do you?"

He did not argue with her about the focus on the last six frames, nor did he question how she could have possibly distinguished a problem even his trained eye—not to mention the eyes of a dozen other anxious, obsessive, desperate-to-please professionals—had failed to detect. He was quite certain that when he went back over the tape with an editor he would find, just as she had noted, a sharpness in the edges of the last six frames.

He got to his feet as she turned, a glass of champagne in each hand, a smile on her face that made him think of summer mornings and eyelet-trimmed pillowcases. "My dear," he said, accepting the glass she offered, "I have been drinking to that very thing since the moment you hired me. After all, you have never failed at anything you tried, have you?"

She cocked her head in an engaging way, as though pretending to consider that. "No," she agreed, and raised her glass to him, eyes twinkling.

His name was Peter Rierson, and he had built a reputation as one of the most talented men on Madison Avenue over the past five years. Since he had won the Nefertiti fragrance line account the previous year, however, he had been plucked from the herd of heavy contenders and deposited into the rarefied realm of unqualified supremacy. Nefertiti engaged only the best. Nefertiti had touched him, and he was golden. His future was assured; he would name his price from now on. There was nothing he desired that could not be his . . . except, of course, the one thing every man who had ever seen her wanted.

She sipped from her glass, and said, "You know, men have gone blind from staring at me like that."

He said, "Was I staring? I apologize." But he did not alter his gaze, did not appear embarrassed.

She looked amused. "I find your apology a trifle insincere. Please don't waste the champagne. It's very expensive, and quite good."

He tasted the champagne. "It's excellent," he agreed. "But in comparison with your own rare splendor, it tastes like dust."

"Ah." A faint and pleased smile touched her lips. "Very nice."

She moved past him toward the window, where the glittering nightscape of Manhattan was spread out below them. A flutter of white silk brushed him as she passed, a vapor of powdered moonlight. He felt the thrill of it on every surface of his skin.

"An enchanted land," she said softly, looking out.

He came to stand beside her. "Most things look enchanted when seen from above."

She laughed. It was an unexpected sound, and not one he had come to associate with her. But to his ears it was like music. "I like you, Peter. You've amused me longer than most men of my acquaintance."

"I'm glad to hear it. You know I'm quite smitten with you."

"Yes, I know." He watched the long curve of her neck as she sipped from her glass, and her reflection in the window revealed nothing of her expression. "You've probably heard some foolish rumor that I occasionally take lovers from among my colleagues."

"I wouldn't believe a word of it," he assured her.

She turned. Her smile seemed to collect all of the ambient light from the room—candlelight, starlight, distant traffic lights, and diffuse it into gentle radiance across her face, and within her eyes. "You are the most adorable man," she said. "So earnest, so self-assured . . ."

She lifted her hand, and caressed his temple. His eyes fluttered closed beneath the intense pleasure of her touch, and he drew in a sharp breath. "So perfectly male," she said.

She kissed his lips as though she were sipping champagne, savoring the taste on the tip of her tongue, testing the flavor delicately at first, questioning, and then more boldly, enjoying. He stood as though mesmerized, breathless and still, and when she moved away he reached instinctively for her.

She stepped out of his reach, watching as a drop of blood appeared at the corner of his closed eyelid and traced a thin path across his cheekbone. He opened his eyes, squinting, and an opaque film of blood obscured them. He blinked hard, dashing a hand across his eyes. Twin streams of blood made their way down his face on either side of his nose.

"Oh my God," he said, staring at his bloody hand.

The glass in his other hand tumbled to the floor, and she frowned.

An expression of terror came into his blood-streaked face as he looked at her, but it was short-lived. He clutched at his eyes and blood welled through his fingers like a flood that refused to be dammed; it dripped down his sleeve and splattered like heavy rain on the white carpet. "Oh my—"

But a sudden seizure of the throat prevented him from uttering any sound other than the desperate, croaking gasps for breath. He sank to his knees, and there was a dreadful moment of convulsive movement upon the floor, but soon even that ceased, and he was still.

"Unfortunately," she said, sipping again from her glass, "you are also beginning to grow rather tiresome."

She finished her champagne and moved to refill her glass, stepping carefully over the stains on the carpet.

# Sixteen

I saw her in London, as I was getting out of a cab. Her face was two stories high, and her kohl-painted eyes looked directly down at me. She was wearing a gold headdress and squash-blossom necklace that I remembered from her days in Egypt, and gold-circle earrings that touched her shoulders.

This was formidable magic to me.

Five hundred years ago I had cast all that remained of her physical body into the flames, and had destroyed forever any chance, however small it might have been, of her resurrection. And for five hundred years I had been haunted, tormented, and damned by the everlasting *what if*? What if I had not allowed my righteous anger to control my actions, what if I had listened to Akan, truly listened to him, for even if he was mad wasn't he still my friend? What if I had treasured our past more than I treasured the high-handed notions of right and wrong I carried, and what if—just what if—Akan had been able to perform the Dark Rite? What if Nefar might have been brought back to life?

On that long-ago night in Venice I had obeyed the wrong mandate, and the intervening five centuries had been filled with bitterness.

Carelessly I had walked through history. I had served as general to Hitler and spy to Napoleon. Should one peer through a window in time, it would be my handwriting on the chalkboard of the Manhattan Project, filling in the blanks in the formula for the atomic bomb; my breath that raised the wind to sink the Spanish galleon, my hand that loaded the pistol that killed a prince and set the world at war.

I should like to say that in all these actions there was purpose, that with the accumulation of years there was also an accumulation of wisdom. But in fact there is no magic for predicting an ever-changing future, and the days of my life were as random as those of any normal man. I acted from rage, disappointment, boredom, or curiosity, or occasionally from hope or guilt or the desire to right a great wrong, and I suppose, in my own way and without intending it, I kept the balance.

But in the year A.D. 1952 I looked back over the millennia through which I had lived and I saw, as I had seen so many times before, how very pointless it all had been. Nothing I had done had made a fundamental difference in the state of mankind, nothing I had seen had surprised me or given me cause to think anything at all would ever change. Men and women continued to be born and die, to go to war, to kill at random, to waste and pillage, to learn and forget, to create and destroy. And I was as eternally alone as I had ever been.

An eternity ago Darius had warned me I would one day yearn to die, and he had been proven right a thousand times since. I thought of Akan, and whether I might find him again, and if I did what madness might possess him now, and whether he could be trusted to perform the final kindness for me. I wondered, as I had done many times throughout what is called the Modern Age, how much of the chaos that afflicted the world was simple chance, and how much was Akan's dark magic. I wondered, but I was weary to the bone with life and the effort of living, and I did not seek the answers. Instead, I merely . . . went to sleep.

Deep in the jungles of Brazil there is a root with such a strong narcotic effect that merely touching it will kill an ordinary man. When harvested, distilled, and infused with a paralytic known at that time as curare, then mixed with twelve grams of crystallized venom from a certain African viper, it produces a toxin strong enough to inhibit my vital functions, shut down my brain, and give me rest.

I buried myself in one of my favorite mausoleums in Paris—one, in fact, in which my remains had supposedly rested for over a century—and there I slept for fifteen years.

I awoke to color television and fiber-tip pens, to men in space and powdered breakfast. I awoke to the face of Nefar, calmly smiling down at me from a billboard two stories above the St. George Hotel. Below her image was written, in flowing script, "Enchantment . . . the fragrance for all time."

I paid the driver with pound notes that were issued in 1949, I went into the lobby of that venerable establishment, and I approached the desk clerk. He looked at a man with long gray hair and craggy features, in rumpled linens and sandaled feet and a snarled beard, and he saw a smartly dressed gentleman of forty or so with thick dark hair and a Monaco tan, and he smiled. "Welcome to the St. George, sir. Do you have a reservation?"

I gave him my name, and he looked chagrined. "Of course, Mr. Sontime, I beg your pardon. I didn't recognize you. Welcome back."

I had of course never stayed there before—not in that young man's lifetime, at least—and that was the first time I had ever used the name Randolph Sontime.

"Your suite is ready sir, if you'll just sign here. Will your luggage be following?"

"It should have already arrived."

He looked embarrassed again as he checked his book. "And so it has, sir, I apologize. Everything seems to be nicely unpacked and pressed for you, and a bottle of your favorite is chilling. Enjoy your stay, sir."

He snapped his fingers rather frantically for a bellman's attention.

I said, "I wonder if you might tell me who is that lovely young lady on the placard across the street?"

He looked confused, but I nudged his mind along. "Ah, you must mean Nefertiti, the cosmetics diva. You have been away a long time, sir."

"And where do you suppose she might be found?"

Again a blank stare, but even with my help the poor fellow could not tell me what he did not know. "Why, in New York I should imagine sir. That's where most of that sort dally about, isn't it?"

It was a start.

# Seventeen

I found her not in New York, but in California, at a party for some film star or another. There is a certain irony in the fact that our reunion should take place in this modern land of fantasy and make-believe, where magic is handled by the special effects department and illusion is their stock-in-trade. The house to which I was admitted was decorated to fulfill the fantasies of a thousand Arabian nights, and once I left the architectural monstrosity the producer called home and stepped out into the back garden, I might easily have convinced myself I had gone farther than that. What I had not been able to achieve in almost three thousand years of study—travel through time—Hollywood had mastered overnight.

The desert sky was illuminated with a canopy of artificial stars; the flames of torches were whipped back and forth by the warm wind. Brilliantly colored silk canopies and striped tents had been erected across the lawn, sheltering long tables laden with food and wine. The swimming pool, that perennial feature of the California landscape, had been transformed into an oasis lagoon with floating petals and water grasses, and the oddly dissonant strains of a sitar wafted through the air. Those who called themselves the Beautiful People floated about like desert flowers in brightly colored garments that twinkled and shone, flashing jewels that could have put the treasures of Tutankhamen to shame.

She wore a silver gown that clung to her figure like a mermaid's skin, and a gossamer silk scarf with tiny diamonds caught in it like dew in a spiderweb. Her hair was drawn up high on the crown of her head, and tumbled over a small tiara in cascading curls down the length of her bare back. When she tilted her head, as though in particular attention to something someone said, darts of fire caught the diamonds that dangled from her ears and spun out a blue aura.

Suspended from a silver chain of such fine and delicate craftsmanship it could only have been wrought by master craftsmen was a triangular pendant formed of three interlinked globes.

I watched her for some time before I made my presence known. When she happened to glance my way she saw a boy with long blond hair and a Pacific tan, or a waiter with a silver tray, or a palm swaying in the wind. But as I looked at her I saw a woman with extraordinary power to captivate men and women alike—the men flocked to her in unabashed lust, the women in envy and awe. She was like an exotic creature captured from an alien place and set free to roam among ordinary men, and her courtiers had hungry, adoring eyes.

I made my way through the crowd, brushing shoulders with the film producer whose home this was, pushing past a bevy of scantily clad young women, setting aside the brash young film star who was bold enough to think he could enchant the enchantress. He started to sputter an angry protest, but I looked at him and he forgot what he meant to say. One by one the crowd of admirers who surrounded her dropped back a step, looking around in bemusement, and I came forward.

She turned slowly, and we gazed upon each other for a long moment.

I said, "Who are you?"

Slowly she smiled, and extended her hands to me. "Han," she said. "What took you so long?"

I felt the stirrings of wonder within me for the first time in over a thousand years.

We left the party of the anxious producer and the annoyed film star to the flash of camera bulbs, and when the long silver car pulled up to take us away she rested her hand upon it for a moment and looked at me with laughing eyes. "Or would you rather fly?"

I knew she did not mean in an airplane.

We did not talk in the car. I wanted only to sit with her, to stare at her, to be with her. And there was nothing, at any rate, I could have said, not then.

I didn't care where we were going, but eventually we arrived there, another house on a craggy hill with a swimming pool lit by floating lights and decorated with abstract paintings of bold swirling colors on the walls. We went inside this empty house and lights blossomed to illuminate our way as she waved her hand; I came to realize after a moment that it was not magic but an electric eye that caused this.

We were in a large room with black and white tiles and white furniture and an enormous window that overlooked the desert night. She stood before the window, pivoting to face me so that the light spilled over her from above and diffused shadows around her from below and caught the luminosity of her eyes like ball lightning in a fortune-teller's globe. I said then what had to be said, what I could not delay another moment in saying, although I feared the answer, and dreaded it.

"How is it possible?" I demanded quietly. "How can it be you?"

She pressed her hands together as though embracing her own excitement between them. Her eyes fairly danced with delight. "Oh, Han, I have so much to tell you, so much I want to show you. So many memories I've saved up for you, so many things I want to share with you. But look." She waved her arm and the window behind her shimmered and lost its opacity. Through it I saw brilliant blue skies and soft white terraced cliffs from which trickled a gentle fall of water that pooled in a deep pocket of perfect blue before spilling over to the next terrace, where it formed another bathing pool, and the next, until it spilled at last into a sea that was unmistakably Mediterranean.

"Crete," she said softly. "I think of you every time I go there. Oh, Han, do let's go now. Let's transform ourselves into mighty eagles and fly across the ocean—"

I said, "Is it a television screen?"

She looked momentarily startled, and then she laughed. "Ah, Han, look at us—two ancient magicians in an age that has no need for magic. And I suppose it would be more practical to call my private jet than try to cross the ocean as a bird, wouldn't it?" The window resumed its opacity as she crossed the room. "What can I get you to drink? I've developed a taste for California wines recently. They remind me of the raw fruit wines of our youth, and make me nostalgic."

"I don't want anything to drink."

"Neither do I, in fact. Nothing made by human hands could be more intoxicating than this moment. Ah, but Han, you look so fierce. Do you still doubt that it is I?"

She had been speaking to my reflection in the mirrored wall that overhung a low chrome bar decorated with crystal decanters and sparkling glasses. She turned now, in as smooth an illusion as I have ever seen performed, and she was no longer the sleek, silver-garbed icon of sexuality whose face had been reflected in the mirror, but a young girl with long dark hair and sun-darkened skin dressed in a white muslin shift. She was my Nefar.

I was before her in an instant, and my feet did not touch the floor as I moved. I seized both her arms roughly, fingers sinking into soft flesh, and though a flash of alarm crossed her eyes she maintained the illusion. I tightened my grip on her upper arms; I shook her once, harshly. "Tell me," I demanded. "Tell me who did this dark magic. I saw you die in Amarna. I saw your blood on the floor." My voice was hoarse, and the anger that made it so surprised me. "I myself tossed your bones into the fire and watched them as they were consumed! Tell me how this is possible!"

She did not struggle in my grip. Instead she placed her hands upon my chest and she fixed her eyes deep into the heart of mine, and she whispered, "Han, I've searched the world for you, waited centuries for you. I've come back to you. Come to me now. It was you, always you . . ."

I shook her again, filled with a sudden powerful rage that had been centuries in the making. "Were those the words you spoke to Akan when you plotted to betray me? Did your false promises sound as sweet to his ears? Damn you, Nefar, have you risen from the dead only to torment me with more lies? Tell me how this thing was done!"

"If I could take back the choice I made, don't you think I would?" she cried. "Don't you think I regretted it, hated it, suffered because of it every day and every night of my time in Amarna? I beg you, Han, don't hate me still. This time I have made the right choice, I have come back to you! Please don't turn me away."

She lifted her face to mine, her mouth to mine, in a kiss that was long and hungry and a thousand years in the making. I felt her flow into me, the pure sharp essence of Nefar, thick and invasive, electric with power. I felt her intent; no, I inhaled it. I let it wrap itself around me and thread my will into hers, and yes, it was my choice. I could have resisted had I desired. But my desire was only for what I had longed for these past millennia: to be alone no more, to be a part of the whole once again. Resist? The very notion was alien to me at the moment. I embraced what she offered to me as a hungry child will embrace its mother's breast, with no thought except that my emptiness would be filled.

I felt again what I had not known for centuries uncolumned, the entwining of wills, the blossoming of power, the surrender and the control. Potential swelled within us like lava and erupted through us like blue fire; we were filled with it, masters of it. I closed my eyes, sinking into the deepest, focused center of it, and wherever I touched her, or she touched me—my fingertips, my chest, the tops of my thighs—small sparks of electricity tingled and crackled in the air. *Fly,* I thought, and with a sound like a muted clap of thunder we melted through the plate-glass window, skimmed the sandy ground with our feet, and soared into the air.

We spiraled over the flagstone pool, and its still blue waters rippled with the breeze of our passage. We leapt high above the neat green lawn with its artful landscape lighting, over the clay-tiled roof, above power lines and telephone lines, spinning like leaves caught in the wind, higher and higher, until the house in which she lived and all its neighbors, with their grand high gates and curving drives and glittering windows, were mere matchbox toys, playful shadows and pinprick lights.

It is not so complex a thing, this defeat of gravity for a leap into flight, nor was the magic particularly rare. Shamans and priests of focused intent have achieved it in some small way in almost every culture around the world. It is ordinary magic. But to fly as we flew then, to soar high above the earth with the stars as your canopy and the sturdy breath of the wind your only bolster . . . that was not ordinary. That was a kernel of intent magnified to its fullest possibility; it was the kind of magic that was possible only when we, together, became one. It was the kind of magic I had not practiced in twenty-five hundred years, the magic I was born for, and I reveled in it. She was a masterful seductress, and she used her power well.

The wind streaked through my hair and plucked at my clothing; it had an odd electric taste at this altitude, cold and devoid of the thickness of the air closer to earth. I turned on my back so that my face was to the stars and felt the heat of Nefar's fingers linked with mine; I heard the fluttering of the wind through her garments and the rushing of exhilaration in my ears, but there was no other sound. I laughed out loud from the sheer delight of it. And she laughed too.

We soared across the desert and dived between canyon walls, we glided on undulant currents of wind and were tossed by turbulence. We were one with the stars and with the shadowed clouds; we were one with one another.

We came to rest at last atop the Bank of America Building high above Los Angeles. Had we stayed aloft much longer, our fingers and toes would have begun to freeze, and the compulsion to go ever higher into the oxygen-thin realms was a dangerous temptation. So we perched above the city like the rare avians we were, I in my tuxedo and she in her silver gown, our hair tossed by the wind and our clothing rumpled and well used, clinging to each other in the wonder of it all, as breathless as children. The city spread below us in a network of lights as far as the eye could see, but we were masters of it all.

"Do you remember," she said, "the first time we flew? You and Akan and I?" Her breathing was quick and shallow, her words soft, her eyes brilliant and intent. "It was me—I gave you power. But you and Akan flew away—and left me."

"I will never leave you again," I said, and I kissed her mouth, hard and long, and I held her close to me, and my joy and her joy surged together until starbursts exploded behind my eyes and seemed to cascade into the night sky and I laughed out loud. It had been centuries since I had laughed so. It had been a thousand lifetimes since I had felt such gladness.

"Nefar," I said, and there was wonder in the sound of her name, magic in the syllables. "Nefar."

"I'm so glad I found you," she whispered, and pressed her face into my coat. "Thank you for coming back to me."

I threaded my fingers through her hair, tilting her face to look at me, and I saw all of the night reflected in her eyes, alive and dancing and thrilling with energy. I could feel that energy within me, like the buzz of a thousand insects beneath my skin, like the ache of a fever before it breaks into wild delirium, the thrum and rhythm of jungle drums calling to the hunt. There were things I knew even then, in some deep reluctant part of my knowing, and I won't deny it; questions that teased the edge of my consciousness and spun away before I could capture them, impossibilities I dared not look in the eye, dangers I refused to acknowledge. But twenty-five hundred years had led us to this moment, and I held the answer to the emptiness of all my endless lifetimes between my two hands. I wanted no questions, I needed no answers. All I needed was in the words she spoke next.

"It should have been us, Han," she said. Dark eyes searched mine, drank from mine, begged of mine. "All along, it should have been us."

"I think," I replied, with a chest so full of things I hardly dared feel that the act of speech seemed almost beyond me, "that all along, it was."

I felt the cadence of her joy like music in my blood, I felt the sweet warm threads of her adoration winding through my soul, binding me, binding us. I felt the wonder of male and female, of children awakening, of morning spreading over the cold dark places in my mind where no one had touched in so long, so very long. I felt Nefar inside me, drifting through my secret places, caressing my deepest pains, and I was reflected in her thoughts; I was full of her and she was full of me, we dwelt within each other and reveled in the delirium of one another and the sexual energy that lashed between us like wind in a storm was but a shallow expression of the power that roared and tumbled through us, sweeping us up and casting us down like pebbles in the tide.

I think that we began our lovemaking there on that windswept rooftop overlooking that glittering city of make-believe, though I cannot say for certain. It would have been appropriate that what was born of magic so long ago amidst the ragged cliffs and shimmering deserts of Egypt should be consummated at last upon a man-made cliff in a land where magic was just another form of currency.

My memories run together like droplets of water in the great swirling vortex of a waterfall, each a crystal of individual marvel that sparkles and shines in the sun, yet merging altogether into a thundering cascade that even the power of ancient earth cannot stop or diminish.

I recall the slow-turning dance of stars and the vermilion glow of sunrise, the acrid taste of desert wind and the sweet salt of passion on my tongue. There was the ache of longing and the fury of desire and the sweet and swelling glory of her presence, her essence, the taste and touch and feel and smell of her, so rife with all that was familiar and all that was dear, making me whole again. She came to me, my Nefar, and she brought back all that was lost. Though the price might be all the world, I would count it well paid for that moment.

Did days pass, or hours, or perhaps even weeks in this magnificent amalgam of sensation and exploration, of union and reunion? I would tell if I could. Within the scope of a lifetime that had already covered over two thousand years, the difference between days and hours was unremarkable to me . . . even though those days, and those hours, were the most important of all that I had lived before, or that I would ever live again. I think I knew this even then, and it was for that reason that I surrendered myself so completely to the sensual feast that was spread before me. I was drunk with longing, yes, I raged with need; yes. But no one seduced my will, and the only spell I was under was my own.

What began upon a rooftop in Los Angeles was renewed upon a mountaintop in Majorca and celebrated in the crystal springs of Crete, and found us at last in a penthouse in New York. I cannot tell you of the magic we made together, of the power we harnessed when our wills were linked and our emotions unleashed, for it seems in retrospect an insignificant matter, children embracing a plaything that had been put away and almost forgotten. Trains ground to a halt at our raised hand, crystal glasses danced in midair at our pleasure, storm clouds scattered before our breath. Child's play. What I can tell you is of the love we made; the shallow thrill of physical pleasure, the slow drugged euphoria of our deepest union, the mating of minds and bodies, needs and wills. We two, in sexual union, found the power between us I thought I would never know again. Forever I had waited to be part of the whole again. And forever was not long enough to immerse myself within it.

I knew, in the deepest part of my heart that had waited and wanted too long, that tomorrow would come. And I knew what that day would bring. The choice was mine.

The choice was always mine.

# Eighteen

✣

In New York we slept, I cannot say how long, tumbled together like young cubs exhausted from play, and the sun arose upon a world we could no longer keep at bay. It was a world in which telephones rang and impudent young men knocked rudely upon the door and called out to Nefar with urgency and demand in their tones.

She smiled beneath the veil of hair that had fallen across her face, and stretched her arms over her head, and she said, "I am quite in demand, I'm afraid. Goddesses so often are."

I waved my hand before the door and made it transparent. This is a simple process that involves the concentration of intent and the mastery of physical principles that govern the world of things unseen; it is one of the first elements of magic an aspiring Practitioner must learn, and by then it came as naturally as a thought to me.

Outside the door stood not one, but a half dozen or more harried-looking men, some with briefcases, some with photographic equipment, some with boxes and file folders. Nefar lived in the penthouse above her offices, which occupied four full floors of one of Manhattan's finest skyscrapers. I suspected the crowd in the corridor to represent some aspect of her enterprises.

"Shall I make them all disappear?" I offered, only half-teasing.

She laughed, a sweet sleepy sound that held the echo of temple halls and jasmine-scented courtyards. "Don't squander your magic. I can accomplish the same with a single phone call. Just as . . ." She reached for a pointing device on the low long table and directed it toward a television screen mounted on the wall. "I can see through doors without the use of sorcery." The television reflected the same view of anxious young men that I had made visible through the transparent door, only the machine's view was from a much higher angle, and in black and white. "Closed-circuit television," she said.

I let the door resume its solid shape.

She arose and swirled on a robe of shimmering white silk, lifting the cascade of her hair to tumble over her shoulders as she walked toward the door. "Have you thought how odd it is? What passed for magic a thousand years ago is science today. The deadliest toxin we could devise is used today to keep swimming pools fresh. We could spend months collecting the materials for a few moments of the kind of rare magic that today is racing across tiny wires into every household in the civilized world. Once we called ourselves powerful magicians if we could cross the ocean from the old world to the new in two days. Now we need merely to give money to an ordinary human at a counter and we can make the same crossing in hours."

She pushed a button on the wall near the door, and said, "Daniel, go away, and take your troops with you. I will be occupied the remainder of the day."

The young man to whom she had spoken began to sputter, "But, Miss Azure, you have appointments all day, and we're starting design meetings for the new magazine and—"

He ceased to speak, and the camera showed him clawing at his throat as though it burned him. The clutch of papers he held fluttered to the floor and others began to gather around, their voices sharp and alarmed as he sank to the floor, gasping and coughing. Abruptly the babble of voices ended, though I could not be certain whether she had merely released the intercom button or performed some more severe magic.

I stood and clothed myself in an instant in the fashion of the day—a high-collared sweater and woolen trousers—and remarked, "It must be difficult for you to keep employees."

She turned from the door, a small scowl marring her features.

"These silly games we're required to play. Don't you ever find them annoying?"

"Do you mean the ones where we establish our place in the society of the times, pretend to earn money and keep a household and try our best to do as little damage as possible with the magic we know, and then pretend to die and begin it all over again? I find it, in fact, my only defense against boredom."

The annoyance fled her features. On the monitor above her head, it was clear to see that the face of the young man on the floor had begun to swell, and darken in color. Someone was jerking at his tie, someone else running for the elevator. Yet another was pressing the door-chime button on Nefar's door repeatedly, but no sound was audible from within.

"I was an actress last time," she said. "A star of stage, of film. That was entertaining. Tragically, I lost my life beneath the wheels of an automobile. I enjoyed the drama, come to think of it."

I said, "The young man Daniel will die in another moment."

She shrugged. "He can be replaced." Her silk robe fluttered becomingly as she crossed the room toward the dining area. "I have a taste for strawberries today. But not just any strawberries—only those grown on the side of a certain cliff in Corsica. Will you help me?"

"The police will come."

"They won't bother me."

"Release him, Nefar," I suggested gently.

She looked surprised. "This from one who once earned the name Dark Warrior?"

"That was in a different time."

"Will you tell me now, Han, that you have never killed another man because he annoyed you, or for sport, or simply because you can?"

"I have done so," I admitted calmly, "but I do not any longer. I don't choose to debate this matter with you, Nefar. Release him."

I saw resistance flash across her eyes like storm clouds racing across an horizon. But only for a moment. "Perhaps you're right," she said with a shrug. "It would probably cause more trouble than I care to deal with at the moment."

I glanced at the monitor, and I saw the knot of terrified men begin to part, and the one called Daniel staggered to his feet, still rubbing his throat as though it pained him. A few of them cast worried eyes toward Nefar's door, and I sent them a gentle suggestion that they were all to go away and resume their normal activities, remembering nothing of the incident except that Daniel had suffered a mild coughing spasm. They began to wander toward the elevator.

Nefar was smiling at me. "Now you will tell me that with age comes wisdom. Or is it simply boredom that has given birth to such restraint?"

"A little of both, I think."

She cocked her head toward me in an expression of bemused interest. "And so tell me, dear brother, with all the great magic that you have mastered over the centuries, how is it that it has never occurred to you to declare yourself a god before all the world, and take it under your command?"

"The world is rather a large responsibility for one man," I replied. "I'm not certain I wish to make that kind of a commitment. Besides . . ." I gave an ironic nod toward the telephone, which had begun to ring again. "Gods lose a certain amount of anonymity, as you have no doubt noticed. That is a sacrifice I'm not particularly interested in making."

Nefar cast an impatient glance toward the telephone and it ceased in mid-shriek. The air was tainted with a bitter burned scent as the black plastic casing began to melt, spurting tongues of fire across the lacquered table.

"I suppose," she agreed, "it would be rather more difficult to be a god today than it has been in times of old. More, as you've said, than one man could manage, even with a thousand years of magic at his control."

"But not," I suggested, watching her carefully, "for two?"

Her smile was unsurprised, beautifully reminiscent of the girl she once had been. "You know me too well, beloved, and my ambition is as great as it has always been. But I have ruled the world already, and if you do not think I'm a goddess already, ask anyone on the street."

"It was never your ambition to be merely worshiped, Nefar," I observed.

She inclined her head in agreement. "I wanted to bring change. I wanted to use the gift we were given for a purpose."

"You and Akan were alike in your dreams."

"No," she said simply. "We were not. Akan's dreams were small."

I walked to her, embracing her face with my hands in a tender, brief caress, stroking the silk of her hair between my fingers. "Nefar," I said. "I have taken many wives. I have lain with uncounted women. All of them were you. And all of them were mere shadows, without form or substance, because they were not you." Unbidden, there came to me the memory of the walls of Akan's house and the dozens of portraits of his dark-haired, dark-eyed wives. I pushed the vision aside, but it remained crouched in a corner of my mind, watching me like a tiger in the dark. "Tell me how you came to me. Tell me how you were made."

Such light in her eyes. Such wonder. It filled me like sunshine, it washed through the very fiber of my being and made me new. She said, "Don't you know, Han? Haven't you understood it by now? Our magic has always been the science of the future. Even now ordinary scientists work with their electron microscopes and their petri dishes to map the structure of human DNA, and in only moments they will be able to do in their laboratories what Akan did in his all those centuries ago to create me."

I understood, but only partially. Upon awakening from my long sleep I had made a point to quickly read the books and view the films that chronicled the major developments, discoveries, and trends of the past two decades. Only the term DNA was new to me; I had known of the existence of the chain of life since my days at the House of Ra. But what properties had Akan discovered that would allow him to create human life from ashes? What perversion of science and magic was now being unleashed into the hands of ordinary humans?

She said, her eyes aglow, "The entire pattern of a human life is contained in each and every cell of his body. Hair color, eye color, size, shape, the timbre of the voice, the way one holds one's head, the smile . . . the capacity to perform mind magic. The ability to live forever. This was how applicants were chosen for the House of Ra so long ago—the Masters would take a paring of fingernail or a prick of blood or a strand of hair, and place it in a reactive agent, and if the subject had the necessary genetic structure to become a Practitioner, they would know it. It's all written in the books, that and so much more."

I said carefully, "What books?"

"The Dark Arcana. The copies the priests made and scattered throughout the world so that the knowledge would never be lost. I told you, I found them!"

"You told me nothing, Nefar." Quietly. Calmly.

She was excited now, and the radiance was in her face and glowing on her skin. She shrugged away from me, moving across the room simply for the sake of movement. "All that was needed was a scraping of bone, a single cell, fed on blood and brewed in the semen of a man, and transplanted at last into the womb of a living woman. . . . By the time you tossed those musty bones into the flames, Han, I had been born and had lived for fifteen years!"

In an instant the image came back to me from Akan's muraled "Wordless Book"—a woman, large in pregnancy, chained to a bed while the alchemist works. The formula for creating life.

"Whose blood?" I asked quietly, "Whose semen?"

"Why, his own of course. Akan's. So you see in many ways he is my father as well as my brother." This seemed to amuse her, but then she sobered. "But never my lover, Han," she said softly. "Never that."

She came to me on a breath of floating silk and tropical ginger, and she curved her hand around my neck. Her eyes were tender, luminous, penetrating. "It was I who begged him to find you, Han, to bring you to us and make us whole. I was the one. And all these years since I have spent trying to find you again, trying to grow and remember what I had lost . . ." A shadow came over her eyes, and her hand slipped from my neck, curling like a wounded bird upon my chest. "His magic was imperfect, you see, as it so often was. I was resurrected, but not intact. Not complete. My magic was weak. I could remember what I had been, but I could not *be* that again. I stumbled about like a child, struggling to piece together my memories and my power, learning it all over again, desperately hoping for you, looking for you . . ." And she smiled, wanly. "And shall I tell you a secret? This great century in which we live, the age of high-speed travel and telephones and televisions and radio broadcasts that circle the globe . . . my small magic, snippets of memories from my past that I made known to the right people at the right time for one reason only: that the world might grow smaller, and make it easier for me to find you. Or you to find me."

"I am flattered," I said. My heart was still, waiting, listening. "And Akan? Why did he desert his creation? Why did he leave you alone?"

But she did not answer directly. "I have been a courtesan of wide renown, a songstress, and as I have said, in my last life an actress of great acclaim—all in an effort to attract your attention. I've worked mighty spells of forgotten lore, trying to find you. But of course they were worthless. All I could do was wait, my love, my friend, and trust in the teachings of our youth. That time and nature would bring balance. And so they have. You have found me at exactly the perfect time."

"Akan," I repeated. "Where is he?"

She turned away from me. "He was a genius, it's true, but also a little mad. We are better served without him."

"Without him," I said slowly, for they were words I dreaded to say, dreaded even to think, knowing, as I think I had from the very beginning, what the truth must be, "we cannot perform the great magic. We never could. And that's why you wanted him to find me all those years ago, isn't it? You knew that he alone could not give you what you needed."

She said sadly, "He was a vain man. He wanted to share his triumph with you—and I think he loved you, Han, I truly do—but he would not share *me*. He let you leave. He refused to tell you the truth, and he let you leave."

"You might have come for me yourself," I reminded her. "Venice in those days was not so large you couldn't have found me. Or you might have made yourself known to me while I was in Akan's house."

"Yes," she agreed, but it was a slow and reluctant syllable, punctuated with a vague confused frown. "I can't think why I didn't do that. I should have known that."

But then she smiled. "It was a long time ago. All that matters is that I've found you now. *Now,*" she repeated. "This perfect time."

The smile radiated into sudden brilliance, the delighted excitement of an idea first captured or a dream long realized. She grabbed my hand and tugged me toward the window. "Han, look. Look at the world below us, look at this magnificent city! Not Thebes or Babylon or Constantinople at the very peak of its glory could compare to this!"

But I was not looking at the busy street below, which held her so enraptured. I looked instead at her. "You died before Constantine was born," I said. "What do you know of his city?"

She gave an impatient shake of her head, and her fingers tightened on mine. "Han, just look. Look at what ten thousand years of civilization has built. Look at the opportunity it has given us!"

I brushed a strand of hair behind her ear, swept by a wave of infinite tenderness . . . and sorrow. "Didn't you say you had no more wish to be a queen—or a goddess?"

Her sigh was encased in a bubble of laughter and she turned her face to my caress like a cat seeking a stroke. "Ah, Han, you misunderstand. The world is filled with goddesses, and there are too many queens already. I was born for something more." She turned in my embrace and lifted her arms, slipping the pendant she wore from around her neck. "*We* were meant for something more," she whispered.

She dropped the necklace over my head, and the pendant felt cold where it settled just below my collarbone. Infinite power. I could feel the beat of my heart, hard and slow.

She turned her eyes again to the window that overlooked Fifth Avenue, and because I knew her words before she spoke them and because I could not bear to look into her eyes as she said them, I turned my attention to the street as well. Taxicabs and limousines, and throngs of people moving this way and that, traffic lights that turned from green to red without visible cause, a subtly shifting quilt of color stitched with threads of asphalt and glimpses of humanity.

"Our time has come, Han. That is our world. All of civilization is united beneath the rule of a single God, and all mankind stands in awe of the notion of magic. They seek it in the stars and in columns in the backs of magazines, in the offices of psychiatrists, in the teachings of ancient religions and in the rantings of modern cult leaders. We can bring them the magic they seek, Han. We can show them those miracles. We are the guardians of the future, my love, the keepers of civilization. We cannot ignore our destiny."

I said, with dread tainting every syllable I spoke, "I have heard those words before."

She placed her hands upon my chest, searching my eyes with all the dark intensity that was within hers. "Will you turn your back on your heritage now, as you did then? Oh, Han, don't you understand Amarna should have been yours! I know that now. Akan knew the magic and remembered the Arcana, but he was weak. I only chose him because I thought he would be easy to control, but I needed a warrior, not a poet! And I never thought you would leave us. Everything would have been different if you hadn't left us."

She drew a quick sharp breath, fingers tightening in the fabric of my shirt, and the light in her eyes flared with a sudden fever of conviction. "But now we have the chance to do it all again, to bring the dream that was Amarna to life—but to do it *right.*"

I made myself step away from her, to turn and cross the room. "A world that can send men to orbit the moon and talk to one another across an ocean has no need for the minor miracles that awed ignorant peasants three thousand years ago."

She laughed. "Don't you understand it, Han? Don't you know the secret yet? There *is* no magic—only remembering! The Masters of old, the ones who wrote the Dark Arcana—they had lived a thousand lifetimes, just as we have done, they had seen a hundred civilizations rise and fall, just as we have done. And the only difference between them and ordinary humans was that they accumulated knowledge over all their lifetimes, instead of losing it to death. We do not perform magic, we simply remember what was forgotten. Electricity is not new. Nuclear power, machines that fly and compute data, bridges that soar on a single support, potions that cure the lame and cause the blind to see—none of this is new to us, nor was it new to the Old Masters.

"Imagine," she said softly, "to what heights mankind might have already risen if no one ever died. Imagine what price any one of those frantic, desperate people out there might pay for an opportunity like that."

I said, "Ah." And it was a gentle syllable, barely breathed.

Her smile was quiet and confident. "Akan had the right idea, when he proposed to bring his method for cloning life into the world. But he didn't take it far enough. He never did. He never understood the true scope of our potential—or of our responsibility. *This* is what will make us gods, Han. This is what will give us all the world."

I said nothing, waiting.

She came toward me, but stopped just a few steps shy of the distance that could be closed in an embrace. Her hands were pressed together lightly, her tone musical and filled with reason and well-considered rationale. "You have turned your back on fortune before, Han. Once in Amarna, and once in Venice. Tell me now—will you desert me again?"

I replied in the same composed tone, "It would take three of us to perform that kind of magic. Where is Akan?"

A brief impatience crossed her features. "Look at the magic the two of us have performed already without him! We don't need him, I tell you!"

"And the formula?" I inquired, still very calm. "The method for rearranging the chain of life so that it includes the gene for immortality?"

Her face grew suddenly radiant, as though with a delightful secret, and she extended her hands to me. "Come," she said.

Her fingers closed on mine, her will wrapped itself around mine, and suddenly we were in a large cathedral, awash in the blue glow of stained glass and the smell of wood polish and the hush of reverence. We were wrapped in the slightly distorting bubble of invisibility, but I could see the sacristy was almost empty. Two or three sat quietly in the pews, another genuflected and departed. I recognized the place as St. Patrick's Cathedral in New York, not far from the building in which she lived, and I noticed with an absent, almost automatic part of my mind that this was not great magic, that this was as far as she could transport us without my concentrated help.

It might have been Rome, but it was not.

She released my hands, looking around. "One before us promised eternal life," she observed. "How very ironic that it should be his Church that has sheltered the secret that will enable us to deliver what it could not." She turned back to me, smiling. "The City within the City of Rome, sanctified and protected for centuries unchanged, where all the arcane knowledge of the world eventually ends up. It was Akan who first realized the power of the Church, shortly after the Basilica of St. Peter was built, when the first of the minor writings was brought there from the East. He used an entire lifetime to maneuver himself into the position inside the Vatican, and he used his authority to send out knights and couriers and secret searchers across the known world to retrieve the rest of them—some of them in original papyrus, some carefully copied on pressed paper with brilliant inks. Many a crusade was fought for the sake of them, many a city fell because of them . . . and many a treasure was brought back in place of them. It required, of course, more than one lifetime, more than one high-placed cleric. And then an eternity of reading, of discovery, of experimenting . . . But finally the code was broken, and the formula for the most forbidden of all the Dark Arcana was proven."

She spread her hands in a gesture that was both subtle and dramatic. "I am the result. And the formula for creating life—for creating *immortal* life is forgotten in a vault in the heart of the Holy City where Akan left it six hundred years ago. We have only to retrieve it."

I said, "Then why haven't you done so already? Why hasn't Akan?"

"Because *knowing* and *performing* are two different things!" she cried. "Because I can't do it alone! You know that. You've always known it!"

In her agitation, the invisibility shield began to waver. I took her hands. "Let's return."

Once again in her white apartment, with its high window overlooking Manhattan, I kissed the top of her head tenderly, and I said, "It's because Akan is dead, isn't it? Tell me why you killed him."

A shadow passed over her eyes, but she seemed to consider the matter and decide it unworthy of debate. She touched her fingers to her lips in a thoughtful way, walked a few steps away, and turned back to me.

"I never passed through the fire," she said. "In my other life, I never took the Passage. I don't know whether I would have passed or not, I don't know whether I had the gene. That's why Darius, beloved father . . ." Her lips quirked a little at this. "Was able to kill me so easily. It takes a great and sudden trauma that affects all of the body systems at once—like a fire—to activate the gene that immunizes us against death. I had never had that.

"When Akan made me—remade me—he used his own genetic material to nourish mine. I was the same, but also part of him. The part that was immortal. On the night you came to us in Venice, it was time for my Passage. We were to be together again, the three of us, but as equals this time, performing the greatest magic of all time. But Akan was selfish. He told you too much, and he told you badly. He drove you away. Everything was ruined. And that was when I realized I didn't really need him. I only needed what he *knew*."

The interplay of emotions across her face was fascinating to watch as her mind searched back through time. "Amazing, isn't it," she murmured, "how time will dull the memory of pain, but keep the taste of triumph alive?" She looked at me. "It was quite magnificent, Han. I wish you could have seen it. I called forth the fire from the pit, just as I did in the House of Ra, and I survived it, I mastered it. I became what you are, what Akan was. I claimed my birthright. And Akan, cowering and whimpering from the pain of the flames . . ." A brief shadow of disdain crossed her features. "He tried to escape. He was a coward."

Her attention, which had been so focused on the past that she seemed almost to be reliving it, now returned to me. She finished in a matter-of-fact tone, "It is true that the same physical chemistry that makes us immortal also allows us to assume certain qualities by ingesting the essential flesh of one who possesses them, you know this. That is why the great magic we performed with the Pharaoh was possible."

I said nothing. I watched her eyes. They were calm and implacable.

"I consumed his brain," she said. "So you see Akan is not dead. A part of him lives within me. His intent, his memories . . ."

*His madness,* I thought.

Once again a scowl of impatience flitted across her features. "But it wasn't enough. His memories were scattered and his power was fragmented. It took me lifetimes to relearn what I should have known, to integrate his power into my own. And still I was nothing without you." She looked up at me, open, waiting.

I said, "So this is how you remember what you weren't alive to see. This is why we two can perform the magic it has always before required three to make."

"Now," she said softly, "we *are* three."

I looked at her solemnly for a long moment. "Yes," I said at last. "We are."

"Oh, Han, don't try to tell me this isn't what you've hoped for, dreamed of, longed for all these centuries! You and I together—you and I in *power*! Tell me," she repeated urgently. "Tell me that you do not want to be a god!"

But I could not.

Yes, I wanted to be a god. I had wanted it since Amarna. Yes, I hated Akan for stealing what was mine. And now I had a chance to reclaim it all, to put right today what had gone so dreadfully wrong in Egypt. This was more than a temptation. It was the fulfillment of a promise.

She knew my thoughts and her triumph embraced me. "We shall burst upon the world in a blaze of splendor," she said, and she began to pace excitedly. "It will be the most magnificent PR campaign ever designed. Of course, we will have to discard our present identities. I have a particularly spectacular death planned for myself—I think I shall be murdered, the apartment streaked with blood, no traces of my body ever found." And suddenly she whirled toward me, laughing. "Perhaps you will murder me! And leave a delightful confession note just before you commit suicide by—by drowning I think."

And the delight in her eyes sharpened into victory as she continued, "Then we will set ourselves up as religious icons. We'll lull the world into submission with the trappings of familiar ways, and then we will do something spectacular and dramatic, like leap from a tall building and land unharmed on the ground, or walk through flames, or take an assassin's bullet and arise from the dead. They will flock to us. And upon those who prove themselves worthy, we would bestow the gift of eternal life . . . but only for a price of course."

I said softly, "Never to be lonely again. To know there were others of your kind, wherever you went . . ."

"Others who were loyal to you," she amended, "devoted to you . . . indebted to you."

I returned my attention to her. "And subservient to us, of course."

She smiled. "We would be gods."

"And the state of mankind would be advanced immeasurably."

"Just as it was at Amarna."

I came to her, threading my fingers through her hair, settling my palms against her temples. "And you and I," I said softly, "together for all of time."

"Yes," she whispered.

I caressed her face, her cheeks, her lips. I dropped my fingers to her neck, the thumbs stroking either side of her windpipe. And she held my gaze, unafraid.

I said, "What will you do if I say no to your grand plan, my love? Will you kill me as you did poor Akan?"

She said thoughtfully, "No. I don't think I'm strong enough to kill you. You have lived longer and you have more protective magic. But it will not make any difference to my plan if you refuse to help me. Already I have taken what I need from you." She took my hand from her throat, and guided it gently to her belly. "In mere months we will be three again."

Her features softened, and became almost imploring as she looked at me. "The blood of the child will give me the power I need to perform the great magic without you. But I don't want to do it alone. Please say you are with me, Han. Please make this our triumph, together."

I pressed my fingers against the softness of her belly, and I imagined I could almost feel the faint throb of a tiny heart. I raised my eyes to hers. I drew her slowly into my embrace.

"I am with you, my love," I said. "Of course I am."

# *New York City*

✣

## THE PRESENT

# Nineteen

✣

"She gave birth almost effortlessly," Sontime said, "on a three-hundred-year-old bed in a château on the Loire." His tone was easy and matter of fact, as though he were relating nothing of more consequence than the sports scores. "The child slipped from her body in a rush of blood and fluids and she cut the cord with her teeth, sucking out the blood. I remember the fury and the hunger in her eyes as I snatched the infant from her, but I had spent months perfecting the skills that would be required to perform this, my most important magic. Her scream of greed and rage could be heard across the river valley as I vanished with the child before her eyes."

His expression grew thoughtful as he added, "I'm not at all certain in all those months that she ever really trusted me, or believed I would keep my promise to her. Of course I knew from the beginning that she would dispose of me as soon as she grew strong enough to no longer need me. She wouldn't want to, and it would have made her sad, but Nefar has always served a much greater god than self-interest. All else paled in the light of her own grand design for the perfect world, and what she did, she did always for the greater good as she saw it. The same girl who risked the safety of us all to save a child she didn't even know from dying in the streets would consume the flesh of her own child in order to advance the state of mankind. She was from the beginning the perfect embodiment of power and ambition, of danger and design, the nexus from which all our dreams were spun. Nefar always knew this, and she was strong enough, and wise enough, to wait until the time was right to make her move. I think I always knew it too.

"But in the end it didn't matter. The nourishment she could not take from the flesh of her own child she received in another, simpler way. Though she did not know I was there, I watched as the placenta was delivered, and as she stuffed the gory mass into her mouth, tearing at it and swallowing it like a woman starved. I could almost feel her power grow before me.

"Perhaps I should have killed her then. I've often asked myself why I did not. I think the answer is . . . hope." For the first time since he had entered her office there was something very close to vulnerability in his eyes. "Eternity is a very long time to live without it."

After another moment he seemed to come back to himself, and his face, and his tone, resumed its impassive expression. "At any rate, I did as I have always done—the best I could manage at the time. I hid the infant away in a place as safe as I could make it, and I stood back to watch, and wait for Nefar to make her move."

It was fully dark outside now. This Anne could see from the arc of sky that was visible above the stone courtyard wall outside her window, and from the graceful play of leafy shadows that were created by automatic landscape lighting that came on each night at dusk. No sound reached her through the window; not the whisper of a tire on asphalt nor the warble of a siren nor the rattle of a delivery van in the alleyway. Restlessly she fingered the chain at her neck, stroking the links. What time must it be? It seemed to Anne only moments had passed since he had begun his incredible tale, and yet it must have been hours. Had all the world stopped in the interim?

"You mustn't assume," Sontime went on, "that I have developed a conscience, or a moral imperative concerning the rest of mankind. About one thing Nefar was right—the only difference between me and an ordinary man is that I have lived longer, and learned more. I am still at heart a very ordinary man, and I tell you that if I believed for one moment that the scheme Akan and Nefar had devised would work, if I could have found a way to end the loneliness and restore the balance between mortal man and immortal god, I would not have hesitated to do so. Because I am a man, I am selfish and needy and concerned now as ever with my own comfort. But because I have lived too long, I have learned that the progress of history cannot be forced, for to attempt to do so robs humankind of the element of free will. The gift of civilization—of freedom from war, disease, and suffering—cannot be bestowed; it must be earned. And the power of magic belongs only to those who are willing to pay the price for it.

"My mistake," said Sontime, "was in assuming she would make her bid for power through the world's financial, communications, or trade markets. I expected the obvious. I had forgotten she was also now Akan."

A heaviness came into his voice with the last, and an odd expression ghosted across his eyes—a sort of puzzled annoyance, as though even now he could not understand how he could have made such an error. But it was a fleeting thing, and his features rearranged themselves into their previous pleasant neutrality even as the hint of a wry smile touched his lips. He turned his attention to the television set, whose muted picture still flashed blue-and-white shadows on the walls of the office.

The television was tuned to an all-news station, and the picture showed St. Peter's Square, thronged with people. Anne tried to calculate the time difference between New York and Italy, but her head felt fuzzy and slow. Was that a live shot? How late could it be?

Sontime made a small gesture with his fingers, and the volume abruptly returned to the television. Anne found she was not even startled.

The female voice-over was respectful and subdued. "We're live outside the Vatican, where, as you can see, hundreds of thousands have gathered to mourn the passing of Pope Innocent X. Most of these people have been here since the Pope's death was announced Friday afternoon, and as you will see from the helicopter shot the streets leading to Vatican City are just as thronged with mourners as the Square itself is. All of Rome has come to a standstill today.

"Although the Pope had only been in office ten days before his brutal murder, he had already been hailed as a leader for the millennium, a progressive, forward-thinking man whose personal charisma had enchanted millions around the world and whose courageous ideas were expected to breathe new life into the Church."

The sound was muted again. Anne could hear the sound of her own heart, and feel it, like the timpani of a parchment drum, in her throat.

"The details of her plan must have taken years to perfect," Sontime said. "She took on a male persona, and it must have been Akan's influence that persuaded her to clothe herself in the trappings of the god-priests of old. She might have obtained the books from the Vatican's vaults in a number of ways, but the spectacle and pageantry of the office of the world's greatest religious leader—that appealed to her vanity.

"On Friday the newly elected Pope was to fly to Paris, where he would begin a highly publicized tour of Western Europe. The first of the miracles would have no doubt been performed there. In a matter of months, perhaps a year, all the world, civilized and savage alike, would have been in the thrall of a new god. And her own kingdom on earth would have been well established.

"Two days ago, while hundreds of people in New York believed they were watching me give a speech, I stood in fact on the steps of the Vatican where no one could see me, and I ripped out the heart of the woman I have loved for almost three thousand years."

The silence was long and thick. Even their breathing, hers and his, seemed to have been swallowed by it.

"And so," said Sontime softly, "the world now mourns the savage assassination of a Peacemaker, a Bringer of Hope, the Holiest of Holies, and they are angry, shocked, and confused. But it wasn't the Pope who fell beneath the killer's blade. It was simply a magician from long ago whose dream had outlived its own possibilities, and who must never rise again."

He met her eyes, and held them. And that was when Anne realized she was not looking into a stranger's eyes, but her own.

"No," she whispered.

He leaned forward and slipped his fingers beneath the chain she wore, lifting it so that the pendant it held was revealed. His touch was cool, his skin smooth. "Infinite power," he said, and let the triglobed pendant drop gently to her chest, where it shone softly in the lamplight, almost as though it were emitting energy, instead of reflecting it.

Anne said again, "No." Her voice shook.

He sat back. "I placed it around your neck when I left you in that despicable orphanage in London. I knew Nefar wouldn't think to look for you in such a place, and I couldn't keep you with me for fear that she might seek her revenge on me through you. I needn't have worried. She had all that she wanted, from both of us, and she never imagined that I, who have loved her all my life, would stand against her. She simply never imagined it.

"Nefar was the most powerful of Darius's children, and the most flawed. He knew that, of course, which is why he could not allow her to live. Had Akan's magic not been flawed, who can guess at the greatness she might have achieved?"

The smile that curved his lips seemed touched with genuine affection, and even regret. But it faded as he looked at Anne. "Look what she was able to accomplish," he said. "Look how close she came to changing the history of the entire world and the state of all mankind. And she did not even have the birthright of two immortal parents. You do."

Anne's fingers felt like wood as they moved beneath the desk, fumbling for the button there. She found it, pushed it. Hard.

He said, "You are of my blood, and of hers—and even of Akan's. Three of the most powerful Practitioners who ever lived have combined in you all the genetic mystery that makes us what we are, that empowers us above all other humans on this planet, that leaves us, in fact, hardly human at all."

"I want you to leave, Mr. Sontime," Anne said hoarsely. She pushed the button again. And again.

He smiled. "Your security devices won't work, I'm afraid. And even if they did, what chance would your building guards have against me?"

He stood in a single fluid motion that was almost too swift, too graceful to be real, and he swept his arm toward the window. A burst of flame erupted from the curtain, lapping greedily up the wall.

The cry that escaped from Anne's throat was more like a dry gasp, and she spun away from the desk, staring at the blazing curtain.

"Have you ever considered," inquired Sontime gently, "that counseling is a form of alchemy? You seek to transmute minds, perhaps even souls, just as I do. And soon you will be able to. Soon."

Anne screamed, *"No!"* as the great magician swept a curtain of fire through the air, igniting books and papers and carpets and wood in a single magnificent *whoosh*. The flash of heat seared her face like sunburn and stung her eyes. She tried to draw in a breath and gagged on smoke. She stumbled toward the door, and a wall of flame sprang up before her, causing her to fall back. On the other side of the blaze she saw Sontime, standing serenely, watching.

She screamed, "Stop it! Don't do this! Help me, please!"

A crystal vase on the bookcase exploded from the heat and Anne threw up her arms to shield her face. The spines of books began to melt and crumble, and pages floated through the air like fiery magic carpets. The heat was intense, and so was the light. Everything was dancing, leaping through the black mist of smoke, casting shadows on the ceiling and on the floor where it wasn't already consumed by flames. In the distance there was a sound, high and steady and shrill—a fire alarm. It meant nothing to her now.

Another explosion—the television set?—and Anne dropped to the floor, choking, gagging on the thick gray smoke. She tried to crawl toward the window but she couldn't see; her eyes were streaming, blinded, and the bright red-gold light from the fire was all above her; here there was nothing but foggy darkness and the heat, the *heat*. Sharp pain flashed up her leg and she screamed as her stocking began to melt into her skin. Her silk blouse caught in a flash and she rolled over and over on the floor trying to smother the agony that ate away at the flesh on her back. But there was no floor, only flames. Her hair caught. Her lungs could not draw breath for screams. The last thing she saw before her eyes fused shut was Sontime, bending through the flames to swing the pendulum on the antique clock.

Four units responded within three minutes, but by the time they arrived the building was completely involved. Two more pumpers, a ladder truck and a rescue unit were there well inside the six-minute safety zone, but it was already too late. The building was unsalvageable, and the paramedics stood helplessly by, knowing the only ones they would be treating from this call would be firefighters. No one inside that building could have survived.

It took two hours to secure the adjacent property and bring the blaze under control. The small crowd that had gathered behind the police tape in the bleak predawn began to disperse, for there was little more to see. A few random flames sprang from the rubble and were reflected in the puddles on the street. Flat gray fire hoses were stretched across broken asphalt and sidewalk and the remains of the blackened stone walls, and weary firefighters lifted their helmets to wipe their faces. The air tasted like soot for blocks, and the smoke had mingled with a low morning mist to form an ugly gray smog that swirled around knees and ankles like a slow-stirred soup. Radios crackled. Engines rumbled.

And then someone said, "Hey!"

Later, several witnesses would passionately insist that she came *from* the ruins of the smoldering building, walking across crushed glass and treading on superheated charcoal beams as though she were strolling through a park. Others would claim that she clearly came from the alleyway behind the building where, it was obvious, she had been trapped during the fire. They all agreed that her appearance was so startling that for a moment, no one did anything at all except stare.

She was nude, her face and body streaked with muddy fingers of soot. Every hair on her head had been singed away, but otherwise she appeared perfectly unharmed. She had an odd, dazed expression on her face, and yet she walked with purpose, her eyes scanning her surroundings as though she was looking for something. One of the paramedics recovered himself and ran to her with a blanket. She accepted it, holding it around her shoulders, but when he tried to lead her toward the truck for treatment, she twisted away.

He would remember how strong she was.

She moved past the fire trucks, the police cars, the rattle and babble of official services; she pushed through the crowd, she pulled away from those who reached for her, and oddly enough, no one tried to restrain her. Later they would not be able to explain, exactly, why.

On the other side of the street she stopped, staring intently into the fog. The crackle of radio voices receded, the swirl of flashing lights slowed, and when the fog parted there was a man there, waiting for her.

She walked toward him, and it seemed as though she was walking toward the edge of the earth. The mist swallowed up the sounds of the engines and the voices, the smell of ash, the glow of streetlights, even her own footsteps. When she stood before him there was no one and nothing else in the world.

Her voice was raw and hoarse from newly healed tissue and harsh emotion. "What have you done to me? Look what you've done to me! I didn't want this, I didn't ask for this. Look at me!" She gestured to her face, her torso and legs, which should have been covered with burned oozing flesh; she touched her scalp, which was now covered with a crown of soft, downy hair. It horrified her, and she jerked her hand away. "My God!" It was barely a gasp. "I should be dead but—look at me!"

Sontime said softly, "You are your mother's daughter."

"No!" She took a stumbling step backwards, her bare foot catching on uneven pavement. "No, I'm nothing like her."

He lifted a hand as though to touch her face, and she jerked away. She was shaking, inside and out, every muscle quivering with a high fine awareness, neurons shifting and adjusting to new sources of power, metabolism racing to keep up with the demands her newly created body was placing upon it. Her consciousness seemed a step out of synch, dragging through a suddenly accelerated time stream.

"Why did you do this to me?" It was a plea, low and desperate. "Why couldn't you leave me alone? I never wanted to know, I didn't need to know. I have nothing to do with you! *Why?*"

He said, "There are always two of us. Else, how should we ever die? I've lived so long, and done so much. It's your time now."

She stared at him. Her heart was fast and strong in her chest, pumping waves of adrenaline through her bloodstream. Adrenaline, or something more? Fingertips tingled with it, skin crawled with it, surges of energy arced from cell to cell. If she lifted her arm, would streetlights explode? If she turned her gaze upon a rat in the gutter, would its heart seize? Would engines die when she touched them, would batteries burst?

Ah, she could feel it. She could feel it growing inside her, a network of power, mending a body that had once been only mortal, strengthening a will that had once been frail. Changing her. She wanted to deny it, to fight it somehow. She wanted to . . . and she didn't.

She raised her hand before her eyes, fascinated by its shape, its texture, the faint radiant glow that surrounded it, which was no doubt visible to none but her eyes. Not her hand at all, but a weapon bursting with potential, thrilling her; terrifying her. The protests that had seemed so passionate and real a moment ago lost their urgency as she felt this new and wondrous feeling saturate her.

A shape moved in the mist, startling her. Instinctively she whirled, her eyes seeking and capturing it with a single hard thought, like a slap or a bullet from her mind. She didn't plan it and wasn't entirely certain she intended it, but with a choked-off screech the alley cat fell dead against the curb.

Her heart was roaring, pounding, and she could taste burned energy in the back of her throat like bitter smoke. A cat. Only a cat. Once living muscle and rhythmic pulse, seized in mid-breath by nothing but her thought. Horror filled her. And a great, glowing wonder.

*Look what you've done,* a voice whispered inside her, faint with condemnation. *Look what you can do!* cried another in unrestrained amazement. Life and death. She had the power over life and death. Only a cat, but . . .

Sontime watched the play of emotions across her face, read the cacophony of her thoughts. His expression gentled, and his eyes were almost tender. "Impulsive," he observed indulgently, "just like your mother."

Anne snapped her head around to look at him harshly. "I'm nothing like her!"

"She is in every cell of you, as am I. What an interesting mix that will make."

*The most powerful wizard in the world.* From out of nowhere the thought came to her. She tested it, tentatively at first, and then more boldly. She let it fill her. *The most powerful wizard in the world.*

Anne looked at him steadily. "I won't kill you."

He smiled. It seemed a weary thing, but kind. "Yes, you will. It is your destiny. But first . . ." He lifted his arm, inviting her to join him. "You have much to learn."

Anne turned away from him, searching hard through the mist for the lights of the city, the emergency beacons, the remnants of her office building. They were there; she knew that. But even if she could have seen them, they would have been irrelevant, like someone else's dream. All of the years that had gone before were like that: someone else's dream, fading fast. Nothing had ever happened to her, not really, until this moment. Until he came, and opened the door to her future.

Somewhere out there was her home, her husband, her friends. Her life. She wanted to mourn it, but she could barely remember it.

Before her was all the world.

She looked back at Sontime, at the lifeless shape of a skinny cat on the ground not far from his feet. *Must learn to do better than that,* she thought. *Must learn to control it.*

But the energy inside her felt hot and kinetic, aching to burst free. If she lifted her feet from the ground, would she continue to soar straight up until she touched the sky? Oh, yes, she would learn to control it. She would master it. She would *use* it. She would revel in it.

She looked back at Sontime, and cocked her head thoughtfully. "Perhaps I will kill you someday," she said. "But not until you have taught me everything you know."

"And that," he replied, "could take a very long time indeed."

She smiled, and walked toward him.

He dropped his hand lightly upon her shoulder, and together they disappeared into the mist.

## About the Author

**Donna Boyd** lives in a restored turn-of-the-century barn in the heart of the Blue Ridge Mountains, where she is now working on her next novel.

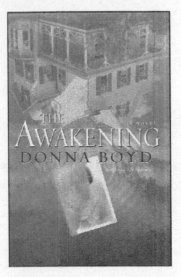